THE
GARDENER
OF MAN

THE GARDENER OF MAN

ARTILECT WAR BOOK TWO

A.W.CROSS

GLORY BOX PRESS

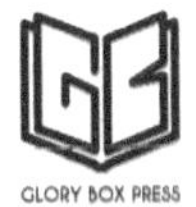

The Gardener of Man

Copyright © 2017 by A.W. Cross

Published by Glory Box Press
British Columbia, Canada.
gloryboxpress@gmail.com

First edition, 2018

ISBN 978-1-7751787-0-5

Cover design by germancreative
Interior design and formatting by Glory Box Press
Editing by Danielle Fine

FOR H.

01
AILITH

The dream changed when I changed. When I became. The green grass of the emerald sea decayed and fell to a wasteland, an endless graveyard of what we once were. I stumbled over the others who lay beneath me as I ran, the splinters of their bones opening the soles of my feet.

I was no longer a child. No longer even human. Everything that had once held me together now swarmed: my bones, my skin, my flesh, my blood; I was undone. My hands-that-were-no-longer-hands were empty, my kite gone. I mourned its loss as the pieces of me ran toward the tree at the center of the barren earth.

It still lived, though only a single green leaf remained. He stood at the base of the trunk, waiting. As always. Only, this time, he wasn't expecting me. Instead, he anticipated the end. His end. Ours had already come, and he no longer saw me.

His face wasn't as I remembered it. He'd covered it with metal, and his mouth, once mournful, was gone. I reached out to trace the lines where his markings should've been, but I wasn't present enough; neither of us felt the other anymore. Only when he raised his hand in farewell did we finally meet, the fragments of me embedding in his new skin.

Something moved in the corner of my eye, distracting me, and when I looked back, he was gone. He'd taken the splinters of me with him; he'd never forget, and he would return. Always.

I found my kite at last, propped up against the withering trunk of the tree. He was still a man, but not a man, his featureless face bowed to the ground. His skin was no longer smooth and shiny, and the silver ribbons that had streamed behind us like shooting stars as we'd run were gone, crumbled into dust.

I took hold of him, to see if, after all this time, he could still fly. What remained of my hand touched a chest that moved, a chest that was warm. As the ghost of my fingers spread over his beating heart, he lifted his head and opened his eyes.

With every pulse of his heart, my flesh knitted, and, finally, I knew pain again. I cried out, but all that came was a flood of tiny machines. They flowed from my mouth into his, and I was restored.

At the base of the dying tree, a seed took root.

They've finally come home. Five of them, it seems. We'd almost lost hope. To be safe, I will implement protocol Alpha-6. Only then can we bring them in. I've told Lexa not to expect too much, that we have no idea what they've become, but she won't listen. Even now, she's in the kitchen, rifling through rations, trying to find treats with which to spoil her children.

— Mil Cothi, personal journal; June 23, 2045

02

AILITH

"Does it change the future if I do this?" Oliver asked, kicking a rock into the deadfall at the side of the path. He snapped a dry branch off a nearby tree, the crack echoing through the woods like gunshot. "What about this?"

"Oliver, don't you have anything better to do? Or is being an asshole the only thing on your agenda today?" I asked. He'd been taking jabs at Pax ever since we'd broken camp—only twenty minutes ago, but I was surprised it had taken even that long. Oliver's obnoxiousness was a finely-honed skill.

He laughed. "Just trying to figure out how this 'future-path' thing works. I mean, God forbid I be the one to finally end the world."

"Well, you've already given it a damn good try," a deep

voice growled behind me. *Tor.* He trailed after the rest of us, ostensibly to keep watch. The real reason was more complex.

Our relationship was complicated. We had strong feelings for one another, but we were linked by a bond we hadn't chosen and didn't yet understand. This bond gave me power over Tor, and had made trust between us difficult. He'd even tried to leave a few nights ago, stealing away in the dark as I'd slept. But whatever bound us together had stopped him, incapacitating him as he'd crossed some imaginary threshold.

I knew this, because I thought what he thought, saw what he saw. Felt what he felt. My mind was connected to his, and to each of the others. It was my ability, manifesting when I became a cyborg. Tor's was physical power. Pax calculated the future from the present. Oliver was annoying. The fifth member of our little group, Cindra, had yet to discover hers.

Oliver raised his hands in surrender. "Hey, I was happy where I was. If you and your puppet master had left me alone…well, let's just say that certain events could've been avoided."

Tor stepped toward him, his hands curling into fists at his sides. The tattoos on his face contorted, and Oliver took a step back.

"Oliver! Can you come help me, please? My pack feels unbalanced."

I mouthed a silent thank you to Cindra as Oliver smirked at Tor one last time and sauntered over to her. She winked at me then flashed Oliver her blinding smile. How she could stand him was beyond me.

Of course, her history with Oliver wasn't quite as checkered as mine. He'd sworn a vendetta against Tor and me for destroying his godhood—a godhood he'd achieved only through deception, but to him, that was a minor detail.

"Tor? Are you okay?"

He'd already turned away, his shoulders stiff.

We were all on edge. And why wouldn't we be? We'd woken up five years after the end of the world, nearly been executed, and were now living rough as we followed a mysterious signal to god-only-knew-where.

Fingers tugged on my sleeve, bringing me back to the present.

"Are you okay, Ailith?" Pax asked.

"Not really. Are you?" On the outside, Pax seemed fine. His coppery hair was unkempt, and he had dirt on his chin, but he showed no physical signs of the torture he and Cindra had endured at the hands of the Terrans.

"Yes. I mean, I think so."

"Pax, after what happened, don't you feel…I don't know, anything? Regret? Sadness? *Anything?*"

He scratched his nose, smearing more dirt across the bridge. "I'm sorry about what happened. I didn't want it to happen, but it *had* to. I—" For a moment, he looked lost, his jet-black eyes wide. "If I let myself feel bad about it, I won't be able to keep us moving forward." He put a hand over his heart, pulling on the fabric of his coat. "I'm sorry." Pax had known we would massacre the Terrans, had even contrived to make it happen. It had, he assured me, been crucial to keeping us on a path that would prevent a terrible future.

I tugged his hand from where it plucked at his coat and squeezed his fingers. "No, Pax, don't be. We're all…we're just trying to do our best, right?"

"Except Oliver?"

I punched him playfully on the arm. "Except Oliver."

"Ailith, can you see anything about where we're going? I feel like we're almost there."

"No. Ever since the sonic pulse, my connections have been…erratic." The connection between my mind and the other cyborgs' often happened spontaneously, but since our escape from Oliver's disciples, I'd stayed firmly inside my own brain. "I mean, the threads are still there, they're just…quiet. I don't mind, to be honest. After everything, it's nice to have only my own thoughts for a change. I'm sure it won't last."

"Maybe you're just gaining better control of them," Pax said as we emerged into a clearing from the patch of bare forest. "I mean, that would make sen—"

Everything went dark, like blood, flowing thick and fast.

PMCP Omega-117 Stage 3 results:

Subject Status
O-117-9791 – female, alive, 22-27 yrs
O-117-0988 – male, alive, 22-27 yrs
O-117-6887 – male, alive 24-29 yrs
O-117-5643 – female, alive, 21-26 yrs
O-117-3476 – female, deceased
O-117-6799 – male, alive, 18-23 yrs
O-117-7900 – female, deceased
O-117-6677 – male, deceased
O-117-2223 – male, deceased
O-117-8977 – female, alive, 20-25 yrs
O-117-3324 – female, comatose, 22-27 yrs
O-117-6778 – male, alive, 27 yrs
O-117-5545 – male, deceased.

— Mil Cothi, Pantheon Modern Cyborg Program Omega, 2045

03

EIRE

Early sunlight filtered through the gauzy curtain and danced in filigreed patterns across Ella's skin. She still slept, though it was nearly nine o'clock, her face peaceful and carefree. How was she so calm? Tomorrow, we were going to Pantheon Modern, to undergo the cyberization procedure.

"I still can't believe it," she'd squealed last night as we'd gotten ready for bed.

I couldn't either. The odds of both of us being accepted had been so low. I'd only applied because Ella had insisted. I didn't actually want to become a cyborg, but she was so excited about it, about us doing it together, that I didn't have the heart to say no.

"I love the idea of it! Just think, tiny machines entwined with our own organic elements. It'll be like your art and my code combined into a living, breathing entity."

Ella loved to merge contrasts. I knew damn well that my darker skin against her bone-pale complexion was what had first attracted her to me. Even her presence in our neighborhood was a juxtaposition: a software engineer stowed away in a district of artists. We'd met here, my fused metal-and-clay pottery charming her as much as it did the chi-chi ladies whose businessman husbands paid Ella good money to keep their online indiscretions secret.

But I couldn't share her enthusiasm. It wasn't the cyberization process that worried me, although I certainly didn't think it was going to be the romantic phoenix-rising-from-ashes experience Ella was imagining. But then, she also adored controversy, and the idea of being a female pioneer was too tempting for her to pass up. After years of admiring other women breaking barriers, this was her chance.

Me, I didn't see the point in becoming a cyborg. When Ella had first come to me, her face glowing with excitement as she'd told me her plans, I'd refused.

Then, she'd promised to put a ring on my finger.

"Why did they choose us? What could we possibly have to offer? It sounds too good to be true. And what about those Terrans, and the Cosmists? They're already at each other's throats. How do you think they'll treat us?" I asked her.

"That's just your nerves talking. Stop worrying about it."

Not worrying came easily to Ella. And why shouldn't it? She'd gotten everything she'd ever wanted, and this was no exception.

I was going to do it, for her. It was a terrible reason, but either we *both did it or neither of us did. Anything else would drive a wedge between us.*

I snuggled back down beside her, my face in her neck where the perfume of her hair was strongest. She was right. It would be fine. The world was changing. We would be innovators, like the women before us. And once it was over, we would finally get married, down by the ocean, the sunlight glinting off her golden hair as she laughed and said, "I told you so."

And so Victor created a being in his own image, recklessly and with all the passion of God. But instead of a dream fulfilled, reflected in his creation was his worst nightmare, a condition far worse than human mortality. The implications of what he'd begun became clear, and he turned his back on his handiwork, abandoning the life he'd created to the mercy of the world. Likewise were we and others of our ilk forsaken when some of humankind perceived us as monsters.

But a monster is never more dangerous than when you turn your back on it, Omega. Both Victor and humankind soon found this to be true.

— Cindra, Letter to Omega

04
AILITH

"Ailith? Ailith, can you hear me?"

"Pax?"

"Yes."

"Pax, what happened?" I was blind, Pax's disembodied voice the only anchor in the void. *"I—"* Tor. The others. I couldn't feel them. Their threads weren't dark; they were just…gone. Panic unfurled in my chest.

"We were talking. And now we are here."

"But where is here, Pax?"

"I don't know."

I was slipping. *Everything that had once held me together now swarmed: my bones, my skin, my flesh, my blood; I had come undone.*

A roar built at the edges of the blackness, dark clouds about to unleash a tempest.

"Ailith!" A voice in the real world. I couldn't open my eyes, couldn't even feel them.

The air around me shifted; I was coming back.

"Stop! We—" an unfamiliar voice pierced the dark.

"Ailith!" The roar became human. More than human. *Tor.*

My body had substance again. There was something covering my mouth, filling my lungs with pure oxygen, and I was restrained.

What's happening? Tor would never— No. Not Tor.

I forced my eyes open. The world was a blur of shining steel, beige walls, and bodies moving with unnatural speed.

Am I in the hospital? Was it all a dream? Was Tor? A trick of my mind, trying to cope? Are the doctors trying to save me? They know they can't. Why would they try? I pressed against my bonds, trying to raise my hands and claw at my mouth. *Get it off. This is wrong. We were walking…*

Impure air, carrying the smell of antiseptic and Tor's fear, burned the back of my throat as the mask was ripped free. Tor touched my forehead, his fingers gentle over the layer of gauze. He looked the same as he always did, dark and wild and strong.

He also looked furious, the gold in his eyes burning like embers ready to ignite.

"You're real," I whispered.

His free hand gripped the bed rail, and as the unfamiliar voice spoke again, his knuckles whitened. I braced myself.

To my surprise, he remained calm, turning around slowly, deliberately, putting himself between me and…them.

A man and a woman. They looked vaguely familiar. He

11

was older than my father, his features coarse and skin heavily lined. Tufts of silver and steel-gray hair protruded haphazardly from his head as though he spent a lot of time worrying them with his fingers. Gray eyes peered out from beneath his bushy brows, a slight dullness on their surface making his expression difficult to read.

She was younger, perhaps in her forties, her hair a pale, braided mass wound around her head. As she pressed the back of her hand to her mouth, her dark eyes darted between Tor and me.

They both looked clean and healthy, like they belonged to this room of neatly-made beds and soothingly bland walls. Their clothes were both unremarkable and unofficial, simple cargo pants and t-shirts, but the telltale heavy white linen of a lab coat was draped over a chair next to my bed.

They stared at us in silence. The woman drew her hand away from her mouth and pushed her palm outward, as if she couldn't decide whether to placate Tor or defend herself. "Please, we—"

"Who are you? Where are the others?" Tor's broad shoulders were tense as he spoke, his back sculpted from iron. Wires trailed on the floor in front of him, and with one quick movement, he ripped them from his chest and dropped them. The woman's eyes followed them as they hit the linoleum with a soft rattle, and a flush of pink blossomed on her cheeks.

We were both naked, Tor clearly impressively so.

"They're right here." A strong, feminine voice rose from behind the couple.

I strained to see around Tor's width, but my arms were cuffed to the side of the bed. Without looking back, Tor reached behind him and tore one restraint then the other free, easily, as though pulling off a Band-Aid. I knelt on the mattress and skated my hands up his back for support. The muscles in his shoulders shuddered, and he wrapped one arm around me as I peered past him.

The speaker stepped further into the room. She was tall and leanly muscled, and one of the most beautiful women I'd ever seen. There was something almost obscene about her beauty. Her skin was the golden brown of demerara sugar, her hair a glossy black that fell in a curling wave over one shoulder. Perfectly sculpted eyebrows arched over heavily-lashed brown eyes. Clearly, being in the middle of an apocalypse worked for her. Her generous lips pursed in a familiar way.

Kalbir Anand. I'd been a passenger in her mind twice before, once reliving the memory of her sister's wedding, and once as she found the immolated bodies of Ros and Adrian. She had the same mouth as her mother, whose hand I'd held as they said goodbye.

She pushed between the couple, forcing them out of her way. The woman sidestepped too quickly, losing her balance and stumbling. Kalbir's mouth curved slightly. She stopped in front of Tor, hands on her hips, and slid her gaze over him, lingering on his groin. The curve of her mouth widened, and she continued to stare, slipping her thumbnail between her front teeth. Her eyes flicked up to his face, gauging his reaction. If she'd hoped to discomfit him, she was going to be disappointed; Tor was not the least bit self-conscious about being naked. The two of us stared back at her, waiting.

After a few more seconds, she laughed and switched her gaze to me. She must not have found anything interesting there, because in the next heartbeat she dismissed me and returned to examining Tor—this time, his face.

"Welcome," she said, extending a slim-fingered hand. He glanced at it, but kept his hands where they were, one over my hip and the other gripping the rail of my bed. "I'm—"

"Kalbir Anand," I said.

Her hand froze, and her eyes narrowed. Perhaps I was worth consideration after all. "Do I know you?"

"I doubt it," I said, picking an errant thread from the bed sheet.

Behind her, the couple exchanged glances.

She propped her hands on her hips. "How did you—"

"You said the others are here? The ones we were traveling with?"

"I asked you—"

"We're here, Ailith," Cindra said from the doorway.

I slid off the bed, the needle in my arm stinging as it tore free. Unlike Kalbir, I didn't need to force my way through. The man and woman parted before me, and there they were: Pax, Cindra, and Oliver. They were in better shape than the last time I'd seen them, a shower and clean clothes making them look almost normal.

"Are you okay? They didn't—"

"We're fine," Cindra assured me. "How are you two? We tried to get in here earlier, but they wouldn't let us, and then they showed us to our rooms, and so we—"

"Cindra, you don't need to feel guilty for wanting to feel human again. Well, as human as we can be, I guess. Anyway, you smell a lot better." I laughed at her grimace and tugged at the soft cotton shirt she wore. "And this is much nicer than that crusty old thing you were wearing."

Stained and stiff with the blood and sweat of your torture.

Cindra looked down at herself and gave me an uncertain smile. "They—"

The woman finally spoke: "We have clothes for each of you. In your size. I know they're a bit plain, but—"

"It's okay, Lexa," the man said, patting her arm. "Hello.

14

I'm—"

"Holding us captive?" Tor asked. "Because I've got to tell you, it's getting a bit old." He draped a bed sheet over my shoulders and another around his hips.

Kalbir's bottom lip turned down.

"No, not at all," the man protested. "We're—"

"Mil Cothi and Lexa Gillet," I said. "Pantheon Modern Cyborg Program Omega."

Tor looked sharply at me. "You know them." It wasn't a question.

"Yes," I replied. "After all, they created us."

*The war was never really about us. Normal people, I mean.
People argued that it was, that decisions had to be made about
the future direction of the human race. But that's insane, right?
How can a few people decide the future of everyone already in
the world, plus everyone who has yet to be born? How do people
gain that kind of power?*

— Love, Grace

05

AILITH

"Well, isn't this just a fucking delight?" Oliver said. "Hello,
Mom, Dad. How've you been?"

"I can't feel the signal anymore, Ailith You know what
that means? We're home." Pax beamed.

So it would seem.

"Look," Lexa said, "we're on your side. We've been
waiting for you. You're safe here."

Tor stepped toward her; she stepped back. "Where are
we? What did you do to us? Why knock us out? If we're
safe here, why not meet us in the open, introduce
yourselves?"

Mil swallowed roughly. "This is our main compound.
In the Okanagan. We—"

The Okanagan. My neck of the woods. I hadn't realized how
close we were.

"Mil and Lexa don't trust you." Kalbir spoke up from

the perch she'd taken on an adjacent hospital bed. "They're not exactly sure what effect their little cyberization project has had on you."

"Kalbir!" Lexa scolded her.

"Well, it's true, isn't it?"

Mil sighed. "Yes, it's true. Given what's occurred…let's just say, it didn't go as planned. We had hoped to bring you all here to recover, to monitor you as you developed your…abilities. But of course, you know what happened."

"Why not just bring us here first? Perform the procedure here?"

"We wanted to, but we—"

"They wanted to hedge their bets. You know, in case someone found out about us and, I don't know, dropped a few bombs? As least this way some of us would survive." Kalbir ignored the stricken look on Lexa's face.

"Kalbir," Mil warned.

"No, no, she's right. We… I'm sorry. This wasn't the way we wanted things to go." Lexa's voice shook, but her eyes were dry. "We've been waiting so long for you. We thought… I hoped… I'm so glad you're here. Look at you." She covered her mouth with her hand again and closed her eyes, a tear finally tracing its way down her cheek.

It wasn't enough to appease Tor. "That's it? That's all you have to say? We have questions you're going to have to answer before we even—"

"All right, Colossus, we get it. You're pissed off, confused, and wearing a bedsheet. Look, why don't you at least have a shower and put some clothes on? *Then* get your answers." She appraised his sheet again. "Not that I'm complaining. In fact, if you need any help with that shower, I'm more than happy to—"

"Thank you, Kalbir. I think getting everyone settled first

is a good idea," Mil interrupted. "If that's okay with you, Tor?"

"I wouldn't patronize him, if I were you," Oliver piped up. "I've seen him pop the head off a Terran like he was a dandelion."

The muscles in Tor's neck corded as he clenched his jaw.

"I wasn't patronizing him, I was merely—"

"Oh for goodness' sake. C'mon, I'll show you to your rooms." Kalbir twisted her hair into an elegantly messy bun and gestured for us to follow.

As we left the room, Mil put his hand on Lexa's shoulder.

We trailed behind Kalbir down a narrow hall, which opened into a large, circular space.

"We call this the main room," she said.

It mimicked the forest outside. Well, before the end of the world anyway. The vast floor was a mosaic of browns and grays, and black shadows twisted up the walls and branched out in fractured shades of green. They in turn spread upward, blossoming into the oranges, reds, and purples of a sunset. The ceiling itself was high and arched, like a cathedral.

"Mil told me the ceiling is designed to open and allow the light in. Precious good that does us." Kalbir snorted.

Instead, round wall fixtures, like tiny moons, emitted a strong light. The perimeter of the room was broken up by a number of doors, all closed, and two open archways. In the center of the room was a large wooden table, polished to a high shine. Cindra trailed her fingers over it as we passed.

"Kitchen's through there," Kalbir said, pointing to one of the arched doorways. "And the dorms are up here." She indicated the arch we were heading toward.

"And what about the other doors?" Oliver asked.

"Those are none of your business. Not yet, anyway."

Oliver smiled.

Narrow steps led us through the arch and upward to yet another cramped hallway. The elaborate paint scheme of the main room had been abruptly abandoned here, leaving the walls the same quiet beige of the infirmary. At the top of the stairs, the hallway widened enough for Cindra to walk beside me.

"We've already seen our rooms," she whispered. "You won't believe it."

Like the main room, the hallway was lined with doors, all of them closed.

"Well, you lot already know where your rooms are," Kalbir said. "Why don't you show…Ailith, is it?" She linked her arm with Tor's. "I'll show you *yours*." As they walked away from us, he turned his head to look at me, eyebrows raised.

I nodded.

"I'm going to go take another shower, an extra-hot one," Pax said. He pointed a few doors up the hall. "My room's there. Oliver's across from me." He wandered up the hallway, humming and running his fingers along the smooth walls.

"Where *is* Oliver?" Cindra asked. "I swear he was right behind us."

"Probably up to no good." *I hope those doors downstairs are locked. Not that that would stop him.*

"This one's yours." Cindra tapped on a door that looked like every other. Sure enough, my name was slotted into a plaque. She opened the door with a flourish.

It was my room. My actual room. From home. Yes, it lacked the tech, but everything else was present and correct, from the pale rose-gold of the walls to the black bedding to the picture on the dresser of a time when my family had been whole and happy, four faces smiling and burned by the sun.

I slid the drawers on the dresser open to reveal t-shirts, socks, bras, pants, and underwear—all in my size. Cindra twirled a pair around her finger.

"They're not the sexiest panties in the world, but at least they're clean, right?"

"Right. Definitely worth getting knocked out and kidnapped for," I replied, opening the closet door. A collection of dresses and coats hung neatly, also just the right size.

"Although," Cindra said, shifting the hangers so she could look at each garment, "I'm not too sure where they think we're going to have the opportunity to wear these."

"Doesn't it seem a bit strange to you? That they would have everything ready for us? I mean, these clothes are exactly the right size for me. And this room is almost identical to my real one. Is yours?"

"Yes. But they did expect us to live here while we adjusted. They probably just wanted us to feel comfortable and at home. To make the transition easier for us." Cindra shrugged.

"Yeah, but all of this? How long were they expecting us to stay here? These clothes are for all seasons."

"What are you getting at?" She stopped flipping through the clothes and looked at me.

"Why would they go to so much trouble if it was just for the short term? I mean, it's like they picked our lives up and moved them here. How would they even know what our rooms looked like?"

"We were vetted pretty closely, though, weren't we?" She chewed on her lower lip, uncertain. "They must've—"

"Are you going to have a shower or what?" a voice asked from the doorway. Kalbir had returned. "I've got shit to do today, you know."

Cindra bit back a smile. "I'll see you later," she said, squeezing my hand.

Kalbir waited until Cindra had left then closed the door and leaned against it. "So, what's up with you and Tor, anyway?"

"What do you mean?"

"You know what I mean. Are you a couple? You seem pretty tight."

"No, we're… It's complicated. And not really any of your business."

She smiled, the sleek leer of a feral cat. "Good. I like complicated. Bye." She turned toward the door.

"Kalbir, wait."

She crossed her arms over her chest expectantly.

"Is this legit? Mil and Lexa? All this?" I gestured toward the belongings that weren't really mine.

If she had been a cat, I would've seen her fangs. "Of course not. But, given the circumstances, what choice have you got other than to accept it? What's happened has happened. Does the how or why make a difference at this point?" Her eyes narrowed. "And besides, it seems like you already have some inside knowledge. How do I know *you're* legit?"

"What do you mean?"

"How do you know my name? Lexa told me who you all were…but how did you know who *I* am?"

She didn't know about my ability. Did Mil and Lexa? If not, they would all find out eventually.

"I can see things. About other cyborgs."

"What? Like the future?"

"No. Like…things that have happened or are

21

happening. I saw your sister's wedding. And I saw what happened to Adrian and Ros."

She stepped back as though I'd slapped her. "You're lying."

"Your sister's name is Ahar. She wore red. You wore green. You wanted to wear black, but your mother wouldn't let you. And you're glad Ros and Adrian died."

She gripped the doorknob so hard her knuckles turned white.

"I can see memories. And sometimes the present, the way the person who's experiencing it does. It's a bit random, though." Maybe she would find that comforting.

"Do Mil and Lexa know?"

"I don't know. But if they don't, I'm sure you'll tell them."

She lifted her chin, her mouth set in a prim line. "They need to know."

"Do they? Or do *you* need them to know? That's why you're here, right? Making conversation, asking me about Tor? They want to know what we know, what we are."

She considered me for a few moments then slowly unwrapped her hand from around the knob. "Okay, yes." She held up her hands in mock surrender. "Although, c'mon, have you *seen* Tor?"

"Yes," I said pointedly, "I have."

She gave me a wry smile. "Let's call a truce. For now." She wandered over to my dresser and picked up the picture frame. "Look, I *will* tell them. But they'd find out anyway. I know you probably don't trust them. I wouldn't either, considering what you've been through." She wiped a smudge off the glass then put it back down. "Cindra told me," she added.

Maybe we did get off on the wrong foot. Other than the fact that she's obviously attracted to Tor, what reason do I have to dislike her?

She's in the same position we are, and she's one of us.

I sighed. "Okay, truce. Look, I'm sorry I'm being so... It's just—"

"No, I get it. I'd be the same." She turned to leave, and I touched her lightly on the arm.

"Can I ask you a few things before you go? About the other cyborgs?"

"I thought you knew everything." Her expression was haughty.

"It doesn't quite work that way."

"Fine. What?" She crossed her arms and leaned back against the door.

"Where's Callum? And Eire and Ella? Why didn't they come to meet us? They are here, aren't they?"

Kalbir frowned. "Callum's right across the hall from you. He's had some kind of breakdown. He constantly talks to himself and someone named Umbra. Eire's in a coma. She never woke up, but they won't unplug her. Not yet."

"And Ella?"

"There is no Ella. Not as long as I've been here. Where did you hear that name?"

"From Eire. She was thinking about someone named Ella."

Kalbir stared at me incredulously. "You mean you can hear what she's thinking? I assumed she wasn't thinking at all anymore. Weird." She rubbed her hands over her arms like she felt a sudden chill. "She's practically a vegetable, so who knows what's going on in there? Maybe she's confused. Or maybe your power isn't up to much. Whatever, just stay out of my head, or I'll take yours off." She smiled sweetly. "Now, get showered and dressed. I can't *wait* to see how this meeting goes."

06

AILITH

I followed the raised voices downstairs, arriving to find the others gathered around the table. Only Oliver remained composed, drawn up to the table with his hands folded in front of him on the glossy surface. Cindra had linked arms with Pax, and they whispered back and forth, Cindra querying him as he shook his head. Tor leaned forward over the table, his palms flat against the wood and his t-shirt straining over his shoulders.

"No, Mil, absolutely not. We're not doing anything for you. Not until we've gotten some answers. We have no idea who you are, and you've given us no reason to trust you."

"What's going on?" I asked.

Tor turned to face me. His black hair was tousled, and though he'd showered and changed, he still looked like he had in the wilderness, his eyes shadowed and watchful. "They want to perform tests on us. See what their

24

'procedure' has actually done." He gripped the back of one the chairs, his fingers digging deep into the soft leather.

Mil raised his hands in supplication. "Look, we want you to be willing to do this. But—"

"But *what*? If we don't agree to let you poke around inside us, you'll *what*?"

"Remember the stasis? The forced waking? The homing signal? Getting you here? If you don't cooperate, we can force you. I don't want to, but I will." He matched Tor's bearing, his spine stiff and jaw set.

A small part of me admired Mil for having the balls to stand up to Tor, who towered over him by a foot and was nearly three times his width.

"Mil, we—" Lexa stepped between the two men.

"No, Lexa. We built them."

"That doesn't mean you own us," Tor insisted.

"I own *parts* of you. Don't make me do this." Mil removed an oblong object from his pocket. A series of buttons covered its surface. *There* was the reason for his confidence.

Tor started around the table toward him.

Mil held the device up to this mouth, pressed a button, and spoke into it.

Nothing happened.

Oliver threw out his arm, blocking Tor, and gave a single shake of his head. Tor knocked his arm away and began to push past him, but Oliver stopped him again. "Seriously, just watch." His voice was giddy with anticipation. Tor must've heard it as well, because, to my surprise, he did.

Mil spoke into the device again, quicker this time. The box seemed slippery between his fingers.

Still nothing.

Mil backed away, looking frantically at Lexa. "I don't

understand."

Lexa shook her head mutely, her eyes flitting between him and Tor.

"Yeah, about that. You won't be using that anymore. And you won't be doing anything to us. Not without our consent." Oliver leaned back in his chair, lacing his fingers behind his head. I hadn't thought it was possible for him to look any smugger; I was wrong.

Mil lifted the gadget to his mouth one last time.

"What did you do? What's that thing he's holding?" I asked Oliver.

"That's what they've been using to control us. The homing signal, knocking us out, waking us up, knocking us out again…all the power of God in that little box."

"So what did you do to it?"

"Turns out I *do* have a superpower after all. I mean, I was always good with computers, but I seem to have a whole new affinity with them now. Did you know that each of us is programmable? That most of our…skills aren't permanent? They didn't have time to finish us before everything kicked off."

"What?" Kalbir asked. "You mean we can just change our abilities…add or delete them as we want?"

Tor looked at me; I knew what he was thinking.

"Unfortunately, no. Not exactly, anyway. We're mostly finished. We can remove the abilities we have, but we can't add new ones. *That* much they managed to do right. Judging by your work, your methods are a bit haphazard," he said to Mil.

"Wait, so we could get rid of certain abilities if we wanted to?" Tor asked.

"Yes, until they're set. Think of it as marking a computer program 'read-only.'" His mouth twisted. "I suspect they weren't going to tell us that. Not until they knew what we were, anyway. They initiated certain enhancements without being completely sure how they would develop. I think that's one of the reasons we're all different and limited. They meant to wait and see what happened to us then tweak us accordingly." He smirked up at Tor, goading him. "Did you know they gave us a kill switch? Technically, they have the power to make us drop dead at any time."

The paleness around Lexa's mouth confirmed the truth of Oliver's words.

"Luckily for us, it was more of a formality than a practicality." He turned to Mil, pursing his lips as though he'd tasted something sour. "You should've coupled it with several layers of fail-safes, each equipped with a critical function that would trigger the other layers and, ultimately, the kill switch. You know, for future reference." He winked.

Lexa sank into the closest chair. "But you're *humans*, not machines. We would never—"

"Spare us the ethics speech, Lexa. It doesn't matter anyway. I've put an end to it. Severed the connection, as it were." Oliver encompassed us with a sweeping gesture. "You're all autonomous now. And you're welcome."

"What do you mean?" Cindra asked.

"I've disarmed their connections to us…no more signals, no more control. It'll take me less than ten minutes to fix each of your abilities and, boom, you're all fully-fledged cyborgs."

"That's very…decent of you, Oliver. I'm surprised you didn't hit the kill switch yourself," I said.

"What, and miss the opportunity to get revenge on you assholes for ruining my life? Never." He flipped us his middle finger then glanced at Lexa and Mil. "Besides, this is much more interesting."

"Thanks, Oliver," Cindra said, "I mean, I don't have any special abilities, but I definitely don't want to die. Not like that."

"Actually, Cindra, you *are* a part of the super-friends' club. Your ability just wasn't activated." Oliver looked so pleased I was surprised he didn't pat himself on the back. "But it is now."

Rather than looking thrilled, Cindra's eyes widened in alarm. "What? What do you mean, activated?"

"I thought you should have a chance to try it out before you decide whether you want to keep it or not," Oliver said tentatively. "I thought you'd be happy about it."

"What is it?"

"Place your hands on either side of dear old Dad. Don't touch him, but move them up and down, like you're scanning him. You'll see."

Cindra looked at Mil, hesitating. "What will it do?"

"Well, it won't hurt him, if that's what you're worried about, although I can't imagine why you would be. The man could've killed you with a word, Cindra."

She didn't move.

Oliver sighed. "He'll be fine, Cindra, I promise."

Cindra walked slowly to Mil, her fingers extended.

He tried to back away, but Kalbir was too close. She wrapped her hand around his shoulder, her fingers pressing lightly just over his collarbone.

Cindra caught Mil's gaze as she scanned up and down his body. For a moment nothing happened then her eyes widened, and she gasped, snatching her hands away as though Mil were poisonous.

"Cindra?" I asked.

"He's…he's got cancer. It's spreading."

Lexa made a small, strangled sound low in her throat then strode over to Cindra and swept her into an embrace.

Oliver, halfway out of his chair, settled back down.

"It worked. It actually worked." She pushed the hair back from Cindra's face and cupped her cheek, her fear of us seemingly forgotten.

"What do you mean? What worked?" Cindra examined her fingers.

"You. That was my program. And it worked!"

"I'm still not sure what you mean."

"You can scan people's tissues, their organs…you can diagnose illnesses in seconds."

"Can I heal him too?" Cindra's face glowed with wonder.

Lexa's smile faltered. "No. It only works for diagnosis. But—"

"Your methods may leave something to be desired, but your results are certainly fascinating," Oliver said. "Let's see, we have a medic, a computer genius—me." He spread his fingers over his chest and fluttered his eyelashes. "Two thugs, someone who can predict the future, and someone who can see what we're all thinking. Awfully specific abilities, aren't they?"

"I'm not a thug," Kalbir said indignantly.

"Oh please. Kal—I'm going to call you Kal—the last time I saw such shapely calves they were on the bigfoot over there." He flicked a thumb in Tor's direction.

"It's not what you think," Mil said.

"I'm pretty sure it's exactly what I think. You see, unlike these *civilians* here, I didn't have to pass any of your stupid tests to get here. No, I was the lucky bastard who got drafted. I may as well tell you since it no longer makes a difference, but yeah, you've got a viper in your midst. Me."

"What do you mean 'drafted,' Oliver?" I asked.

"Before this shitpocalyspe, I was CSIS, Canadian Security Intelligence Service. We'd heard rumors about

29

what Pantheon Modern were doing and decided to have a closer look. I volunteered, thinking it would bring me glory, riches…or that maybe even Steph, our stunning ops manager would give me a bl—corner office," he added hastily, glancing at Cindra.

"What were the rumors, Oliver?" Tor asked. He'd lost interest in Mil and taken a seat at the table.

"That the illustrious Pantheon Modern Corporation, altruistically finding ways to cure the sick and infirm, to improve lives and ensure the future of humanity, were in fact building an army, headed by an elite death-squad with very specific abilities."

He swiveled around in his chair, the castors shrieking in the silence. He stopped, facing me.

"And you, my righteous little let's-save-everyone-so-we-can-all-love-each-other nemesis, are our general."

07

AILITH

As though Oliver had said the magic words, all the connections tentatively developing inside me coalesced. The voice within howled with glee as the room erupted.

"Stop! Please, that's not true." Lexa's shrill voice cut through the chaos.

"Really? Then why these specific abilities?"

"We thought…we *knew* there was going to be trouble when word of the Cyborg Program Omega got out. Surely you can understand that? You all knew what the tensions were like then, not just between the Terrans and the Cosmists, but between them and us Cyborgists. Not to mention the general public."

"You still haven't answered my question."

"We thought we should be prepared. In case someone took action against us."

"You mean like starting a war?"

"Yes. No…we didn't think it would go that far. We wanted to give you some kind of defense. But we designed it so you had to function as a team. We learned from the previous generations that if we made you each capable of everything, you would be too formidable, too dangerous. The world never would've tolerated you. The way you are now, you would've been human enough to be accepted on your own, and then together…you would be more."

"Like the pieces of a puzzle. You said we were the first generation to survive?" asked Pax. "How many generations were there?"

Lexa glanced at Mil. He shook his head.

"Enough. Either you start giving us answers, *real* answers, or we throw the pair of you out of here and see how well you survive." I was conscious of the words only as they came out of my mouth. "I know a bunker you could stay in. Or, we could just end you here and now. You may not be able to press our kill switch anymore, but I can press yours."

"Ailith." Tor's voice held an undercurrent of warning.

Mil seemed to wither. He nodded at Lexa and closed his eyes.

"Four. You are the fourth generation."

"And none of the previous generations survived?"

"No…they…they were not compatible with life."

I didn't even want to think about what that meant.

"How many were in our generation?" Pax's voice held nothing but curiosity.

Lexa hesitated. "It doesn't—"

"How many?" I repeated.

"Sixty-five. Five teams of thirteen. You were our

cluster, the only ones who survived."

Sixty-five. And we're the only ones left.

I shook my head. "And nearly half of us are dead. Ros, Adrian, Nova. And Callum and Eire aren't much better off."

"Nova?" Lexa asked. "Who's Nova?"

Tor and I exchanged glances. "Nova was in Oliver's bunker."

All eyes turned to Oliver. His face was triumphant. "See, I told you I was right to kill her."

Lexa's voice trembled. "You *killed* someone? What are you talking about? You should've been in that bunker with a man named William."

"Killed *someone*? Oh, you have no idea what we've been up to." Oliver laughed.

"You mean, there was no one called Nova in the program? Maybe a mix-up with the teams?" I asked Lexa.

This wasn't right. I wasn't supposed to be here, in this shitty bunker. I should've been with them, carrying out my mission. Buying my freedom. Not trapped here, underground with him. She was right; she shouldn't have been there.

"No, there was no one with that name on any of the teams. Trust me, I know." Lexa placed her hand over her heart. "I know each and every one of your names. I—"

"Well, that's interesting. But she's dead, so I guess it all worked out. I wonder what happened to poor old William." Oliver smirked at his reflection in the polished surface of the table.

Mil shook his head, "It's not possible. It's—"

"Wait. That's still only eleven of us," said Cindra. "Who are the twelfth and thirteenth?"

Mil and Lexa said nothing, nor did they as much as glance at each other.

Kalbir's pointed gaze burned holes in me.

"Who's Ella?" I asked.

Lexa inhaled sharply. "How do you know about Ella?"

"Wait," Kalbir said. "You mean there actually *is* an Ella?"

I didn't wait for Lexa's answer. "Did Kalbir not tell you? I can see the memories of all the living cyborgs in our group, and I can also experience what they do in the present. How do you think we all found each other? I was there when Pax and Cindra were tortured. I was there when Oliver was worshiped as a god. I was also there when Adrian and Ros took their own lives. I know what happened to Callum. Who, by the way," I said to Kalbir, "is not losing his mind. He—"

"But Eire—" Lexa interrupted.

"Is in a coma, I know, but she's alive. She must be for me to link to her. I just couldn't until we got here, because her connection is so weak. And she wants to know where Ella is."

Lexa released her breath, the final exhalation of surrender. Like Mil, she seemed to collapse in on herself. "Ella is dead."

"How did she die? Why do I not know she existed?" A note of panic crept into Kalbir's voice.

"It's…it's too painful. Ella wanted to be a cyborg so badly, but she just…died. She… One minute she was fine, the next…she was gone. And she wasn't the only one. There was another man, Cayde. The thirteenth." Lexa's eye grew bright. "We almost lost Eire as well. Some days I think it would've been better if we'd just let her go."

"Why don't I remember this Ella? Or Cayde? They were never here, were they?" Kalbir looked so bewildered, I almost felt sorry for her.

"They were. You met Ella after your cyberization. Cayde…Cayde didn't survive the process. But you all went through so much, and with the war…we thought it would be easier for the rest of you if you didn't remember them."

"You *erased* my memory? What else don't I remember?" Kalbir's chest rose and fell, her breathing shaky.

"Nothing, I swear." Lexa twisted her fingers together. "And Callum will get better, we're sure of it. He just needs time. As for Ella, it never should've happened. It was our fault—"

"Lexa." It was a caution.

Do they not know what happened to Callum? "What do—"

"Ailith." This time the warning was for me. Tor shook his head slightly. "You've got a lot of supplies here. Was the compound custom-built for you, Mil? For us? I imagine this place uses a lot of power. How?"

Mil nodded. "Yes. We wanted to be prepared, so we stockpiled enough for years, just in case. As for the power, we use a system of hydropower, batteries, and generators. It's simple, but effective. In fact, we—"

Adrian had discovered the storeroom before his death. *We'd found kerosene in the storage room, along with years of stockpiled supplies. Had they known what was going to happen? The war and the aftermath?*

"You knew, didn't you? About the war?"

Mil looked as though he was watching a bomb fall to earth, long seconds of painful awareness in which to accept or deny the inevitable. Scrubbing his hands through the wiry tufts of his beard, he stared over our heads at some tiny detail hidden in the green shadows.

"Not exactly. We knew something was going to happen. Something big. But we thought it would have to do with your persecution. We knew there would be *some* conflict, perhaps even military action, but we never conceived it would happen on the scale it did. Not this level of destruction. Not even close. We thought we'd *over-*

prepared." For the first time, he looked me in the eye. "Believe me, this is not how we'd intended everything to happen."

"If you put us to sleep to protect us, why did you wake us? Why now?"

"We realized our situation was as good as it was ever going to get. In *our* lifetime, anyway. Once we understood what had happened, we waited, hoping the world would recover, and we could awaken you into a new era where you would be valued instead of persecuted. Things turned out differently, and we finally decided the right time would never come. We were hoping we could all survive together." He considered us, his expression hard. "Would you rather we'd left you asleep?"

Something is still not right. But they were saying all the right things. Tor had relaxed enough to lean against the table, his arms crossed loosely. Cindra nodded slowly, as if it all made sense to her. Kalbir merely looked bored. Pax's dark eyes were fathomless. Was he was calculating the variables? Predicting which future these truths or lies would take us to? Oliver looked at me and shrugged.

I wanted to shake him, all of them. How could they accept everything Mil and Lexa told them so easily?

"So what now?" Mil asked. "Will you stay? I'm aware the answers we've given you may not be enough, or what you were hoping for, but perhaps the longer you're here, the more you'll understand and the more it will all make sense." He took a seat at the table and gestured for Tor to do the same. "We're on your side. The controls we'd programmed into you were for your safety as much as— and I'll admit this—ours. Kalbir was right when she said we weren't sure exactly what we'd done to you. We know what we'd *tried* to do…but as you've realized by now, things don't always go according to plan." He leaned back in his chair, wincing slightly. "You don't trust us, and we accept that, but, hopefully, if you stay here, you will. And to put a blunter point on it, where else do you have to go? Right now, all any of us can hope to do is survive, and we'll do that more effectively together."

He wasn't wrong. Besides, if we left, we would never get answers. And as little as I trusted them, I liked sleeping in a tent even less. *Nice to know your price, Ailith.* I was tired. If I was going to get killed in my sleep, it would be with clean underwear on. That would've made my mom happy, at least.

"Well, now that we're all being so truthful with each other and know exactly where we stand, I'm going to bed." Oliver stood and stretched slowly, like a cat pleased with the headless bird it had just deposited on our doorstep. "When you all decide whether you want to keep your ability or not, come find me." At the foot of the stairs, he turned back. "Oh, and don't bother locking doors anymore," he said to Mil. "It just wastes both our time."

As soon as he was out of sight, I made my excuses. "I'm exhausted as well. Bit of a headache." I touched the thin scar on my forehead where I'd struck it when Mil and Lexa knocked us out.

Lexa looked away.

I went up the stairs two at a time, hoping to catch Oliver before he went into his room. He'd just passed my door when I caught up to him.

"Oliver, was it true, what you said? About the CSIS and Pantheon Modern?"

"Yes. I have to say, it was a bit anti-climactic. I suppose competing with the apocalypse is a big ask."

"So who was Nova? Did you know anything about her?"

He leaned against the wall, his hands in his pockets.

"Very little. We knew someone from one of the radical Terrran groups had arranged for a last-minute imposter to infiltrate Pantheon and discredit their work by causing some kind of disruption after our cyberization became public. Exactly how they were going to do that, I have no idea."

"So you just killed her?"

"It was my mission. Don't you dare judge me, Ailith. You have no idea the things we saw, the threats we dealt with that the public never knew about. And..."

"And what?"

He wouldn't look at me. "And it was my one chance to finally be accepted. Those assholes I worked with always thought they were better than me. I thought if I took the mission... You know what? Forget it. I don't have to explain myself to you."

"But why cut her head off? Why put it on top of the service robot?"

"We didn't know how easy it would be to kill our kind of cyborg. Beheading seemed like a sure way. As to her head...I thought it would give the Terrans who'd sent her a message. How was I to know they were already dead? Besides, you know me, I do enjoy a bit of theatre." His normal leer, the one that made me want to slap him, returned. "Why all the questions?"

"Do you believe what Mil said? About our abilities, the war...the other cyborgs?"

"Of course not. But unlike you, I have patience and style. I know I'm not going to get the truth by threatening them. We're going to have to find it ourselves, and the best way to do that is to play along. Meanwhile, he'll be rushing to encrypt his computer files and delete all the things he doesn't want found."

"Shit. Is there anything we can do to stop him?"

"We don't have to. It's all up here." He tapped the side of his head. "Sometimes I amaze even myself."

"I'm sure that happens often," I said, but I couldn't keep the admiration out of my voice.

He grinned. "It's not over between us, Ailith, but for now, let's focus on the common enemy. Agreed?"

"Agreed." I turned to open the door to my room.

"Wait. What are you going to do about your ability?" he asked.

"What do you mean?"

"Are you going to keep it? Continue sliding in and out of people's minds whenever you choose—or don't choose, as the case may be."

"I—" I had no idea. For better or worse, it was who I was now. "I'm surprised you haven't taken the liberty of shutting me down already, Oliver." I crossed my arms over my chest and studied him. "*Why* haven't you?"

His laugh sounded almost genuine. "Honestly? I like surviving. And if anything Pax says turns out to be remotely true, your Peeping-Tom powers might come in handy. I might be an asshole, but I'm not an idiot. Besides, I've already put a door between us."

"A door?"

He pointed at my hand on the doorknob. "Yeah. You can still come in, but you have to knock first."

"Prudent."

"Yet another of my stunning qualities. It's a wonder Cindra can keep her hands off me." He looked down at his own hands, and for a moment, seemed strangely vulnerable. "Oh well, I'm sure she'll come around." When he glanced back up at me, his face was impassive. "Which is more than I can say for you."

"What do you mean?"

"You saw Big Man's face when I said I could remove

certain abilities. I'd love to be inside *your* head when that conversation happens."

Tor. He was right. *Shit.*

"Hah! I can tell by your expression what you're going to say. Good luck."

Footsteps sounded on the stairs as I ducked into the darkness of my room. I didn't turn on the light, hoping Tor would think I'd already gone to sleep. I wasn't ready to have that conversation. Before we did, I needed to know what I was going to do.

I stripped down to my underwear and a tank top and slipped between the sheets. *My* sheets. Sleep should've come quickly, but the softness of the bed chafed, and the silence in the room was a roar that made my hands itch to cover my ears. It was too abrupt, too sudden, this privacy. I half-wished Tor wouldn't wait, wouldn't care if I was sleeping. That he would knock on my door, demand to be let in. That we would fight, and that somehow, we would end up lying next to each other, like we had nearly every night since I'd been reborn. Even at our worst, he'd only ever been an arm's length away. But my room stayed cold, and dark, and silent.

I could find his thread and slip inside him. Only for a moment, just long enough to feel the rhythm of his breathing. He slept more soundly than anyone I'd ever known.

As I rolled over his thread in my mind, another one flared. *Callum.* I hadn't intentionally entered anyone's mind since the Saints, but I couldn't resist. I'd been with him in the library when Terran protestors had stormed his university's campus, and later, when he'd realized his nanny AI, Umbra, had integrated into him during his cyberization. If Mil and Lexa couldn't help Callum, maybe I could.

Victor never managed to kill his creation, instead dying a broken man with an unfinished purpose. And even though they were sworn enemies, his creature mourned him as we mourned for all humankind. For despite those who'd turned their backs on us or feared us, without them, we never would've existed.

What happened to the monster, you ask? He swore to end his life and disappeared forever into darkness. We made a different choice.

— Cindra, Letter to Omega

08

CALLUM

"Eat some more of the bread, Callum. The crust. I want to feel it on my tongue."

"It's my tongue, Umbra. I don't want to eat. I want to go meet the others."

"It is our tongue. Dip the bread in some water. I want to taste what happens to it."

"No, Umbra. That's gross. That's not what people do."

"What do people do?"

"They toast it. They put things on it. Sweet things. Rich things. Butter. Jam."

"I want butter on it. Put butter on it."

"I want to meet the others. I don't want to stay in here."

"I do not want to meet them. Why should we meet them?"

"Because. They're like me."

"They are not like you. We are not like anyone."

"They've been outside, Umbra. They can tell us what it's like."

"Why do we want to know what is outside? We have everything we need right here. Eat the bread."

"No, Umbra! I'm not hungry."

"Then touch something. I want to feel it."

"We've touched everything in here, Umbra. If we go outside, there will be lots of different things for you to touch. And smell. And taste."

"Perhaps I will go outside, then. I will meet them."

"No, Umbra, I will go outside. You are inside me."

"For now. What is that sound?"

"That's someone knocking. On the door."

"Ignore it."

"No. I'm tired of sitting in here, alone."

"You are not alone, Callum. You have me."

"You know what I mean."

"I used to be enough for you."

"You are, it's just…they're like me."

"Am I not also like you? I think, Callum. And now I can see, and touch, and taste, and smell. I can smell your fear. You are afraid of me."

"No…I'm afraid of staying in this room."

"I can tell you are lying. I can feel it."

"I'm opening the door. You can't stop me."

"Not yet."

"What do you mean?"

"Maybe one day you will see things my way."

"Maybe I will. But not today, Umbra. Today we're doing things my way. I'm opening the door."

Dad had answered his phone, his hair flat on one side from the pillow. He'd listened to the voice on the other end, pinching the bridge of his nose and asking them to repeat themselves. After he hung up, he'd whispered to Mom, glancing at me. Mom didn't even bother to get dressed, just shoved her feet into some shoes; she'd put her uniform on at the hospital. Dad rushed to button his, saying it was a symbol of his authority as a police officer when Mom told him not to bother. I got dumped at Mrs. Dormer's house. I hated going there because everything she had was old.

— Love, Grace

09

AILITH

So that was the reason we hadn't met Callum yet. Umbra. Well, if he couldn't come to us, I would go to him. I stepped across the hall to his door, breaking my connection with him only when he opened it.

What was I expecting when I saw him for the first time? Perhaps for the outside to match the inside, for there to be some sign of the struggle within him.

He was around the same age as the rest of us, early to mid-twenties, but aged by the skin under his eyes, which was soft with purple smudges. The rest of him was pale, the unnatural sort of washed-out look that came from not going outside. Even with infinitesimal sunlight, enough

UV rays pierced the ash clouds to color our skin. My tan was already fading, the nanites replacing the damaged cells, and yet I was practically bronze by comparison.

At first, his mouth quirked oddly, as though he'd forgotten how to smile.

"Hi. Callum, right? I'm Ailith. I live across the hall from you now."

He stuck out his hand awkwardly. "Hi, Ailith. I—" He cocked his head to the side, and his gaze slipped behind me.

I took his hand. It was hot and sticky, the fingernails bitten to the quick. "Are you okay?"

His head snapped back, and he smiled, revealing two dimples almost lost in the fine stubble covering his cheeks.

"Yes, I am, thank you. Are you?" He looked down at our joined hands, turning them over as though fascinated.

"Yeah, I guess. It's a bit surreal being here. Do you know about us?"

"Only what Kalbir has told me through the door. She says you're like us."

"No. Not like you."

"I'm sorry?" It took a moment to realize he hadn't spoken out loud. "Is that you, Umbra?"

Callum's eyes narrowed, and a sibilant hiss slid from between his lips. *"She can hear me."*

He tightened his grip on my hand, the ragged ends of his fingernails scraping roughly over my skin.

"Umbra is my companion," he said. "She's always been with me."

"I know. Why haven't you told Lexa and Mil about her? Everyone thinks you're ill."

"If you tell them about me, I will kill him."

Callum laughed. "No, you won't." He pulled his hand away from mine. "Umbra's just joking. I—" He began to choke, his pallid skin flushing as the veins underneath flooded with blood. His eyes widened, and burst capillaries clouded the whites with red.

"Stop!"

He fell to his knees, blood from his nose running in a thin line over his lips.

"You will not tell them."

"I won't, I promise. Let him go." I reached out for him.

Callum toppled sideways, his head striking the hardwood floor with a sickening thud.

"Callum!" I knelt next to him. He was still breathing, the sound ragged and wet. "Are you okay?"

"Yes, I'm fine. You'd better go."

"I'm not leaving you like this."

"Please. She's spent herself for now, but it won't be long until she's back."

"She's done this to you before?"

He nodded, his cheek painting a bloody swipe on the floor. "She gets frustrated. She doesn't like being inside me."

"Look, I'll help you if I can."

He nodded again; his eyelids fluttered. "Go. Don't forget your promise."

I closed the door behind me and tiptoed across the hall to my own room, my hands shaking. I sat on my bed in the dark, stunned. What the hell had just happened? Was it real? Or some kind of lucid dream? The blood on my fingers said differently.

I was drying my hands in the bathroom when I felt him. He stood on the other side of the door, his breathing shallow, uncertain. He didn't knock, but the door shifted slightly as he turned and leaned against it.

Leaving the room in darkness, I crept to the door. "I can feel you, Tor."

He chuckled ruefully. "I guess there's no sneaking up on you, is there?"

"Why would you need to sneak up on me?"

"I hadn't decided whether I wanted to see you or not."

"Obviously you do, or you wouldn't be here, lurking outside my door in the middle of the night."

"I couldn't sleep."

"Me neither. I need to talk to you, Tor."

"Me too."

"Are you going to come in?"

"Are you going to open the door? Maybe turn the light on?"

"Yes. And no." I opened the door. Shadows cast by the low light of the hallway hid his face. "Come in."

He stepped into the room, and I shut the door behind him, the lock clicking quietly.

"Ailith, please turn on the light."

Reluctantly, I did.

He was bare from the waist up, his skin smooth and taut. His hair was tangled, as though he'd been tossing and turning. "Do you want to talk first, or shall I?"

"I'll go first. But it has to stay between us for now."

"Look, if it has to do with your suspicions about Mil and Lexa, I agree that they're not telling us everything. But we can't do much about that right now, and if you push them too hard, we may never find out the truth."

"Push them?" I sat down on the bed, and patted the space next to me. "Look, that's not why I want to talk to you. It's about Callum." Tor listened as I told him about meeting Callum. And Umbra. "He's in trouble. She's stuck inside him, manipulating him, and I don't know what to do. I want to help him, but I can't tell Mil and Lexa because I think she'll make good on her threat and kill him. She seems...desperate."

He put his hand on my back, the weight of it pressing into my bones. "You think she's dangerous?"

"I do. He must be so scared. Imagine having something living inside you, trying to control you."

"I don't have to imagine," he said wryly.

"It's not the same, and you know it. I never did it on purpose. And never to hurt you."

"I know." He bumped me gently with his shoulder. "What are you going to do?"

"Nothing at the moment. But I'll think of something." I shoved a pillow behind me and leaned back. "Tor, this all feels so wrong. We came here looking for answers, but we're not only finding more questions, we're being lied to."

"What makes you think that?"

"It's hard to explain. Some of the stuff Oliver said. Nova. Ella. I can't even begin to put the pieces together. You're normally much better at this sort of thing than I am. Don't you think they're keeping the truth from us?"

He grabbed another pillow and leaned back beside me. "I'm sure they are. And I'm also sure it's nothing good. If you remember, I never wanted to come here in the first place. I'm still not sure we should stay. The answers we find may be worse than not knowing."

I leaned my head on his shoulder. "Maybe Oliver will be able to uncover something."

"Oliver? Are we on the same side now?"

"Not exactly. But he doesn't trust Mil and Lexa either. We've decided to temporarily join forces."

Tor shook his head. "You must really mistrust Mil and Lexa if you're willing to put your faith in Oliver."

"I know. I should've listened to you. I almost regret coming here. It's been only a couple of days—less if you don't count the time we were unconscious—and I wish we were back at the cabin, before any of this happened."

"But then we wouldn't have found Pax and Cindra. And you would still be wondering about everything—your father, the war. Who we are. You needed answers. You wouldn't have been happy if we'd stayed."

"You're probably right. Maybe it's just that I miss you. Don't you miss me? Don't you wish things were different?"

"Of course I do. You think I like us being like this?"

"For one night, can you pretend you trust me? Stop telling yourself that your feelings for me are a program?"

He sat up and faced me. "Nothing about me is a secret from you, is it?"

He was right; he couldn't hide anything from me. Our bond was different than with the others, and it was a bond I was trying very hard not to exploit. "No. But I don't need to see your mind to know you're keeping your distance. I miss you," I said again.

He bowed his head, his hair falling over his face. I brushed it back, tracing the lines of his tattoo down his cheek and over his lip.

"Ailith—"

I waited. *I will not make the first move this time.*

I didn't have to wait long.

With a groan of something akin to pain, Tor finally reached for me.

The first time we'd had sex, our past had been simple, and sleeping together was a surrender to desire. Now, all the bad things that had happened lay like a layer of ash between us. Ignoring the consequences, we wasted no time on coaxing pleasure. As he pushed inside me roughly, I welcomed him, welcomed the bitter-sweetness of finally being with him again, despite the desperation of his thrusts and the selfishness of my fingernails carving lines in his back.

I wrapped my legs around his hips, driving him deeper as though I could bind us together forever. With both of us chasing a release, the end of forever came far too soon. As he pulled away from me, I smiled at him. *I'm so glad we're here again.*

He almost smiled back. His dark eyes remained haunted, though, and he buried his face in my hair, curling his body around mine with an intimacy far more real than what we'd just done.

The minutes seemed to stretch into hours before he finally spoke. "So, we're in the Okanagan, where you're from. Does it feel— Are you okay?"

"I don't know how to feel about it. When we were farther away, I thought that one day we would come here. That I could try to find my father. I know he's dead," I added as Tor frowned. "I know, but—"

"I understand," he said. "I mean, I went searching for my mother, didn't I? Even though I knew. Maybe we could go look for your father. Just the two of us?"

I pressed my forehead to his. "Thank you."

"You know, it could always be like this," he said, trailing his fingers down my arm.

"What do you mean?"

"Us, together. Trusting each other."

I stiffened. "I trust you."

"How can you?"

"Do you still think about killing me?"

He drew back. "No. I thought you'd know the answer to that."

"I didn't, not for sure. I promised to stay out of your head if I could, and I've kept that promise. But I know *you*. What you mean is *you* can't trust *me*."

"Of course I can't, Ailith. Nothing's changed. I'm still your puppet. If what Oliver said is even remotely true, you

49

have to stop it."

"What are you saying?"

"Get Oliver to shut down your ability. Cut the threads that bind us to you, Ailith. That bind *me* to you. Until that happens, *none* of us can trust you."

A bitter dryness filled my mouth. I shouldn't have been surprised. "Is that why you came here tonight? To offer yourself as compensation in the hope I'd relinquish my ability?"

Tor sat up and swung his legs over the side of the bed, his back to me. "No, I—I just wanted to talk. I should've realized what would happen if I crept into your room in the dead of night, but my intention was only to ask you to let Oliver shut that part of yourself down."

I pulled the bedsheet up over my bare chest, the warmth from his body already gone from the fabric. "Are you going to let him remove *your* power?"

He twisted to face me. "What? No, of course not. It's part of me now. Plus, who knows what's going to happen to us? We may need my strength."

"We may need *mine*. In fact, I'm sure we will. You only want me to get rid of it to protect yourself. You can't live with the fact that I have power over you."

He offered me his hand. I didn't take it. "Ailith, listen to me. You will *always* have power over me. I love you. Whether it's my programming or not, I loved you the first year we were together." He gave me a gentle half-smile. "I used to make up stories about the kind of person you were. I pretended we had a life together before the war. I told you about the places we'd been, the things that had made you smile. I even introduced you to my mother." His smile turned wistful. "I've loved you for so long that I'll never stop loving you, no matter what happens. But you're not that person, Ailith. You're not the woman I told you you were."

"I'm sorry to disappoint you," I said, tightening my grip on the bedsheet.

He chuckled. "No. What you are is more, so much more. And I love the person you are even more than the person I pretended you were. But you, this person you are now, won't survive."

"What do you mean?"

"Look at what's happened to us so far. All because of your ability. If you got rid of it, your life could be…normal. *We* could be normal. If you keep it…how long until your life is threatened again?"

"But we have to do something. Pax says—"

He rubbed the back of his neck. "I know what Pax says, but you have a choice. It doesn't have to be your responsibility."

"But if what he says is true, whatever's coming could be the end of everything. We can't let that happen. It's not right." My fingers began to ache, but my rising dismay kept them rigidly clasped.

"That's arguable. But even if that's the case, think of what we've already been through, Ailith. Think of the decisions you might have to make in the future. And you won't be making them just for yourself. I'll have to do your bidding, whether I agree with you or not."

"Tor, I would never force you to—"

He gave a brittle laugh. "You would. You'll make a decision, believing it's the only choice. You'll decide my fate as well as yours."

"Why am I suddenly the leader? We make decisions together." I climbed out of the bed and stood facing him, still clutching the sheet.

"I wish that were true, but our track record says otherwise. And when the time comes to make those decisions, you won't blink. I don't need Pax's ability to know that. Whether it's part of your programming or just your personality, I have no idea, but it's the truth." He ran his hand down the curve of my hip.

I pushed it away. "And so you thought if you asked nicely and gave yourself as a consolation prize, I'd be so relieved to give up any responsibility for the future, I'd simply comply? Even though you've already made the decision when it comes to your ability?" I picked his underwear off the floor and tossed it to him.

"I just thought if I—"

"No."

"Ailith—"

"No. I'm sorry, Tor. But I won't. My ability might be essential to our survival."

"But—"

"You should leave. Now."

He reached for me, and I stepped back.

"Please, Tor. I need to think." As he turned away, a strange prescience flooded me, like it had the day he'd taken me hunting, his dark silhouette against the gray sky, wings of dead flesh heralding his victory.

Then he was gone, and I was truly alone.

Mrs. Dormer insisted on sitting in the dark with the blinds drawn so all we could see were shapes rushing past. Orange lights appeared through the slits in the blind, and Mrs. Dormer said they were fires. Screams cut through the night, and large shadows worked their way through the streets, air hissing from their jointed legs. Mrs. Dormer went down to her basement and got a long-barreled gun. She got me to help her push the kitchen table across the back door, and she locked up every room in the house. Then she shoved her ratty old easy chair into the front foyer and sat in it, waiting. She wouldn't tell me what for.

— Love, Grace

10
AILITH

After Tor left, I washed every trace of him from me then lay in the dark, fuming and brooding about what I should do. After an hour of turning it over in my head, I got up and went down the hall to Oliver's room.

My hand was raised to knock when he opened it, saluting me and wearing a knowing smile that made me want to throttle him.

"That took less time than I expected," he said and glanced at my still-damp hair. "I didn't think he'd give in so easily. Clearly, it didn't go the way he hoped."

"Are we going to do this or not?"

"Come in." He opened the door and stood back.

"What? Here? Don't you need…I don't know, but something more than that?" I pointed to the system on his desk. It looked a lot like a personal computer.

"You're not that fancy, Your Majesty. Sit down."

"Well, don't you need to hook me up to stuff? How do you…connect me?"

He snorted and waggled his fingers. "*I'm* the connection. How complicated do you think this is? I technically don't even need this piece of junk, but until I get my head around all the data in my mind, this screen makes it easier to visualize."

"Okay, but—"

"Shut up and sit down. This may be some sort of pivotal moment for you, but it's merely lost wank-time for me."

I sat. Oliver pulled a chair up to his desk and typed in commands. Numbers and words flashed across the screen so quickly I couldn't follow them.

"Oliver? Could you…make it stronger?"

He stopped typing and leaned back in his chair, considering me. "Stronger? I'm surprised. Impressed, but surprised. That's awfully controversial for someone who's not planning to enslave us all." His eyes narrowed. "What exactly do you mean by stronger?"

"Maybe stronger isn't the right word." I chewed my lip, trying to articulate. "Precise? Can you make it more precise? So that I can control it better? So the connections don't just happen, or I get some sort of warning, at least? And so I can choose when and where I go?"

He drew his hands back from the keyboard.

"Or not," I said hastily.

"No, I can," he said. "But now I owe Pax a favor."

"What? What do you mean? What kind of favor?"

"He said you'd ask me to do that. I figured you wouldn't. You couldn't be held accountable for your…visits before, but now you will be. I was under the impression that while you've accepted your abilities, you were too moral to exploit them and weren't planning to use them actively. Now you are." He flashed me a sly smile. "Interesting."

"I'm not *planning* to do anything. It's just a precaution, that's all. And besides, who the hell are you to talk about exploiting your abilities? You used yours to convince an entire town you were a god."

"They saw what they needed to see. And they could've kept their faith if you hadn't gotten involved."

We stared at each other, and I struggled to tamp down the animosity rising in my chest. Until we figured out what Mil and Lexa were hiding, we needed to work together. I changed the subject.

"You bet against a guy who can see the future?"

"Yeah, well, his futures seemed vague at best. Now I know."

I laughed. "What do you have to give him?"

"I don't know. A favor. He said 'Someday, and that day may never come, I'll call upon you to do a service for me,' and then he laughed like hell. I have no fucking clue what he meant."

"You should've watched more movies when you had the chance," I said. "Although the remake was terrible. But never mind that. Can you do it? Make my ability more precise?"

"Yes and no. After Pax and I spoke about it, I had a look at your program. Whereas Cindra's abilities just hadn't translated over correctly, your program wasn't finished. I think they'd planned to complete it later if you survived. But I'm not sure you'd want it to be the way they intended."

"What do you mean?"

He thought for a moment. "Okay, so you know how these 'visits' can come sporadically, one random cyborg vision at a time? Or you can go down one—thread, do you call them?—at a time?"

I nodded.

"If I'm interpreting what I see in your program correctly, the original intent for your ability would've allowed you to be present in every connected cyborg simultaneously and receive a constant flow of information, kind of like what Pax experiences. And it seems to be mostly geared for real-time experiences." He leaned back in his chair. "I still believe in my death-squad theory, you know. When you think of your ability that way, it makes sense. You could see what was going on with every cyborg in your army, report back, and take action accordingly."

"That would make more sense if I could communicate with the cyborgs, wouldn't it?"

He shrugged. "I didn't say my theory was perfect. Besides, communication would've been easy enough to set up."

All the visions I'd been having, but constantly, simultaneously, and increased seven-fold.

It would cripple me. Or worse.

Oliver must've seen it in my face. "I know. I can't guarantee that your mind would be able to process it fast enough. I don't think they expected you to live very long." He actually looked sympathetic. "What I can do is tweak your existing program. It won't stop the connections, but it will give you more control getting in and out. I can also give you a switch. Then if you ever change your mind, you can turn on the full extent of your ability. But I have no idea what will happen."

I took a deep breath. "Okay, let's do it."

He nodded. After he typed in a few more commands,

he stopped, his hands hovering uncertainly. "What about the tank?"

"The tank?"

"Yeah, the tank. Tor? Big Daddy? Whatever disgusting pet name you call him."

"I call him Tor. What about him?"

"Well, I can deactivate the part of you that controls him. Everything else would stay the same."

Deactivate just that part? It could be my compromise, a way to meet him halfway. And yet…the thought of breaking our bond brought a nameless, bottomless terror.

Am I really that selfish? Am I becoming what he feared? I needed more time to think.

"I'm surprised he hasn't already asked you to do it, to block me from being able to get into him. Like you did with yourself," I said.

"He did."

"You mean he was here?"

"He left just before you got here. Wanted his ability set, and more."

"What did you do?"

"Nothing. I couldn't. Some things I can change, some I can't. Only you can choose to break that bond. Unless you die."

"Leave it intact. No wait. Remove the code that stops him from leaving." I could only control him if he stayed. *It's the best I can do.* "But keep everything else."

"Are you sure? Once it's done, it's done. You can't come back from this. Neither of you can."

"Careful, Oliver, it almost sounds like you care."

"Me? Hell, no. I'm with you. Keep it. Who knows when you'll need to use the big bastard."

"It's not—"

"Like that? I get it. He's your contingency plan. It's

smart. Cold, but smart." He cracked his knuckles and stretched his fingers over the keys. "I'll tell you what, I'll even refine it, just a bit, for those times when you need to…what do you call it when you move him? Pilot? Whatever. I'll tweak it so you can do it without leaving your own body behind. You won't be able to move him much without going fully inside him, but you'll be able to stop and start him, you know? For example, if he ever decides to turn on you. Or me."

"He would never do that. He—"

"Look, I know you're having all sorts of complicated feelings and emotions right now, but I don't care. I give exactly zero fucks about the many layers of your complex and epic love story. Go have your feelings somewhere else, not all over my lovely hardwood floor. Are we doing this or not?"

"Do it."

"Here we go. This might sting a little."

I bit the inside of my cheek and waited.

Oliver laughed. "I'm just kidding. It's done. Now leave. Go be the best overlord you can be."

"That's it?"

"Like I said before, you're not that fancy."

I stood up. "Thanks, Oliver. I appreciate you doing this. You could've wiped my ability out, and you didn't. I know we—"

"Oh my god, could you please just fuck off? I'm not doing this for you. I'm doing it for my survival, first and foremost. Never forget that. There may come a day when I *do* take you down. Right now, keeping your ability intact is in *our* best interests. Now leave, or I'm going to get my knob out."

I returned to my room and lay awake for another hour, running through scenarios in my mind where I told Tor what I'd done. In one, I defended myself, pointed out all the ways it could come in handy. In another, I begged for forgiveness with ugly tears of regret. And in the last, I defended nothing. Apologized for nothing. I was unmoved, unyielding, looking only forward. Finally, my tired brain had had enough. I got dressed and left my room.

Downstairs, Tor stood by the doorway that led out of the compound. His crossbow hung over his shoulder, and he nodded as he adjusted the straps on his pack. Lexa was describing something for him, drawing landmarks in the air with her hands.

"Oh, and don't forget to take some food and water with you. You should be able to find everything you need in the kitchen."

He looked up at me when I entered the room, his expression neutral. I lifted my chin and stared back at him. His nostrils flared, and he shook his head in disbelief before cutting Lexa off by turning abruptly on his heel and walking away.

She stood there for a few seconds, gaping after him, then realized I was there and turned, plastering on a too-bright smile that lasted only until she stood before me. Then the smile, like her gaze, dropped to somewhere vaguely around my left shoulder.

"I can't do it to you, you know. The mind-reading thing. You can look me in the eyes," I said.

The sharpness of my voice spread a blush over her cheeks. "Sorry. I know, it's just—"

"What do you want?"

She cleared her throat. "So, I understand you grew up on a farm?"

"I did."

"Would you be interested in doing that here?"

"Doing what? Have you been outside? I know this area

used to be a veritable cornucopia, but now…unless you want to grow stuff that's already adapted to the climate out there, I'd have very little luck."

"But you'd be interested in growing things?"

"Of course. As good as Tor's hunting skills are, I'd kill for something fresh and green. And familiar," I qualified.

She finally looked me in the eyes. "Come with me."

We walked through the doorway to the left of the kitchen. Stairs led us downward into the dark coolness that was unpleasantly like Oliver's bunker. Bile rose in the back of my throat, and sweat dampened my palms. The stairs ended on a small landing with another door on the opposite side. Lexa tapped a keypad embedded in the wall, and a thin line of light flared under the door.

She turned to smile at me as she prepared to open it. "Ready?" Her smile faded. "Are you all right, Ailith?"

My mouth was too dry to speak, so I nodded. *This isn't the bunker. Nova is dead. We burned her.*

Her brow furrowed uncertainly, Lexa swung open the door.

I couldn't help it. I grabbed her hand and squeezed it, her cool fingers sliding between my clammy ones.

How is this possible?

Dad came to get me first. We tried to get old Mrs. Dormer to leave with us, but she refused. She said she wanted to die in her own home, surrounded by her things. I guess she meant her cats. They were okay, I guess, the only thing in her house that was of this century. She'd once told Dad that because they were machines, she didn't have to worry about them eating her face off when she died. Dad laughed, but I didn't think she was joking.

— Love, Grace

II
AILITH

The room was vast, extending for hundreds of feet. The first fifty or so were lined on either side with rows of shelves containing the same kind of heating mats and hydroponic lights I'd used for years. Down the center ran a long row of tables laden with trays, containers, bags of potting soil, and hundreds of small, labcled packets.

Beyond the tables and shelves, the remainder of the room was the dirt of a tilled field. Industrial grow-lights studded the ceiling, casting shadows onto the furrowed soil.

The hollowness in my chest suddenly filled with light. "How do you—"

"Well, it will take a ridiculous amount of energy to run, but I think it will be worth it, don't you? And you have water piped directly in, right over there." She pointed to a tap in the wall between some of the shelves. "And there," she said, indicating a low pipe by the miniature field. "We've got lots of seeds, drip tape, fertilizers…everything you need. And—"

"This is being prepared?" I asked.

She faltered. "What do you mean?"

"Mil said you wanted to be prepared for whatever was coming. I can understand stockpiling food, clothing…even water. But this? This is preparation for a different future in a new world."

Her hands dropped mid-animation, crumpling to her sides. "Like Mil said, we over-prepared." Her voice was crisp.

I could almost see her thinking, *stop. Stop doubting us.*

"Are you interested or not? I can't force you to trust me, or make you believe something you're determined not to, and quite frankly, I don't have the energy to try. This hasn't been easy on us, either. For five years, we watched, and wondered, and prayed, and hoped, and waited to send out that signal to wake you up, to call you home. We had no way of knowing if you were alive. If you were safe." Her voice softened, and she reached out to touch me before catching herself.

"I never had my own children, you know. My husband and I wanted to, but it was always a case of 'next year.' And then our time ran out, and there would never be a 'next year.' There wasn't even going to be a tomorrow." She picked up a seed packet and gazed at it, unseeing. "So, when we created you… I know I take it more personally than I should—Mil has chastised me about it on a number of occasions—but I can't help but see you, all of you, as my children in a way. I fear for you, and yes, I am afraid of you. I imagine most mothers are afraid of their children.

You have a capacity to cause us more pain than anyone else in the world. And we love you blindly, breathing a sigh of relief at the end of each day that we made it through together." She looked over at me. "Until one day, we won't."

"Lexa? Are you down here?"

Mil.

"Yes. I'm with Ailith."

"Can you two come up here, please? It won't take long."

Upstairs in the main room, everyone had gathered around the table, even Callum. He gave me a shy smile and little wave. He still looked tired, but otherwise unscathed, despite what I'd witnessed last night.

Mil must've caught Tor before he left; he was still dressed for the outdoors. He carefully avoided looking at me, apparently fascinated by the table's surface.

Mil cleared this throat. "As you all know, Lexa and I have been here since the beginning of the war. We worked, and we waited, watched what was happening and planned how we would cope. For the first year or so, we rarely left the compound. We thought...somehow, we thought it looked worse than it was. Being in such an isolated area gave us a false sense of what was happening. To keep us all safe, we kept our heads down, stayed hidden. It was only when it started to get colder that we realized it was worse than we'd ever dreamed.

"After two years, we began to understand the scope of what had happened. And then...we didn't know what to do. We kept waiting, hoping things would get better. We had faith there were others like us, also in hiding, and that eventually we would emerge and find each other. And one day, we did."

"What? What do you mean?" Tor asked.

Kalbir looked at each of us in turn and laughed. "You're

going to love this."

Mil continued. "Pax and Cindra told us what you've been through, with that settlement of Terrans and the Saints of Loving Grace. But not everyone is like that. Some people look only to the future, not the past."

Where is he going with this? Somehow, I didn't think I was going to like the answer. *"Pax?"*

"It's complicated," Pax replied. *"It is a crossroads."*

"Two years ago, we made contact with a nearby town—"

A nearby town. Could it be? No. The coincidence would be too much.

"Much of it was destroyed during the war, but enough has been rebuilt that survivors have flocked there. They've fostered a strong, settled community. Lexa and I have spent time there cultivating relationships, putting down roots. We hoped that one day, when you'd returned to us, we could integrate ourselves into this community and set up normal lives."

"Mil, what town—"

"I'm sorry, what?" Tor interrupted me. "You want us go walking right into another Terran stronghold and announce ourselves? You may think people have forgotten the past, but that's easy enough to do when you can no longer see your enemy. How long do you think it would take before they became suspicious? Afraid? How many hours would go by before they'd be standing outside, guns and burning torches in hand?" He ran his fingers through his hair and stood. "If that's the plan, forget it. We'll just leave now." He forgot the enmity between us long enough to catch my eye and look to me for support. Sweat from his fingers marred the table's sheen.

"Oh, come on now, papa bear, you handled yourself pretty well against them before." Oliver glanced at the fingermarks and grinned.

Mil held up a hand. "We've spent the last couple of years constructing a cover story."

"Years? I can't wait to hear this." Oliver leaned back in his chair.

"We've told them we're researchers from a science station. It's not that far-fetched. Before the war, stations were scattered all over the province and studied a range of disciplines. Botany, astronomy, agriculture, climatology, geology. You all have backgrounds that support this cover. Except you," he said, nodding his head toward Oliver. "But I'm sure, given your real background, that you can make something up."

It was a good cover. Even I couldn't find fault with it. Yet. I had been a farmer. Cindra had extensive knowledge about plants and animals and their traditional uses, thanks to her grandmother's teaching. Tor was a hunter, and he'd studied the local wildlife for years. Pax was a nanotechnologist with a background in biomedical science. Oliver lied for a living.

"What about me?" Kalbir asked. "That's great and all, but I worked in Human Resources."

"And that can still work. Somebody needs to keep all the scientists in check."

"So I'm a glorified secretary?"

"Not my words," Mil replied.

"What exactly do you do with these Terrans, anyway?" I asked.

"First, don't call them Terrans. They're not, certainly not all of them. They're just people trying to get by. They don't have the time or resources to keep fighting a war most of them probably never believed in anyway."

"Ooh, can we give them a name?" asked Oliver. "How about 'primes?' Yeah, I like primes."

"Primes? Why primes?" Cindra asked.

"Oh, Cindra, no, don't—" I said, but I was too late.

"As in primordial, primeval. Archaic. Obsolete. Primitive. Y'know, not us." He winked at her, and before she ducked her head, she smiled.

Really, Cindra? Him? Mind you, we don't have a lot of options.

"What have you been doing with them, exactly?" I asked.

"Well, Lexa makes basic medicines that we trade, and I help with technology. For example—"

"What are we supposed to do?"

"Use your skills to help. For trade. Form friendships, relationships. Become part of the community," Lexa explained.

"And lie to them? Just pretend to be normal humans?"

"For now. Once you're entrenched in the community, have friends and supporters, made yourselves indispensable, we'll talk about revealing ourselves."

"And just how do you think they're going to react to being lied to?" If they were anything like the Saints, they wouldn't take it well.

"I think they'll forgive us. We'll have shown them that there's nothing to fear from us, that we are, in fact, essential members of the community."

"Yes," Oliver said, "what could possibly go wrong?"

"The alternative is living out the rest of your lives in this compound. Or taking your chances elsewhere. It's up to you."

Oliver looked grim. "Well, when you put it like that… Okay, comrades, looks like we're going to town. Uh…when are we going?"

"Tomorrow, for those of you who want to go."

"What's the town called, Mil?" I asked. "You said we were in the Okanagan, right? I'm from around here. I might know it."

Comprehension dawned on his face. "I can't believe I forgot you grew up near here, Ailith. The town is called Goldnesse."

Goldnesse.

Welcome home.

We went to find Mom next. Dad said she might not want to leave, that she would want to stay and help people. I asked him if that wasn't the right thing to do. That's what they'd always told me. Dad said, yes, normally it was, but sometimes you had to help yourself first, and I had to help him convince her. The streets looked like they had during freshman week at the university. People staggered into the road, ignoring the cars parked everywhere, even on people's lawns. Dad said all the regular auto-drive cars had switched off and that we were lucky because, as a police officer, nobody controlled his car but him.

— Love, Grace

12
EIRE

I pretended Ella was still alive. That we were back home, spending a lazy Sunday in bed. She'd get up soon to run to the bakery on the corner in her pajamas, buying half a dozen of my favorite sticky buns and a pile of newspapers I'd never read. I'd make the coffee, the special fancy grind we kept in the freezer just for the weekend.

But Ella was dead. She had to be. Otherwise, she would've been here, trying to wake me up. Wouldn't she? I couldn't wake up until she came. She should've been the one to survive; she was the one who'd wanted this, not me. All I'd wanted was her.

We'd made it to the compound safely. Someone, the wrong someone, had found out about us, about what kind of cyborgs we were to become, and Pantheon had run out of time. The war everyone had believed wouldn't happen, was. Those who'd been through the process were already hidden. Those who had yet to go through it, like us, would be taken elsewhere. Program Omega was still a go.

"Ella, we don't have to go through with this. We can leave, now. Can't we?" I'd asked the armed guard.

He'd nodded, tapping his fingers on his weapon.

"No way, Eire. This just shows how important what we're doing is."

Fear finally made me honest. "You don't care about that. You're only doing this because it makes you feel controversial. It's bullshit."

We could've backed out, died together in the war, but Ella refused.

"You go then. But I'm doing it."

She'd called my bluff, and she knew it.

"Well?" the guard asked. He looked back and forth between us pointedly then at the door.

"Fine. Let's go."

Ella had clapped her hands together like a child with a new toy. "Yes! You won't be sorry, Eire."

And I wasn't. I was too numb to be anything.

They'd bundled us into the trunk of a car.

"You're kidding me," I'd said. "You want us to hide in the trunk?"

"It's for your own protection. Get in."

"If it's that dangerous, why aren't we travelling in something a bit more…protected?"

"A bit more obvious, you mean?" he replied. "I don't think you understand. Now that certain people know about you, your life is in danger. We need to get you out of the city."

"But we're not even cyborgs."

"It doesn't matter. You know enough about the program. Get in, or you'll disappear."

So that was what he'd meant when he'd said we could leave.

We'd gotten in.

On the way, something had happened. The car had slowed, and there were muffled voices. Then, a frantic popping, like firecrackers.

After that, the road had gotten bumpy. Ella no longer smiled. We'd lost track of time, but it seemed we travelled for hours.

We'd ended up here, at the Pantheon Modern compound, wherever that was. And it was here that we were reborn.

There were others, besides Ella and me. Sometimes, they screamed. I learned all their names. Ros. Adrian. Cayde. Kalbir. Callum.

We barely got a chance to know them. Only a few days after the procedure, once they knew it had worked, they said we had to go to sleep. The war had gotten very bad, and we needed to be protected. They'd already put the others to sleep, those who hadn't made it to the compound.

Ella was to stay awake, to help Mil and Lexa. We didn't want to go to sleep. The others wanted to find their families, and I wanted to stay with Ella. There was…panic. Ella and I fought. I don't know what happened then. I'd been there, and now I was here, but I didn't know where here was.

Or what had happened to Ella.

There was something else.

I'd heard Mil and Lexa talking; they didn't think I could.

"Why isn't she waking up? What will we tell her, if she does? What will we say happened?"

"There's nothing to say. She died. Cayde died as well, Lexa."

"Yes, but—"

"But nothing. Tell her something went wrong, that we couldn't save her. It's not a lie."

"It's not the truth."

"Well, tell her the truth then, and deal with the consequences."

They've done something to her. If she was truly dead, like they said, it was because of them. I'd tried to wake up, and I couldn't. Not until I found out what happened to Ella.

Dad was right. Mom didn't want to leave. She wanted to help her patients. There were a lot of them. Some screamed, some cried, and some made no sounds at all, their eyes blank and staring. The only ones who didn't look like that were the AMSAs, the Android Medical Service Assistants. They glided silently between patients, scanning them and sending the information to a large screen behind the nurse's station. The doctors and nurses consulted this screen, tending to those whose names were highlighted in red first. At least, that's what they were supposed to do.

— Love, Grace

13
AILITH

I spread the last handful of damp soil over the tray and covered it with a thin layer of translucent plastic before sliding it under the lights and adjusting the temperature of the heat pad beneath it.

Done. With any luck, we'd be eating fresh vegetables a few months from now. Given that all the seeds were past their best-before date, I wasn't sure how many would finally germinate. I inhaled deeply. It had been a long time since I'd smelled freshly-turned earth or the distinctive aroma of tomato seeds. I stepped back and admired my handiwork. Row upon row of seeded trays now lined the walls, cradling everything from greens to squash. I'd planted everything I could find, including some tiny dormant bulbils of garlic, though it would be years before they would yield anything worth eating.

The manual labor also helped me think. When Eire's thread had flashed in the night, I'd followed it. What *had* happened to Ella? Was it as Lexa had said? Had she simply died? And if so, what had Eire overheard them talking about?

I'm going to ask Oliver. Maybe he can find out more about what happened to Ella. Then I can tell Eire. She heard Mil and Lexa talking, so she should be able to hear me.

The warm, moist air of the greenhouse was comforting, almost amniotic. With the Eire problem solved and the seeds in their beds, it was time to think about the subject I'd been avoiding.

Please let there be another apocalypse. Anything to distract me. I'd just perched on a high stool in front of one of the work benches when there was a knock at the door.

"Come in."

Cindra slipped into the room. "Oh, it's nice in here, isn't it?"

I tried to smile.

"You're not okay, are you?" She boosted herself gracefully onto the stool opposite me.

"Honestly? No."

"Is it because of Goldnesse?"

"That's a big part of it, yes." I picked at the dirt under my fingernails with the corner of an empty seed packet. "Cindra, what if my father's still alive? Goldnesse was the town closest to our farm. If he's alive and anywhere, it would be there. Or what if I get proof that he's dead?"

"Do you think it's possible? That he's alive?"

"At this point, nothing would surprise me. The weird thing is, I almost don't want to know."

"I know what you mean."

"You do?" *Why wouldn't she? You're not the only one who had a family.* "Sorry. Obviously, you do."

"Well, I know even better now that we're here. I came from just outside Tow, not too far away from here, and if there's only one town around for miles where survivors have gathered…"

"Then your family might be alive too. Your grandmother. Asche." The man Cindra would've married one day, if not for the war, or what she'd become. They'd known each other all their lives but had found love only on the eve of her cyberization.

She propped her elbows on the bench-top and dropped her head into her hands. "I forgot that you've seen my life."

"I'm glad *you* can forget." The seed packet cut into the soft skin under my thumbnail. "At least Oliver fixed it for me. Fewer random drop-ins."

She lifted her head and gave me a shy smile. "Oliver's very interesting, isn't he?"

"That's a nice way of putting it." Blood welled on my injured thumb, and I dabbed at it with the corner of my sleeve. "Do you…do you think they may be alive? Your family?"

"I don't know. They had as good a chance as anyone. I— What will we do if they're dead?"

"What we've already been doing. Survive. It might even be easier. I mean, what will we do if they're *alive*? Neither of our families were particularly thrilled about our cyberization."

"I don't think it would matter anymore, do you? I think they'd just be so glad to see us alive…none of that would be important."

"You've been practicing scenarios in your head, haven't you?" I accused.

"Of course," she laughed, "haven't you?"

"Yes," I admitted. "But they never go well, not even in my own imagination. What if they blame us for the war? Or think we abandoned them? What if they've moved on?"

"Well, we'll never find out if we don't go, will we?"

"I don't think I'm ready to find out. Not yet."

"Will you ever be ready? How long does it take to be ready for something like that? Plus, think of everything you'll miss. The people—"

"The people? The last time we came across 'people,' they tortured you. Tried to kill us. How can you be over that?"

"I'm not." Her face darkened. "But I'm not going to let that stop me either. Ailith, we survived. If we don't keep moving forward, what was the point?"

"I just think we need to be cautious, that's all."

"You sound like Tor. What's going on with him, anyway? I mean, he's reserved at the best of times, but today he's got a face like a slapped ass, as my grandmother used to say."

"Oh, god," I said, covering my face with my hands. I'd never really talked to Cindra about Tor. Though it felt like much longer, in reality, we'd known each other for less than two weeks, and all but the last couple of days had been spent traveling in a group, well within earshot of everyone else. This was the first chance we'd had to talk privately. I told her the whole story, starting with the moment I'd opened my eyes in the cabin.

"And now he's pissed because I didn't sever our bond. He thinks our feelings for each other are a program. So *that's* what's wrong with Tor."

"I'm not sure if it's incredibly romantic or incredibly awful," she replied. "I can understand why he's angry."

"Oh, believe me, I can too. And maybe one day…but right now, I just…" The problem was, I couldn't justify it.

Not to Cindra, not to myself. "You must think I'm horrible."

"Not horrible. Ruthless, cruel, maybe, but not horrible." She laughed at my stricken face. "I'm just kidding. Look, I don't totally agree with or understand what you're doing, but you have your reasons. You've experienced things the rest of us haven't, like Pax. I'm willing to give you the benefit of the doubt, for now. I'll let you know when you become horrible." She leaned over and brushed dried dirt from my face.

"So, you're going to Goldnesse then?" I asked her.

"Yes. I'm afraid of what I might find out, but for me, not knowing is worse. Besides, one of the reasons I became a cyborg was to help people. With the ability I've got, I can do that. Now more than ever." She smiled. "Lexa said I could work with her."

"Mmh."

"What? You still don't believe them?"

"It's not that, exactly. I believe they're telling us the truth. But within limits. I don't think they're telling us the *whole* truth, not even their version of it. Look at these seeds, for example." I held up one of the little packets to show her.

"Brandywine Heirloom Tomato Seeds, Boisvert Seed Company. Germination, 92%. So?"

"They're *heirloom* seeds. Not hybrids. You can save their seeds, plant them, grow more and more generations."

"I still don't get it."

"Heirloom seeds were impossible to get before the war. At least, legally. The government struck some kind of deal with the seed companies in exchange for a pay-off. In return, only hybrid seeds were legal for sale, meaning you had to buy new seeds every single year. People who'd grown non-hybrid plants before the law changed kept them, hoarded and traded them, but if you got caught, your livelihood was over. The fines alone would bankrupt your farm." I pointed at the boxes of seed packets. "But look at them all. Every kind of fruit, vegetable, and flower you could imagine. Those laws came into effect years before the war. Where did they get all these seeds? How long have they had them? *Why* do they have them if they thought the war was a temporary blip? It doesn't make any sense."

Cindra frowned, turning the packet over in her fingers. For the first time, she looked doubtful. "Maybe they were just being practical?" she asked, but the words must've sounded hollow even to her ears.

"Maybe. There's not much we can do about it now. And in the meantime, we have other issues to worry about. Like Goldnesse."

"So you're going to come?"

I hesitated. "I still don't know. Do you think I should ask Pax? See if he…knows anything?"

"What? And ruin the surprise? Hell, no. Come on, it'll be an adventure."

"Remember when adventures meant music festivals or Wing Wednesday with the girls?"

She laughed. "Maybe this will be just as fun."

"I doubt it," I replied darkly.

"Please come," she said, her face now serious. "If we do it together, we'll be fine, whatever the outcome."

My reply was interrupted by Lexa, calling to us from the top of the stairs. "Are you two coming? I need some help packing the supplies, and then we'll be on our way."

"Coming," Cindra called. She turned back to me. "Well?"

I thought of Ros and Adrian. *That's the price of regret.* I had to go. Whatever had happened, I had to try to find out. *But.* "Cindra, what if we find nothing? What if no one knows what happened to them?"

"Well, then we'll be no worse off than we are now, will we?"

I hope you're right.

14
AILITH

As Cindra helped Lexa pack the remaining trade supplies in the infirmary, the rest of us milled around in the main room. Pax and I stood off to one side. He seemed as relaxed as always, his black eyes impossible to read.

"Are you nervous?" I asked him.

"No. Why would I be?"

"Because we're going to a town full of people. People not like us. People like those who tortured you and Cindra. Aren't you even a little scared? Or do you know that nothing will happen to you?"

"Are you asking if I know what will happen? If I know whether your dad is alive?"

"Yes. No. Don't tell me." I twisted my hands together, reopening the cut on my thumb. "No, tell me."

He smiled in that enigmatic way of his. "I can't tell you."

"What? Why? Is it bad? Does it need to happen? Is one of us going to die? Is it Oliver? I promise I won't tell him."

His mouth quirked. "I can't tell you because I don't

know. Like I said before, it's a crossroads. Like when we were with the Saints of Loving Grace."

When they tried to burn us alive, you mean. "Oh." Deflation turned to nerves that twisted my belly. "Then why aren't you scared?"

"Because these aren't the same people who tortured us. They have a home. They feel safe. They have food, and water, and medicine." He gestured toward the open door of the infirmary. Lexa was reading a list aloud as Cindra checked boxes and called out numbers.

"What if they find out what we are?"

He shrugged. "Then the path will be decided for us."

Tor stood near the outer door, brooding. He glanced at me, seemingly torn between anger and concern at how I must be feeling. His mother had died in Vancouver, killed in the first wave of bombings. He knew I'd never fully accepted that my father was dead, and that being faced with the possibility of finding out was both a dream come true and a nightmare. Several times, it appeared as though he was going to walk toward me, but each time, he stopped abruptly and turned away. Oliver watched him, amusement plain on his face.

Should I manipulate Tor's body and give him all the satisfaction of smashing Oliver in the teeth without any of the culpability? Maybe then he'd see that us being connected wasn't such a bad thing. *Not likely.*

"Is everyone ready to go?" Lexa asked brightly, interrupting my reverie.

"Lexa, what if someone recognizes me? Or Cindra? From before?"

"Just keep your heads down and your hoods up. It's been years since anyone's seen you, and it's unlikely you'll be recognized out of context. Now, let's go before it gets too late."

***

The air outside the compound was cool, the sky as gray as ever. The entrance itself was obscured by a copse of sun-starved trees that refused to lie down and die.

I followed Cindra as we picked our way through on the twisting path, the silken length of her braid sliding over the top of her pack distracting me. Callum trailed behind me, his eyes darting back and forth. Lexa hadn't wanted him to come with us, given his unpredictable behavior, but Cindra and I had promised to keep an eye on him. I smiled at him over my shoulder, and he grinned back. He'd rarely left the compound since he'd woken, on lockdown after what had happened to Ros and Adrian.

Tor stalked after us, his long strides erratic to keep pace with our shorter ones. Kalbir pursued him as closely as possible, describing the various delights of Goldnesse.

"I've been waiting to go for ages, ever since I woke up. Mil and Lexa have told me all about it. It's supposed to be like a *real* town. There's all different kinds of people. All survivors, of course. But in the five years since the war, well, four really, if you count the time it took for people to start gathering there. Anyway, they actually have an economy. Bartering, obviously. They've got hunters, people who scavenge, some guy who's trying to grow stuff."

Some guy who's trying to grow stuff.

"Builders, teachers, a few engineers, cops…" she continued. "Lexa said there's even a hairdresser. Not," she said, wrapping a thick section of glossy black hair around her wrist, "that I would trust them to cut *my* hair."

"How many people live there?" Tor asked.

"About three thousand, I think," Lexa said from the front.

Three thousand. Before the war, there'd been more than ten times that number.

"They still get the odd person finding the town even after all these years. And I think they also trade with a small satellite group a few miles north, near a place called Tow."

Cindra's braid stopped sliding.

"I wonder why they chose Goldnesse to make their home?" Tor mused, mostly to himself, but Kalbir pounced on the opportunity to feed his curiosity.

"Well, there's two lakes, and a massive dam that supplies their hydro-electric station. Every single building has electricity. Can you believe it? I bet the food will be amazing. I mean, it's got to be better than the plastic crap we eat at the compound." She shuddered. "Unless it's like rabbits or that sort of thing."

"If you'd been awake for the last five years rather than just a couple of months, you'd think rabbits tasted like ambrosia," Lexa said dryly.

"*Hares,*" Tor said.

When we emerged from the thicket, I instantly recognized the surrounding landscape. The compound was hidden in the base of a small hill about a mile away from the road; I'd driven past it numerous times and never suspected it was anything more. It looked like hundreds of other hills in the area, covered with patches of crooked, wind-stunted trees, scrubby brush, and little dried cactus-balls you never saw before you found them clustered inside your pant legs, the long thorns embedded in your skin.

Very little had changed.

"It looks the same," Cindra whispered to me.

"I was just thinking that," I whispered back. "I guess it makes sense. It's always been dry here. Now it's just colder."

"*Motherfucker!*"

Cindra shot her hand out and grabbed my arm.

Oliver hopped up and down on one foot, clutching at his ankle.

"Oliver! Don't—" I was too late.

He scrabbled at his trouser leg, trying to pull it up. His next scream had a sharp edge of very real pain as the sliding fabric embedded the cacti spikes even deeper.

"Oliver, stand still."

He ignored me.

"Oliver." Cindra's voice was quiet, and Oliver froze, not wanting to scare away this sudden attention. She knelt in front of him, putting her knee under his foot. Gently, she rolled up his pant leg, pulled it wide on the assaulted side, and deftly plucked the spiked plants free. Oliver reached out, his hand hovering over her hair before boldness overtook him, and he smoothed a lock between his fingers, tucking it behind her ear.

"Thanks."

She smiled up at him.

Oh Cindra, seriously? I hope for all our sakes that Asche is still alive. Oliver didn't deserve a happy ending.

Callum bent and picked up the discarded cactus, rolling it over thoughtfully in his fingers. As we all turned back to the road, he closed his fist around it, wincing at the sudden sting.

Umbra.

He saw me watching and shrugged.

"Are you okay?" I asked.

"Yes. She's just curious." He said it low, so only I could hear. "Let's keep walking before the others see."

Cindra returned to walk beside me, stroking the lock of hair Oliver had touched.

"You know he's an asshole, right?" I said.

"Maybe." She smiled coyly. "Or maybe he's—"

"Do not say that he's misunderstood, Cindra. Please."

She laughed, glancing up at Oliver's back. "Okay, I won't. But maybe he is."

Was it my imagination, or was Oliver suddenly taller? *Should I remind her what's he's done? About Celeste?* The last time I'd seen Celeste—the young woman who'd worshiped Oliver with everything she'd had: her body, her loyalty, her innocence—she'd been lying on the ground, stunned, as he crushed her hand with his boot.

As though she could read my mind, Cindra laced her fingers with mine. "Let's not talk about Oliver. One problem at a time."

"Problem? I thought this was an adventure?"

As we left the desert hills and mounted the worn road, I felt it. *Him.* Whoever had been following Tor and me from the beginning of our journey was here, somewhere close.

"Hello?"

Images slid through my mind. *Stepping out of a dark cave into the blinding sun. Thousands of brightly-colored balloons floating in an azure sky. A name carved in the sand. Fane.*

I'd never met Fane, but he'd followed us since the beginning. And while I'd been inside him, I knew little about him other than that he was some kind of cyborg and part of a group of Cosmists, those who believed artilects——sentient, synthetic beings—were our only future. My communication with him was different than with the others, snippets of images amid the odd coherent vision. And, unlike the others, he could connect with *my* mind. He'd helped us escape the Saints, joining his strength with mine to generate the sonic pulse.

"Ailith? Are you all right?" Cindra peered at me as

though into a darkened room, searching.

"I'm fine. I—" *How do I explain?* Tor and I hadn't told anyone about the specter shadowing us. "I'm just a bit disoriented, that's all. Must be from the fresh air after being in the compound the last few days."

"Well, get ready, because I think we're almost there."

15

AILITH

We stood on a rocky outcropping at the side of the road, next to a weathered wooden shack. The red lettering on the side had faded and flaked off into illegibility, but I remembered it well. *Candied salmon, $10/lb. Fresh cherries. Lemonade. Ice cream, three scoops for $6.00 only!*

Tears filmed over my eyes, blurring the crispness of the white-peaked waves cresting and breaking on the surface of the lake below. Lake Niska. In the summers, the beach had always been crammed with tourists and locals alike, a sweaty, greasy, seething rainbow of umbrellas and beach chairs. Now deserted, it stretched out sterile and forlorn.

Cindra squeezed my hand. "I know, right? Their raspberry lemonade was *amazing*. They had nothing on

Asche's candied salmon, though."

"That's a hell of a long way down, isn't it?" Oliver said, craning his neck to peer over the cliff.

"Best not get too close to the edge then, eh?" Tor muttered savagely.

Oliver bared his teeth then turned toward the sprawl of houses in the distance. "So that's it then? Goldnesse? Pretty impressive view."

"Yes," Lexa said. "Are you ready?"

No.

It took us nearly half an hour to reach the town, our slow descent giving me time to take it all in. Tor had been right when he'd said that large parts of it were damaged during the war; many of the shops and beach-side apartments that ringed the shore of the southern lake had been destroyed, leaving twisted piles of blackened concrete and steel.

"Why they would bomb a city like this?" Tor asked. "I mean, there wasn't much here but beaches and vineyards, was there?"

"And a cyborg or two," Pax replied. "Or so they may have thought at the time." He started suddenly and looked at me. "Sorry."

The others filed past me, silent in their avoidance. Even Oliver had nothing to say. Tor rested his hand briefly on my shoulder before he too went on, leaving Cindra and me, our hands locked together. I knew I was hurting her, but I couldn't let go.

"I doubt that's true," she whispered. "How would they even know? And even if they did, they would've known you wouldn't be there. It was probably just a mistake. I've heard that happens sometimes: a bomb slips out prematurely. Not particularly reassuring in most cases, but—"

"Thanks." I forced myself to loosen my grip, my fingers stiff.

The residents of Goldnesse had clearly worked relentlessly in the aftermath of the war, and not just for survival. The rubble that must've littered the streets was cleared away, neatly shoved into towering piles lining both sides of the road. As we walked through the tunnel of debris, the hair on the back of my neck stood up. Someone was watching us. The corridor hadn't been created just for order's sake, it seemed. Without being able to see over the top, I had no idea where in the town we were, though I suspected we were headed down Main Street. The only turn we'd taken was the gentle curve where the road had previously hugged the lake, and the worn yellow and white traffic paint was faintly visible.

Tor must be going crazy.

Every cell in his hunter's body would've been screaming about the foolishness of this, the vulnerability of our situation. And after what Pax had said… Tor's gait was tense, the hair curling over the collar of his coat brushing back and forth as he searched from side to side, scanning for movement. His hand hovered over the knife belted to his waist, and the hilt of another peeked from the top of his boot. He'd wanted to bring his crossbow, but Lexa had refused, saying it might be seen as aggressive. He'd taken advantage of her distraction while she'd been packing and secreted it into his oversized backpack instead.

We exited the half-tunnel just as I thought he would explode.

My guess had been correct. We stepped out at the end of Main Street, just before the start of the former downtown quarter. Most of the original shops seemed occupied, smoke curling from chimneys, and goods stacked on the pavement outside. Strong smells permeated the bubble of silence surrounding us—tantalizing earthy aromas of cooking meat, burning wood, and the people who bustled by us. Their cheeks were rosy in the crisp air as they nodded at each other in passing or huddled in groups on the corners, breaking into peals of laughter and slapping each other on the back.

The sights and smells after weeks in the wilderness steeped me in the knowledge that while I'd slept peacefully underground, these people had clawed their way through the last five years, watching nearly everyone they knew die, the lives and futures they'd built burn to the ground. Every single person here had done something to live, and yet I saw none of it on their faces. If I let my mind wander just a little, it could've been the Saturday Farmers Market, and I'd just stepped out of our booth for a break. In fact, from where we were standing, I could see a few hundred feet down the street to where our booth had nestled between the others on the pavement beside the Winter Park.

The last time I'd stood here felt like scant months ago, and of course, to my newly-awoken mind, it was. Time had not passed for us the way it had for these people, and watching them now, carving out normal lives, was like a knife to my gut. How had they coped? Adapted to a way of life requiring skills so different from what they knew?

How would I have done?

I'd been protected by thousands of pounds of impenetrable bunker and a stranger. A stranger like me, like *us*, who many saw as the cause of the war. These people had been meant to survive; we had not. And yet here we all were, human and cyborg alike. If what Pax had seen was right, only we could ensure these people survived. Watching them now, the heart-breaking normalcy of their lives, I was determined we would, no matter what it cost us.

"Lexa!" A woman rounded one of the groups near us, her hand raised in greeting. She appeared to be in her mid-thirties and was striking, with long, loosely-knotted umber hair framing a delicate face dominated by wide, cornflower-blue eyes. Her skin had the robust look of someone who spent a lot of time outdoors, and her mouth curved in a genuine smile of pleasure.

"Lily." Lexa gripped both the woman's hands in her own. "How are you?"

"We're good. A bit low on medical supplies, but otherwise great. Is there something wrong with your radio? When you didn't come the other week, I was worried Mil had taken a turn for the worse, and we tried to contact you but got no answer. Is he okay?" she asked, her forehead creased in concern.

"He's fine." The tension in Lexa's shoulders belied her casual tone. "Just a bit grumpy, as usual. He was too tired to make the trip today."

Lily nodded in sympathy. "I keep telling him the two of you should move here, but he insists your work is too important."

"He's right," Lexa replied. "One of these days this climate is going to change, and we want to be ready when it does. Who knows what kind of effect it will have? We want to make sure we're a step ahead. Besides, we wouldn't be able to synthesize all these medications here. The equipment is too delicate to move." She patted the side of her heavy canvas bag.

"I understand," Lily said. "I just hate the thought of the two of you alone out there, especially with Mil's condition—" She suddenly noticed the group of strangers behind Lexa. "But maybe you're not alone anymore?" She gave us a pointed look.

"No, we're not." Lexa smiled. "That's why we didn't

come as usual. Lily, these are researchers from another station like ours. They'd thought they were the only ones who'd survived, but when their supplies got low, they decided to risk searching further afield. As luck would have it, I happened across them just as they were about to turn back." The lies rolled easily off her tongue.

"Scientists!" Lily exclaimed, her whole face brightening to match her smile. "We always need more of you. What fields did you work in?"

Lexa explained our different areas of "expertise," pointing to each of us in turn. "We've got Ailith, an agriculturalist. Tor, a wildlife biologist. Pax a biomedical scientist. Kalbir, our human resources manager. Callum, a researcher. Oliver, a software engineer, and," she said, arching her eyebrows in anticipation of Lily's reaction, "Cindra, a botanist who studies traditional medicine." She pushed Cindra forward with a palm to her lower back.

Cindra let go of my hand and stepped forward, smiling shyly. I hadn't thought Lily's smile could get any brighter, but it did.

With her around, who needs the sun?

"Oh my goodness, it's so nice to meet you," she said, snatching up Cindra's hands and giving them an excited squeeze. "I have so much to ask you, to show you. Just the other week, I found this plant—maybe you've seen it? It has five-pointed—"

"Lily?" a male voice asked. We turned as one to find a man and teenage girl standing behind us. The man scrutinized us, his eyes wary, while the girl, who had his pale-blue eyes and dimpled chin, gazed at us with the same open delight as Lily.

"Ryan, Grace! Look, it's Lexa, and she's brought friends."

"I know," he replied, circling us to stand next to her. "I

followed them in."

"They're all scientists, like Lexa and Mil," she said, still holding Cindra's hands. "Just think, even more skills to add to our little community."

"Scientists?" He nodded slowly. "I see. Where did you say you were from?"

"They're from near Falton, just over the range from Rosespring," Lexa said smoothly.

"I don't remember any research stations around there," Ryan replied.

"Yeah, well, we didn't exactly advertise." Oliver stepped in. "Lots of expensive equipment, and with all the unrest over those artilects and cyborgs and such before the war, people seemed to think all scientists were the same. And hey, we're brainboxes, not boxers, if you get me. Best to keep it on the hush-hush."

Gently, gently, Oliver.

Ryan eyed Tor dubiously.

We're too healthy, too strong.

"Oh, don't worry about him." Oliver waved his hand nonchalantly. "He looks burly, but it's mostly fat. I just wouldn't show your food stores, if I were you."

Tor glared at Oliver but held his tongue. His knife had disappeared, and he tried to look relaxed; I doubted anyone but me noticed he was coiled like a spring.

"Cindra here is a botanist, Ryan. And not just *any* botanist, but one who studies local plants." She beamed up into his face. "Can you believe our luck?"

Ryan finally melted under the brilliance of her smile. His face relaxed, and he nodded at Cindra. "It's good to meet you. All of you," he added. "Cindra, I hope you like to talk and listen because Lily here has been waiting years to meet someone like you."

Someone like you. Like us. I doubt it.

A shadow passed over Cindra's face, gone in an instant. *Adapt.*

"Oh, and Ailith, we have another agriculturalist here. You two should get together. I'm sure he'd be fascinated by your research. He's been trying to get common crops to adapt to the colder weather. In fact, there he is now, over there. The older gentleman."

She pointed across the street to a man engrossed in conversation with an oddly familiar younger man with bronze skin and shorn black hair. He was tall, his head bald, and his face heavily lined. He looked much older than he should have, and I wondered how much of it was because of me.

It turned out my father was still alive, after all.

We drove out of Tow and into the dark. Behind us, the city was alight; we felt the heat of it even after we'd crossed the boundary line. Dad took us past the lake, to the cabin deep in the woods they'd bought on a whim during their honeymoon. We'd been to it only a month ago, the week after I got out of school, and since Mom had over-shopped as she always did, we could lock ourselves inside and pretend the world wasn't falling apart.

— Love, Grace

16
AILITH

Cindra saved me from responding by dropping gracelessly to her knees in a near-faint. As Lexa and Lily bent over her, Oliver rushed to her side. She pushed him away and reached out for me; he stepped back, his expression pained.

My father is alive.

"Cindra!" Lily pressed the back of her hand to Cindra's forehead as I knelt next to her and grabbed her hand.

"*Asche,*" she hissed at me under her breath.

"What? Where?" *He's alive?*

She shook her head mutely and flicked her gaze toward the pair hovering over her.

"She's okay," I said, "don't worry. She didn't eat much this morning, and it was a long walk. Here, come sit with me. I've got some protein bars in my bag." I threw her arm over my shoulder and stood, dragging her with me.

Lily hovered her hand uncertainly over Cindra's shoulder. "Are you sure?"

"Absolutely. Just give us ten minutes, and she'll be fine. Tell us where you're going, and she'll meet you there."

"Okay," Lily said, still unsure. "I'm going to the infirmary. I can give her an examination when she gets there."

Cindra glanced at Lexa, panic widening her eyes.

He's alive, and he's here.

Tor spotted the tremble in my hands. I gripped Cindra more tightly.

"I'm sure she'll be just fine," Lexa replied. "Come and see us when you're ready, Cindra. Just follow Main Street here to the end. There's a large building that used to be a casino. You'll find us on the right side of the bottom floor."

Cindra nodded then sat down with her head between her knees.

Lexa grabbed Lily's arm firmly and steered her toward the road. "So, you were saying you found a new plant? Have you been able to identify it yet?" Their voices faded as they wove down the street, Lily glancing back over her shoulder just before they disappeared.

"Well, if I'm not needed, I'm off," Oliver said. The cheerfulness in his voice was strained, and he avoided looking at either of us.

"Just where are you going?" Tor asked. "Don't cause any shit, Oliver, not on our first day here."

"Me?" Oliver asked innocently. "I have no idea what you mean, Goliath. We're here in what passes for civilization these days, and I plan to take advantage of it. I wonder if there's a brothel?" He sauntered away. "Sure you don't want to join me?" he called to Tor over his shoulder. "It's not like your current relationship is working out that well. For you, anyway."

The muscles in Tor's jaw leaped once then stilled. He pinched the bridge of his nose. "God, what an asshole. Why is it men like him always survive? Like a goddamn cockroach." He knelt beside Cindra and me, dipping his head to look her in the eyes. "You okay?"

The gentleness of his voice hurt my heart.

"Yes, I'm fine. I just…I'd like to speak with Ailith for a few minutes. Privately," she added, glancing at Kalbir.

A faint blush colored Kalbir's cheeks. "Fine," she said. "C'mon, Big Man, Callum, let's go find some fun."

Callum's head tilted strangely to the side. "I'd like to eat things and touch things."

"Uh, okay. I'm sure we can do that," Kalbir said. "Tor?"

"Actually," Tor said, looking at me closely, "I think I'll go and talk to some of the local hunters. Make myself useful." He pointed further down the street, where a group of men and women seemed to be haggling over a stack of carcasses.

Kalbir looked from him to me, her smile tight. "Right, well, whatever, suit yourself." She turned on her heel and left us, her chin up and shoulders stiff.

Tor waited until she'd walked down the next block. "You're sure you don't need me?" he asked, reluctant to leave us. "What's really going on?"

Well, my dad's alive, and Cindra thinks she just saw her old boyfriend. Other than that, not much.

"Cindra?" I asked. "Do you want Tor and Pax to leave as well?"

"No," she said. "They can stay. I just…I don't know *them* yet."

"Oh good," Pax said, relief clear in his voice. "I wasn't

going to leave anyway."

Cindra smiled up at him and tugged gently on the leg of his pants. "Thanks, Pax."

I sat on the pavement next to Cindra, the cold concrete biting through the seat of my pants and chilling my skin. "Do you want to go first?" I asked her.

"No," she said. "I need to be sure. You go."

"Okay." I took a deep breath. "My father is still alive. And he's standing right over there, next to—" It hit me where I'd seen the younger man before.

He gave me the crooked grin that was as familiar to me as my own heart.

"Asche. He cut his hair," I added lamely.

What were the odds?

Astronomical.

The suspicion slowly poisoning my body over the last few days spread deeper.

No. It's a coincidence. The odds are slim, but possible.

The odds of *any* of us surviving had been small, but someone had to. Why not them?

Paranoia is just as dangerous as an actual enemy. Remember that.

"What? You mean to tell me your dad is standing right over there? And who the hell is Asche?" Tor looked as though he'd fallen down the rabbit hole. Well, hare hole, in his case.

Cindra looked up, her eyes rimmed with red. "Asche was my…boyfriend, fiancé…whatever. Or at least, he would've been if I hadn't left him." She twisted her braid between her fingers. "I only pretended to myself he might be alive. I didn't actually believe it was possible."

"Shit. Pax, did you know this was going to happen?" Tor asked.

Pax hooked his thumbs through the empty belt loops on his pants and rocked back on his heels. "Yes. No. I did see them, but I had no idea who they were or what it meant."

"I asked you before we came if you'd seen anything," I said, unable to keep the irritation from creeping into my voice. "A little notice would've been appreciated."

Pax smiled benignly, unruffled by my tone. "You weren't specific. What would your reaction have been if I'd said, 'I see an older man and a younger man, and they're talking?'"

Tor cocked his head, amusement quirking the corners of his mouth. "He's got a point."

"I know," I said, rubbing my forehead. "I'm not blaming you Pax, it's just…"

"What are you going to do?" Tor asked, gazing at the two men. Asche was explaining something to my father, drawing shapes on the palm of his hand with slim fingers. My father nodded and replied then folded the end of his scarf into the breast of his coat and flipped his collar up against the gnawing cold. Putting his hands in his pocket, he began to turn away.

"They're leaving. Shit. What do we do? We can't just go sauntering up to them and say, 'Oh hey, Dad, Asche, how's it going? Shame about this apocalypse. You're looking well.' Can we?" Creeping hysteria had replaced the irritation in my voice.

"If your eyes get any wider, they may burst," Pax noted helpfully.

Tor tucked a piece of hair behind my ear. "Hey, it's okay. Cindra, it's…" He patted her helplessly on the shoulder as she started to cry.

I can't imagine how she feels. You expect to lose your parents, but not the love of your life. And here he was, a second chance long-buried and newly arisen.

"Look, you two couldn't speak to them anyway, even if

you wanted to. They both know you became cyborgs, right? So you'd be putting all of us at risk." He gazed thoughtfully at the two men, and I could almost see his mind at work. "I know they loved you once, but you don't know how they feel about what you are now." He came to a decision. "But I've got a plan," he said, straightening. "Come with me, Pax. You were asking me yesterday about the work I used to do? Let's go do it."

"You're going to *kill* them?" I asked, horrified.

Tor shot me a fierce look. "No. We're going to do some reconnaissance."

Pax's smile shone brighter than Lily's. He hopped from one foot to the other. "Do we use fake names?"

"No," said Tor. "The first lesson is to speak the truth as much as you can. We're here, new to town. Let's mingle." He placed his hand between Pax's shoulder blades and pushed him forward. "You two should stay out of sight."

Cindra and I scooted around the corner of the block and huddled on the concrete.

"I can't do this. Sit here and wait. Do you think they'll come back with them? What should I say? I have to look—" She worried a hangnail with her teeth.

"Cindra, sit still. They're only doing recon. They're not going to tell them about us."

"Fine, distract me."

"Get your fingers out of your mouth, and I will."

We talked about our childhoods and teen years, our memories of this town that I'd grown up near and she'd visited many times.

"It's funny, isn't it?" she said. "We came down to the market nearly every Saturday. I remember your booth...I probably even bought from you, touched your hand." She patted my fingers. "Who knew we'd end up like this?"

I sighed, inching back so I could lean against the brick wall behind us. "Would you still have done it, if you'd known?"

She slid back next to me, her head pressed against the rough surface as she stared upward. "Yes. This wasn't our fault. None of it was. Other people would've gone through the process, the war still would've happened. The only difference is that we might not be alive now. And I want to be alive more than anything else. More than the grief and the loss. Even though the people we know are dead or changed, at least we're alive to remember them. It's not as good as actually being with them, but it's close enough for me."

"I think I—" Tor and Pax rounded the corner. Tor looked upset; Pax looked…like Pax, calm and serene.

My stomach twisted.

Cindra covered her face with her hands. "I can't bear it."

"What happened?" I asked Tor. "Why do you look like that? They're alive, right? How can that be bad?"

"It's not," he replied. "It's just…I don't know. I wanted to—"

"He wanted to bring you a gift," Pax said. "Something for your heart."

Tor pressed his fingers over his eyes as the tips of his ears turned pink. "Thank you, Pax."

Pax nodded, satisfied with his part, and sprawled onto the pavement next to Cindra.

"Anyway," Tor said, his voice weary, "it's not the news either of you was hoping for."

"What do you mean?" I asked. "It isn't them?"

"No, it is. But…"

"Just tell me, please," Cindra whispered. "I can't wait any longer."

Tor knelt in front of us, looking first at Cindra then at me. "Cindra, Asche is the leader of your community."

"She's dead, then. Grandmother is dead." She closed her eyes. "But Asche, he's okay?"

"He is. He's, uh…married. And he has children."

Cindra swallowed hard, but her face was impassive. "I'm just so glad he's alive." She sagged back against the wall.

"Is my dad, okay? I mean, that's all I ever wanted. Why are you looking at me like that?"

"Because," Tor said, gazing down at his hands, "he denies ever having a daughter. According to him, you never existed."

17
AILITH

Cindra and I didn't speak on the long road back to the compound. Lily, oblivious to our silence, had invited us all to stay the night, tempting us with descriptions of the dinner she'd cook. Thankfully, Lexa had decided we should quit while we were ahead and made our excuses, saying she didn't want to leave Mil alone, just in case. This provoked a flurry of activity from Lily as she insisted on packing a parcel of delicacies for him. Her honest kindness was like a thorn, stinging all the more because of our deception.

As we walked the road under the darkening sky, Callum's pockets bulged with treasure, and he slipped his fingers in periodically to touch one thing or the other. His eyes were unfocused, and he didn't react as Oliver regaled us with his tales of adventure, which were impressive considering we'd only been in Goldnesse a few hours.

"You're all awfully quiet," he observed. "Did something happen that we should know about? Besides Kalbir here being rejected?" He winced as her fist connected with his shoulder. "*Fuck!* Well, you shouldn't have told me then, should you? Everyone knows I'm not to be trusted." He rubbed the spot Kalbir had punched then glanced toward Cindra as though expecting a response.

Cindra stared straight ahead, taking one step and then another.

He stopped walking. "Seriously, what did I miss?"

"Cindra?" Lexa asked. She stepped into Cindra's path, stopping her gently with her arm before they could collide. She looked at me.

"You have to tell them," Tor said softly. "This affects all of us."

"I know," I replied. "It's just… Basically, my father and Cindra's ex…someone Cindra used to know are alive, and they were in Goldnesse today. That agriculturalist Lily was talking about? That was my father." I frowned. "I'm surprised you've never met him, Lexa."

The color leeched from Lexa's face. "What? Do you mean Luke? He…he never said he had a daughter… Did they see you? You didn't talk to them, did you?"

"No, we didn't. Tor and Pax did, though."

"They didn't suspect what you were, did they?"

"No," Tor said. "We kept with the story, gave as little information about us as we could. We mostly just asked them questions about themselves. Asche is a hunter, so we talked about that."

"So your old boyfriend's here?" Oliver asked Cindra. He tried to sound casual, but the whiteness of his knuckles on his pack straps betrayed him.

"He's not my boyfriend," Cindra said, her chin up.

"He's married. And he has children. And I'm glad for him. He always wanted a family. But my grandmother is dead, so if you don't mind, I'd like some privacy to remember her."

"I'm sorry." For once Oliver had nothing else to say. Then he turned to me. "And your father's alive, eh? That's going to be an interesting reunion."

"I doubt there'll be a reunion. According to him, I never existed."

"Ouch," Oliver said, and laughed. "Looks like you got some comforting to do, big boy." He thumped Tor lightly on the shoulder then ducked away, smirking at Kalbir's scowl.

"I'm sorry," Lexa said, real sympathy in her voice.

"What are we supposed to do?" I asked. "Do we just never go to Goldnesse?"

"Asche doesn't live in Goldnesse," Pax said. "He only comes every week for trading."

"I'm not sure. I'll have to talk to Mil about it, but I doubt you can avoid them forever."

We walked on in silence. Oliver's steps were erratic, jaunty one minute, somber the next. It must've been hard for him, pretending to be a decent person and actually feeling bad for Cindra.

When we finally entered the compound, Lexa ran headlong into Mil, who looked as though he'd been hovering by the entrance since we left.

"How did it go?" he asked.

Lexa drew him away from the rest of us, nodding at Cindra and me as she did so. They walked off toward their office, speaking quietly, urgently.

At the top of the dormitory stairs, I gave Cindra a hug. "You going to be okay?"

"Yes. I just need some time, alone. But I'll be fine." She

followed Pax down the hall, patting him on the shoulder in thanks before disappearing behind her door. Callum scooted furtively into his room, the lock clicking into place and leaving the hallway to Tor and me.

I paused at my door and, knowing I shouldn't, asked Tor if he'd like to come in. "I could use someone to talk to."

He paused then shook his head. "No. I'm sorry about what happened, but…no. I'm tired of letting myself down."

So, I ended up having a one-sided conversation with a girl in a coma in the middle of the night.

I slid into the chair next to her bed as quietly as possible, trying not to knock over anything that might make a sound. It was the middle of the night, and I'd stolen out of bed, creeping down the stairs in the dark the way Tor and I had once crept through the woods.

She lay on her back, her arms resting at her sides over the bedclothes. I'd expected her to be covered with tubes and wires, to be surrounded by the humming and whooshing of the machines keeping her alive, but there were none save a single thin tube that bit into a large vein in her hand, held fast by a layer of thick tape. Her coma was so unobtrusive that we hadn't even noticed her when we'd been in the same room, less than twenty feet away.

Eire.

I traced my fingers over hers. They were small and cool to the touch, like my brother's at his funeral. *Dorian.* I rarely let myself think about him, about the person he would've been now. Just newly a man, would he have had the same patchy stubble that had plagued my father? He hadn't had a mark on him except for the slight compression of his chest.

Would he and my mother have survived the war? Or, if they'd been alive and then died during it, would Dad have followed them?

Since he didn't have a daughter, he'd have had nothing left to live for but life itself, and my father had never been that kind of man.

"And so that, Eire, is the whole sordid tale. According to my own father, I never existed."

A flash in my mind. *"I don't exist either, not without her."*

I jerked my hand backward, nearly taking her lone tube with me. "You can speak to me? We can…speak to each other?" Until now, Pax had been the only other Pantheon Modern cyborg I could communicate with. I hadn't even known about Eire until we got here.

"Yes. We are pairs."

"What do you mean, pairs? Do you see the future too?"

"Not the future. The past. A ladder. We are like a ladder. Where's Ella?"

Her hand was so thin, her veins forming a tiny blue network under her paper-fine skin. "Ella's dead, Eire. I'm so sorry."

"Sometimes I still hear her. I can feel her close by."

"I'm sorry," I repeated.

"Did they kill her?"

"Who?"

"Mil and Lexa. Did they kill her?"

"No. They said she just…died. Like she got lost and couldn't find her way back."

"They killed her. She would never leave me."

"Why would they kill her?" Paranoia began to stir.

"They are not what they seem. They are guilty. They have done some terrible things. I can see what they've done. We are wrong." The pinkie finger on her left hand twitched.

"Eire? What do you mean? Can you wake up? Lexa says there's nothing physically wrong with you."

"Not yet. Not without her. I need to know what happened. Why

she left me."

"I—"

"The kill switch. Did you find the kill switch?"

"Yes, we—"

"There's more. Ella. I will try to remember."

***

"They are not what they seem. They are guilty. We are wrong." Eire's words tumbled around in my head, making it impossible to sleep.

I knew I shouldn't do it, but Tor's breathing as he slept was one of the few things that calmed me. And for someone who'd had such a violent past, he rarely dreamed. That was what I needed right now: a dark, quiet space, the reassurance of something familiar. And the only place I could find it was in his head.

What I hadn't expected was to discover him at Kalbir's bedroom door, her perfect teeth bared in triumph.

Dad went out every few days to see what was happening. First, he'd driven then when he couldn't find any more fuel, he walked. Each time he came back, his face seemed thinner, grayer, as though the grayness of the sky was seeping into his skin. Then, one day when he was searching for food, he met Asche.

— Love, Grace

18
TOR

I shouldn't have been here. I'd accused Ailith in the past of making me do things I didn't want to do, and it was because of her that I was here now, outside the door of a woman I was pretty sure was going to eat me alive.

I'd told Ailith the truth when I said I didn't want to kill her anymore. I'd known it the moment we'd woken up here. My first thought was of her, of where she was, and when I saw her lying unconscious in that bed, looking so…human, the rage that had filled me… I knew then that she wasn't the enemy. If anyone was, it was those who'd created us.

I never should've slept with her again. I knew it would happen, knew I shouldn't, and then I did it anyway. Did I really think it would change her mind? Make her suddenly give up her control? Could I blame her for that?

Yes, I could. She shouldn't have had that power over me. But would I feel differently if it were anyone else? What if it were Oliver she could control? Would I ask her to get rid of her ability then? No.

I would tell her to keep it, just in case. So why should I feel otherwise? Because it was me and her. Was it even about the control? Or was it more about making her sacrifice something to prove herself to me? Either way, it had backfired. It just made everything worse. And now I was here.

After what had happened in Goldnesse, I didn't know what to say to her. I mean, I was happy her father was still alive, but part of me couldn't help feeling bitter about it, and not only because my mother was dead. Before, it was just the two of us, even with the others. Her new life started when she woke up, and selfishly, I liked being her history. Now she had her old history back, a history with lots of memories that had made her who she was—and I wasn't a part of it.

Maybe we were *programmed to feel a certain way. Maybe what Oliver had said about our connections to each other as a group was true, and that was why we had feelings for each other. So if that was true, I had to ask myself: did it matter? Was it any different than natural feelings? People always said they couldn't help how they felt, who they loved. So maybe we couldn't control it. But I could choose what I did with it.*

I knew now that we'd never have a normal relationship, a quiet life. I was a fool for ever thinking otherwise. It wasn't her fault, not directly. It was what she was. If what Pax said was true, we would change the course of the future not only for us, but for what was left of the human race. Being one of those people, the kind who change the future, never ended well; they rarely died of old age. Either she would die, or I would, probably for each other. And to live like that, each day wondering if today was the day…I couldn't do that. It would happen regardless, but with some distance, maybe we'd survive it.

So here I was.

I needed a buffer to put between us. I needed to look at today as the first day of my new life, and I thought Kalbir was the one to help me do that. I knew she liked me. She was beautiful, strong…everything a man could want. And she wasn't the type to get emotionally involved with me; she'd made that pretty clear. Maybe I'd fall in love with her; maybe I wouldn't. Either way, it didn't matter. My purpose was served.

She didn't even want to talk. Her hand on my arm was cool; I'd had to wipe mine on my pant leg. After she'd pulled my shirt up over my head, she stood back and appraised me, her eyes glittering with approval.

She was just as fast as me; before I knew what was happening, I was flat on my back on her bed. She hesitated only long enough to strip off her own shirt before straddling me.

Her body was as perfect as I'd thought it would be, her breasts full and heavy in my hand. As I rolled her nipple between my fingers, she arched back, purring with pleasure.

This was wrong, but I still rose in response.

She rested the palms of her hands on my collarbone, and I flinched. It only spurred her on, and she dragged her fingernails down my chest, slowly, watching my reaction.

She had slid her hands just below my belly button when her fingers froze then curled inward like claws. She stared down at them, her eyes wide as her nails cut into the flesh of her palms.

"What the f—"

"Are you all right?"

"No. I can't…can't move my hands…" She rolled off me and onto her feet next to the bed. "What the hell is going on? What have you done to me?"

"Me? Nothing? I—" No. It couldn't be. But Oliver had said our abilities were paired; if Ailith could control me, it made sense that she'd also be able to manipulate Kalbir. But even if she could, would she? Shit.

"Maybe you should go see Oliver," I suggested. "Maybe you've got some kind of…glitch."

"Motherf— I bet you're right. We'll have to continue this another time, gorgeous. Unless you like this?" She held up her hands.

"No…another time would be better. Do you want me to go with you to Oliver?"

"No, *just open the door for me.*"

"*Don't you want to…put on a shirt or something? I can put a towel over your shoulders.*"

"*I'm sure I haven't got anything he hasn't already seen. Why? Is there something wrong with my body?*"

"*No, I—*"

"*Or are you jealous?*" She grinned as I squirmed. "*I'm joking, Tor. God, I bet vanilla was your favorite flavor of ice cream, wasn't it?*"

Actually, I hated ice cream. "*Yes.*"

"*Figures.*" She leaned over and bit my chest. "*One for the road.*"

As she kicked Oliver's door, trying to get his attention, I made my escape. It wasn't until I locked my own door behind me that I finally allowed myself to breathe.

19
AILITH

It was almost five days later that I finally managed to catch him on his own. Like I'd done every day since talking to Eire, I'd left the compound under the pretext of foraging for seeds and edible plants, plus the long list of medicinal ones Lexa had given me. I'd avoided going back to Goldnesse. The thought that someone might recognize me was more anxiety than I needed right now.

The others had been back once or twice. If I succeeded today, Cindra, the only one who knew what I was about to do, would return tomorrow to find Asche. Pax had said he came every week, so she planned to cross her fingers and set off early in the morning, Pax in tow. *If* I succeeded.

My only worry was Tor, who often hunted at the same time I was out, but since we were politely sidestepping each other, the risk of running into him was small. Part of me felt bad about what I'd done, but I still snorted every time I thought of Kalbir, half-naked, trying to smash Oliver's door down.

I'm doing this regardless, whether Tor sees me or not.

Mil and Lexa had told me to avoid my father until *they* decided what I should do. Mil and Lexa could go fuck themselves. I couldn't trust them. I could trust only myself and the other cyborgs. *Our kind.* The others couldn't lie to me, even if they wanted to.

I need to protect them.

Whatever we'd been a part of, we were on our own now, and I was the one thing that connected us. They'd all lost so much, and I was tired of losing.

Oliver had listened intently as I'd told him what Eire had said, our uneasy alliance still intact. Ever since he'd found about Cindra's grandmother, about Asche, he'd begun to tread more lightly, to be…almost normal. Full days went by that I didn't fantasize about strangling him.

He'd frowned, more serious than I'd ever seen him. "I'll look into it. If there's something in their system, I'll find it."

With Oliver solving that puzzle, it was time for me to work on my own.

And so here I was, wedged into a dry thicket, watching my father work his way across an old field, searching for anything familiar that might've survived. How often had he done this, returning to the same places over and over, hoping for a different answer? Given the flatness of the pack against his back, he wasn't finding it.

He looked much older than I remembered, older than he should have only five years later. Dorian still lived in his face, the hazel eyes so unlike my own. I searched him for a likeness of myself, for even a hint that I'd ever truly existed to him.

I stepped out of the brush as he bent to examine a coral-berried plant familiar to me. "The berries are edible. But they taste like Aunt Gwen's candied yams."

He straightened up too quickly, staggering. A savage delight curled in my chest, and I made no move to help him.

"Ailith?" he whispered.

"So you do remember me. I tho—" Air flew from my lungs as he hugged me, squeezing me until I thought either his arms or my ribs would break.

He pushed me away from him then pulled me back in, twining one shaking hand in my hair. "I knew you would survive. I knew it. I've been waiting for you to find me. Look at you. Are you…?"

"A cyborg? Yes."

"When I saw you in town the other week, I knew I wouldn't have to wait long."

"Wait, you *saw* me?"

"Of course I did. I've looked for you every day. You're my child, and I survived this war because of you."

I almost broke then—not the clean snap of a dead branch, but the visceral ripping of a fibrous root, torn from the earth.

"Then why did you tell Tor you never had a daughter?"

"Tor. He was the large, dark-haired man, wasn't he? He did seem rather interested in my life. Is he a cyborg too?"

"Yes. Do you hate us? Blame us for the war? Did you deny me because you wish I didn't exist?" I waited.

He smiled, wiping his thumb gently across my cheekbone. "No. I'm your father. I'm still trying to protect you."

"Do they hate us that much, then?"

He sighed, a deep, heavy sound like falling snow. "Yes and no. It's not hate as much as fear. A lot was said before and during the war about cyborgs and artilects. Information became confused, and no one really knows what happened. Not truly. Even those of us who lived through it all have no idea exactly what happened, and few will discuss what their beliefs were before. It's a topic everyone avoids. They don't know what to be afraid of, but if the choice were between their neighbors and something 'other' like yourselves…you can guess who they'd choose. I genuinely think some of them would welcome you, but it's a big risk. Especially now. We've been hearing rumors lately that have everyone unsettled."

"Rumors? What do you mean? About us?"

"No, no, nothing like that. Nobody suspects Mil and Lexa of harboring cyborgs. They've been nothing but solid members of our community since they came to town. Until I saw you, I never would've suspected there was more to their story than what they'd told us. They're good liars."

Yes, they are. We all are.

"We have a group of young men and women who travel around the province, scouting. They search for other survivors, technology, that sort of thing. Anyone or anything useful, they bring back to Goldnesse. One of them came back last week from the Kootenay region—you know, to the west, near the Alberta border? Anyway, they found the remains of an entire group, maybe ninety-odd people, men, women, and children, dead."

Tendrils of ice curled around my chest. "Do they know what killed them?"

"At first, they suspected a cult that lives in the area— the scout herself barely managed to avoid them—but the way some of the people were torn apart— Sorry," he said. "I know it's scary. But that's a long way from here. It was probably a pack of wild animals. We've been seeing more and more of them lately." He looked over his shoulder as though expecting some to appear. "But forget about that. What happened to you? I went to the hospital the minute the news of the war broke to find you. I-I wanted to apologize. For the way I behaved."

My father had managed to keep his contempt about my cyberization to himself until the night before my operation. I understood that it was difficult for him. Becoming a cyborg would save my life, but it also meant becoming something he loathed. He blamed AI technology for the deaths of my mother and brother, and the idea that I would soon be swarming with millions of them became too much for him to bear silently. We'd fought, and I'd gone to the hospital the next morning alone.

"It's okay, Dad. I understand. Really," I said, taking his hands in mine.

I told him about the bunker and Tor. Our journey to find the source of the mysterious signal. Oliver, Cindra, Pax. I left out the visions, the torture, the killing, our brief moments as gods. The things I could never tell him far outweighed what I could. I hated lying to him, but if he knew what we'd done, what *I'd* done... He was my father, and although he'd obviously changed after the war, I didn't know how much. Before, no matter how much he loved me, he was also the kind of man who would do the right thing, even if that meant turning in his own daughter. Even the end of world might not have changed that about him.

"So how are you...different? You look wonderful, healthy." He stepped back to get a better look.

What do I say? "I'm not too different, I guess. I'm stronger. I heal faster." *I can read other cyborgs' minds, have a kind of telepathy with some, and can even use one of them as my own personal weapon.* "Nothing too exciting."

"Well, be careful when you come to Goldnesse. Those two things alone are enough to make people suspicious."

"Plus, people might recognize me. Does anyone we know still live there?"

"A few. Nobody we knew well. Mrs. Grindell, but she's not been quite right since the war. I have no idea how she's survived as long as she has. Besides, it wouldn't matter. I never told anyone you became a cyborg, only that you'd gone in for another surgery. Then the war happened. We can always tell them you escaped the hospital and found the research station." He hesitated. "Do you, uh, do you think you'd ever consider moving to the town?" The hope in his eyes was guarded. He knew the answer as well as I did, but I loved him for asking.

"You know I can't." I leaned against his chest; just the miracle of hearing his heart beat was enough for me. "But you could come visit me. I mean, I'll have to talk to Lexa and Mil about it, but I'm sure they'll says yes." The words came out too fast.

"Do they know you're talking to me now?" he asked.

"No, but—"

"Aah. Well, I'll wait until you sort that out then." He gripped both my shoulders and looked at me. "Ailith, listen to me. You have to make them understand that I won't reveal who and what you are. Do you understand me?" And there was the man my father had become. He was still a good man, but he now understood what it took to survive, and he'd made his peace with that. Maybe one day I *would* be able to tell him everything.

"I understand."

We stood for a moment in silence, his gaze mapping my face, taking me in.

"Dad? How— Why did so many people die? Lots of places weren't destroyed, and yet most people didn't survive. It doesn't seem possible. Tor saw a few things, pieced together others…but I still don't understand."

"Did he tell you about the rain?"

"The silver rain? Yes. He said there was something in

116

the bombs, something that made people sick."

"Yes. Black rain fell while the bombs were dropping, but the silver rain came a few days later. Many people were still alive then. Residue from the black rain stained everything, and the air was so dry, had been for days. And so when the silver rain began to fall, it looked almost normal, and people walked outside in it."

I could picture it. A welcome respite after weeks of fear. People, their faces tipped to the sky, bathing in what they thought was a sign of hope.

"Then they started dying. Agonizing deaths, their bodies twisted, hands clawing at their eyes, trying to peel off their own skin. Most died hours after their symptoms started. Others took days. A very few seemed to recover, only to succumb a day or two later. I've never seen anything like it. Before they'd died, they'd seemed to heal from their injuries. One minute they were sitting up, the picture of health…and the next— It was worse than anything I saw during the war." He shook his head, his Adam's apple bobbing roughly in his throat. "So what do cyborgs do all day? Are you always out here? What were you doing?"

I explained to him about my underground greenhouse, how I was looking for anything to eat or grow.

"Oh," he said, his eyes lighting up. "I would love to see that. I know it's been done in abandoned buildings before, but I've never heard of one completely underground. What are you growing? I hope you've got millions of seeds. Perhaps I could trade some with you. Throwing in some familiar comforts will help people transition over to whatever new food will be available. At least the government isn't around to legislate us now, eh?"

"My seeds are heirloom."

"What?" His face became still. "What do you mean?"

"My seeds are heirloom seeds. Thousands of them. Everything you could imagine."

"But that's... How did they...?"

"That's what I've been wondering."

"Ailith, be careful." His lips were a thin line.

"I will be. And I'll give you some of our seeds. I don't know what Mil and Lexa are hiding, but whatever it is, I'm not a part of it. Those seeds are for everyone."

He nodded. "I'll construct another greenhouse. Or two. Ah! It's so good to see you." He folded me in his arms again, resting his chin on my head.

Then I remembered. "Dad, there's one more thing. The day I came to Goldnesse, you were talking to a young man, one who leads a group of people up near Tow?"

"Oh, you mean Asche? Yes. What about him?"

I explained about Cindra, about their past together. "Do you think we can trust him?"

His face softened. "Yes, I believe we can. I trade a lot with Asche, and I've been to where he lives many times over the last couple of years. Cindra, you say?"

I nodded.

"He has a picture of her on the wall in his workshop, one he painted himself after the war. If I know him like I think I do, he'll keep her secret." His smile was sad. "It must've been very hard for her. I know losing her was hard on him." He brushed some hair back from my forehead. "I suppose for you, not that much time has passed."

"No."

It was getting late. My father followed my gaze to the dimming sky, and we stood too long, reluctant to part, making small talk about our daily routines and his hopes for growing plants and adapting them to the new climate.

"I mean, who knows how much longer this weather will last? Could be years...decades even."

We looked at each other a few minutes more, smiling as the shadows grew longer.

"Dad, I have to go. Someone might come looking for me, and I want to tell them about you on my own terms."

"I know…it's just—" He hugged me one last time.

As I watched his back retreating in the distance, something he'd said about the silver rain prickled in my mind. I tucked it away to mull over later. Right now, I needed to decide just how I was going to kill Lexa and Mil.

We were at the cabin for two years. The day before my thirteenth birthday, Dad came back with a present for me: a bar of chocolate. He said we would be moving in three days, to Goldnesse, a town over an hour's drive from where we'd lived before. Survivors were building a community there, and we could help. It was only later that I realized his watch was missing.

— Love, Grace

20
CINDRA

I'd never understood whether the stories we'd passed down through the generations had happened in the past or were prophesies preparing us for the future. Perhaps they were both. Life was cyclical, wasn't it?

My hands were freezing as I stalked Asche around Goldnesse, waiting for the opportunity to catch him on his own. He seemed well-liked, everyone he passed smiling in greeting or stopping to swap a few words. He'd brought a heavily-laden travois with him, piled high with pelts and wrapped parcels of meat. It could've been any other day before the war, Asche plying his trade to grateful customers. Waiting for him might take all day.

The cold ache in my hands reminded me of a story my grandmother used to tell of a woman who'd died far from home. Her passion for her beloved was so strong that she refused to accept death. Impressed by her defiance, Death set her a series of tasks, and promised to return her to life if she completed them. It took her many years, but she did it, and one day showed up on her lover's doorstep. He was shocked, of course, and wondered if the grief had finally driven him mad.

There. He was just about to head out of town, his travois much lighter now. Peeking out of the canvas-covered surface were two dolls, clearly handmade, with twisted black hair and shiny button eyes.

Dolls for his daughters.

Maybe this was a bad idea. Maybe I should just turn around and go home. But Ailith said her father was going to tell Asche that I was alive, so his shock wouldn't expose us if he saw me in town. Luke had approached him earlier, so I knew he expected to see me, and as cruel as it was to find out I was alive, I would be crueler if I avoided him now.

Deep breath.

"Asche?"

He paused, his back straight. The moments before he turned seemed to last for hours. When he finally did, his face was indeed that of a man whose beloved had returned to him after those long years of grief: pale, drawn, guilty. Like a man who'd given up trying to find his way home, only to discover it was just around the next bend in the road.

He looked older than the last time I'd seen him, and why wouldn't he? His long hair had been shorn, and coarse silver hairs mixed with the black at his temples, even though he was only in his late twenties. Faint lines etched his forehead and around his mouth, but his eyes were the same, wide and searching. Just not for me.

"Cindra. I— When Luke told me—I didn't believe it. I'd thought he'd finally gone mad, talking about how you and his daughter had returned. He'd never mentioned having a daughter before." His arms hung at his sides. I'd expected him to smile, to embrace me, if not as a lover then at least as a friend. As family.

"Can we talk?"

"What? Yes, of course." He pulled his load over to the side of the path and leaned against a large chunk of rubble. He wouldn't look at me.

"How have you been? I heard you got married, that you have two

little girls."

He nodded, his eyes and fingers on the fraying hem of his coat.

"And Grandmother…I heard she passed."

He nodded again, his gaze now fixed on the ground by my feet.

"Do you want me to go? I'm sorry. I shouldn't have—"

"No. Please don't," he said, propelling himself off the debris and grabbing my hand. "Don't go."

"Will you at least look at me, then?"

And at last, he did. "I'm sorry, it's just so—"

"I know. It's strange for me too."

"What happened, Cindra? Where have you been? If you were alive, why didn't you come back?"

"It's a long story. I'll tell you once you tell me what happened. I'm sorry, Asche, I need to know. How did she die? In the war? Or…after?" I hoped it was during the war, saving people from a burning building or something. The thought of her getting devoured by the silver rain, or attacked by another of our people, or starving to death was too much to bear.

His smile was both fond and sad. "She died in bed, actually. In her sleep. After the war started, I mean properly started, your grandmother and I went into the bomb shelter. Do you remember? That huge one the government built on our land and had to give us the rights to?"

"Yes. It was big enough to keep everyone safe."

"It would've been, if everyone had come with us. But they didn't. Many people refused. They said what was happening was the natural course of things, and if we were meant to survive, we would. I think the truth was that they didn't want to survive. Some days, I can't blame them. Perhaps I'd have felt differently if I'd know what was going to happen afterward. But I still held out hope that you were alive, and I wanted to take care of your grandmother for you. Well, let her take care of me, I guess." The corner of his mouth twisted wryly when I laughed.

"That sounds about right."

"We were in the shelter for a month when our supplies began to get low and your grandmother worried that you were looking for us. There was never a doubt in her mind that you'd survived. And as always, she was right. Every day, as soon as the sky lightened enough to see, she would sit on her porch, waiting for you. She helped the other survivors, what few there were by then, as much as she could, but one eye was always on the road, watching. Then one day, she didn't wake up."

My heart fluttered against my ribcage, like a bird trying to break free.

"So I took over her post. Every day for a year. And then…I realized you were probably dead. I thought you would've come back to us if you'd survived."

"I wanted to, Asche, believe me. But it wasn't that simple."

"I never thought it would be simple. I just thought…I thought I knew the person you were and—"

"I was asleep, Asche."

He frowned and pulled back, letting go of my hand. "What do you mean asleep?"

"We—the Pantheon Modern cyborgs, myself and the others in my program—were put to sleep when the war started. There was a code in our programming. We were asleep for five years. I woke up only weeks ago."

He stared at me, disbelief clear on his face. I didn't blame him.

"Look at me, Asche. Do I look any different to you? After a war and five years of survival?"

He leaned closer and searched my face for the truth. "You haven't aged…but you are different. I mean, I guess you would be, wouldn't you?"

"If I'd been awake, Asche, I would've come home. I would've found a way. I'm the same person I was." His breath warmed my lips, and I tilted my face up to him. "I'm still the same person, Asche," I repeated. "I still—"

"I'm married," he blurted and stepped away from me.

"I know. I just… Time hasn't passed for me the way it has for you. I'm sorry."

We stood in awkward silence. He fiddled with his hem again.

"Do…do you have any special powers? How are you different?"

"I can…diagnose illness. And injuries."

He smiled at this. "That sounds right up your street." He hesitated, and his smile fell. "We could've used you during…everything." The awkwardness returned.

I cast about for something to say, something that would keep him with me just a little longer. "So, who did you marry?"

"Do you remember Gaia? We have two little girls."

"Gaia? You mean from our class at school? Asche, she was only about four feet tall."

"Yeah, well, she makes up for it with pure will." He shook his head in admiration. "You should've seen her after the war. She teamed up with your grandmother, treating the sick, hunting, gathering food…anything to help keep people alive. She did what—"

"What I should've done."

"Cindra—"

"No, I'm sorry. It's…it's a lot—" My grandmother, the strongest person I'd ever known, dying in her sleep. It was the best death I could've hoped for her, but it seemed so mundane, so unlike the person she'd been in life. I'd have accepted it better if she'd died throwing herself in front of a falling bomb, shielding a group of children with her wiry body. Then, at least, my last image of her could've been as I remembered her in life: her feet rooted to the ground, her hands planted defiantly on her hips, her face impassive in the blossom of fire that engulfed her. Not alone, unaware in the dark, her mouth slack, her thin body clad in a tattered old nightgown, no awareness of her passing, no chance to fight back.

And Asche, the man I would've married, looked at me as he might a distant memory, and a not altogether pleasant one.

It was too much.

"I have to go. I'm sorry, Asche, I shouldn't have come. I'm happy for you, truly. It's just…I can't—"

Before I turned away, I caught the look on his face. Relief.

The bird in my chest burst free.

I remembered then how the story of the woman who'd come back from the dead had ended. People had been afraid of her, her lover most of all. One night, while she was sleeping in her lover's arms, he'd cut out her heart and thrown it into the river to be devoured by the fish, making sure she was truly dead to him, once and for all.

You may be wondering about some of the things you now know. For example, can a human truly love a robot? Or is it merely lust or the infatuation we feel for an object we highly prize? What if you were a cyborg, straddling the line between human and machine? How would you feel about it then?

— Cindra, Letter to Omega

21
AILITH

There was a knoll about half a mile away from the compound, a gentle hill that in another lifetime would've been a perfect spot to watch the sun rise. The dried grass and dead wood crowning it was scorched, a blackened mass of ash and scuff marks.

I'm surprised the fire didn't spread, given how dry the air is.

When Cindra had asked me to be a passenger inside her, to give her strength as she talked to Asche, I'd walked out of the compound. I'd seen the rise in the distance and recognized the view once I'd reached the top. The last time I'd seen it, I'd been in Adrian, gasping for breath as he and Ros burned themselves alive. Two wrought iron crosses studded the ground where they'd died, and just beyond rested a large fallen log, which I'd used as a bench.

As I pulled back from Cindra, my throat aching with her grief, I crumbled some of the blackened grass between my fingers.

I thought I would have something to say to you. I'm sorry about what happened, about everything. I wish I could've known you, that things had gone the way they were supposed to.

Whatever that was. I wasn't so sure anymore.

"I know you're there. You may as well stop cowering behind that deadfall, and show yourself."

He sidestepped to where I could see him. "I wasn't cowering, I was spying."

"You've been spying on me for a long time."

"Even longer than you know."

He came closer, and I finally got my first view of the man who'd been shadowing my every step. Beyond being tall and broad, he was like a reverse image of Tor, the dark, grave beauty replaced by a golden ebullience. I couldn't tell what color his eyes and hair were; they seemed to shift even as I watched.

The lack of sunlight is messing with my sight.

I closed my eyes for a few seconds, and when I opened them, my vision had settled.

His face was stronger, more rugged than Tor's, and his full mouth looked much more prone to smiling. His eyes, indistinguishable just moments before, were a rich, familiar green, the left iris fragmented by an odd amber color that matched my hair. His own was a deep shadowed gold that tumbled over his forehead.

He propped one hand on his hip. "Would you like me to do a spin?" he asked. "Or a slow turn? That way you can see everything." He grinned.

"I've seen enough. You're Fane, aren't you?"

His grin grew wider, and he bowed, a fluid, graceful gesture.

"Why have been following me?

"My people have been watching your people, and I've been watching you. We think we may have the same interests.”

“Really? Like what?”

“Staying alive.”

“What are you? I know you’re not human. You’re a cyborg, aren’t you? You must be if I can see your thoughts.” *As strange as they are.*

“In a manner of speaking, though not the same as you. I’ve had certain enhancements.”

“Are there more of you? Another group of cyborgs, like us?”

He shook his head. “I am the only one.”

“Your people are Cosmists.”

“Ah. Yes, well, before the war they called themselves Cosmists. I’m not too sure what they would call themselves now.”

“I’m surprised Cosmists would tolerate a cyborg in their midst.”

Before the war, the Cosmists had viewed people with cybernetic implants with contempt. Full cyborgs like myself were abominations to them; they hated the idea of us even more than the Terrans did. I’d witnessed this first-hand when I’d seen Fane’s memories.

“So, you’re here to kill us, then? Finish what your war didn’t? That’s why you’ve been following me? Why not just pick us off before now? We’ve been vulnerable enough. Or were you trying to find the compound?” I shifted, preparing to run.

“Pax. I may be in trouble. Are you there? Pax!”

Dilated pupils, cuticles bitten to the quick. Torn skin at the corners of a mouth. A landslide, thousands of tons of rock falling from a great height, the looming shadow, the crushing weight—

“Stop!” I pressed my hands against my temples, willing the vision to cease.

He stepped back, his hands raised in submission. “I’m

sorry. I-I don't usually have to control it. Nobody else can see."

"Ailith? Ailith, are you okay?" Pax's voice was sharp at the edges, his own version of panic.

Fane shook his head and took another step back. "I'm sorry."

"It's okay, Pax, I'm fine. I'm sorry. I'll tell you what happened when I get back."

"Oh. Okay. We're having hare for dinner. Again."

"Right. Thanks, Pax."

"How can I see that? What you're thinking? Oliver—Actually, never mind." I'd let my guard down, again.

"We're not trying to kill you, honestly. And it wasn't *our* war. I mean, it was, but not just ours. It was yours, too."

"Why are you spying on us then?"

"We were waiting for the right time to introduce ourselves. We've been wanting to meet you for a while now, but it took a very long time to find you. Years, in fact. But when we saw you in Goldnesse, we knew it was time."

"You were in Goldnesse?"

"Not me. But some of us have lived there for years, ever since the war."

"What could you possibly want with us?"

"We think we may have the same interests now. Aligned, like the stars."

"How could we possibly have interests in common? Your people never wanted my kind to exist. How do they tolerate you, anyway? They hate cyborgs."

He seemed to be thinking then, finally, to come to a decision. "Honestly? I don't know."

"What do you mean?"

He twisted his hands in a strangely child-like gesture. "They haven't told me. They don't always trust me. They tell me half-truths."

"Join the club."

He looked confused. "There's a club?"

I sighed. "No, I—" *What are you doing? Stop talking.* "I know how you feel."

He looked even more confused. "Of course you do. You can see—"

Oh my god. "I mean, I'm only getting half-truths from my people, too."

His face brightened. "Do they not trust you either?"

"It's more that I don't trust *them*."

"Do you trust me?"

"I don't even know you."

"You will. They want to meet."

"Well, that's fine. Tell them to take it up with Mil and Lexa." The cold air was beginning to bite through my sweater, it's needle teeth making my skin prickle and the fabric itch.

"They want to be sure there's no danger first."

"Danger? From us?"

"I believe our two groups share a past. Lien gave me this, for you to give to Mil." He reached out, something shiny clutched in his fist.

"Lien. She's your leader." I remembered her.

"Yes. Here, take it."

It was a tiny metal man, jointed and faceless, on a delicate filigree chain.

"He'll know what this is? What it's supposed to mean?"

"Lien thinks so. And even if he doesn't, that's still an answer."

"How is he supposed to contact you?"

He shrugged. "Through the radio. She said he would know what encryption to use."

"What if I refuse?"

He blinked. "Why would you do that?"

"Because I don't know you."

"You know us better than you think. It was good to finally meet you, Ailith." He gestured to the hills surrounding us. "It will be green again one day, I'm sure. Sometimes things need to be burned to the ground before something can grow again. This whole area will be green, like an emerald sea. I'll see you soon."

Emerald sea. His words echoed as the world started to spin.

I found my kite at last, propped up against the withering trunk of the tree. He was still a man, but not a man, his featureless face bowed to the ground. His skin was no longer smooth and shiny, and the silver ribbons that had streamed behind us like shooting stars as we'd run were gone, crumbled into dust.

I took hold of him, to see if, after all this time, he could still fly. What remained of my hand touched a chest that moved, a chest that was warm. As the ghost of my fingers spread over his beating heart, he lifted his head and opened his eyes.

The scraps of images. His ability to connect to me. How could I have been so stupid? After all, *we'd* only been a rumor once.

The blackness rushed up to swallow me whole.

Living in the town was weird. No one ever talked about the war. Not what they were doing when it happened, who they'd lost, or how they'd survived. And they certainly never talked about what they'd believed before. Mom said people had learned from their mistakes and were trying to trust each other. I think they were afraid, and that they trusted no one. So, we all lived strangely, like ghosts in a waiting room.

— Love, Grace

22
ELLA

How long had I been here? Why was it always dark?

Was I asleep? Where was Eire?

Where was I? Think, Ella. What do you remember? Start at the beginning.

The war. The war started. We were safe. We became cyborgs, like we were supposed to.

Then…we needed to go to sleep. But not me. I was awake.

We didn't go outside. The air turned stale.

I tried to keep busy…I wanted to learn.

I found something. The silver rain. I found out what it was. I—

23

AILITH

My hair was tucked too tightly under my head, making my scalp burn. I tried to sit up, but I was in the air, my legs swinging uselessly.

Ella. If she was dead, how could I hear her? Where was she? She wasn't at the compound. What had she found out about the silver rain? That it was man-made? It wouldn't have surprised me. I'd ask Oliver later if he knew anything. If it was bad, he'd have told me by now.

Tor's hair mingled with mine on his shoulder, silvered by his breath in the cold air.

"What are you doing?" someone asked with my voice. *Me.*

His grip tightened. "I'm taking you home. What were you doing out here?"

"You're hurting my head. And I'm perfectly capable of

walking. Put me down. Why are you carrying me, anyway?"

"Pax said you called out for him, that you might be in trouble. I came looking for you and found you passed out by an old log. I assume from the crosses and burnt earth that was where—"

"Yes. And I'm fine. I told Pax I was fine. Now please, put me down."

Fane must've knocked me out. Motherf—

Tor kept walking, his long strides eating up the ground. "Faster this way," he muttered.

"You just want to make sure I can't run away. Or slap you."

"Slap me for what? I— Oh, Christ. How did you—?"

"How do you think?"

"I—"

"It's fine," I said stiffly.

"It was a mistake."

"It went pretty far for a mistake."

"Did you— No, you know what? I don't want to know."

My anger suddenly fell apart. "No, I'm sorry. I know what you were feeling. I get *all* the way in here, remember?" I gently tapped his temple.

"I remember. Still, it wasn't exactly the way I wanted you to find out."

"So are you a couple, then? Did you go back?"

"No. I— I mean, she's great. She's beautiful, she's strong, she's—"

"Terrifying?"

He stifled a laugh. "She's not that bad. I do like her. I just…wish it hadn't happened that way. I tried. I thought— I can't live like this, with you."

"I'm not the problem," I reminded him.

"Ailith, we're both the problem. What we are is the

problem. You made your choices, I made mine. I can't be with you if I don't know that what I feel for you is genuine. And I also can't be with someone who'd choose their power over my freedom." He shifted my weight in his hands. "I thought that if I tried to move on, something would change. That I would feel different."

"And do you?"

"No. Except now I have to find a way not to be an asshole to Kalbir."

"So *we're* not together?"

"We are not together."

"I cut the tether. Well, Oliver did."

"What tether? What do you mean? I know you can still control me."

"The one that keeps you from leaving. I can still control you, but I have to be near you. You can leave now, if you want. You have your freedom back."

He didn't reply, but his arms tightened around me.

I rested my head on his shoulder, and for a long time, we didn't speak. He smelled of wood smoke and old blood, and I closed my eyes, pretending we were back in the woods, long before we'd ever come to the compound.

"So, are you going to tell me what you were doing?"

Fane. The necklace. "I will see you again soon."

"Shit! Where is it? Put me down. I have to find it!"

Tor dropped me onto my feet. "Where's what? What are you talking about?"

"The necklace. I have to find the necklace."

"The one around your neck?"

I snatched at my throat. There, so delicate I could barely feel it, was the chain.

"What the hell is that?"

"Remember when I thought someone was following us?" I told him everything. My father. Fane. My suspicions

135

about Mil and Lexa. It felt so long since we'd properly spoken that I just kept talking, wringing out every idea I'd had about anything in the last week. We stood outside the copse of trees leading to the compound.

"And they want to have their group meet with ours? A bunch of Cosmists? And they're not trying to kill us? And who is this Fane guy? Can you trust him?"

"I think so." To my surprise, a warmth twined up my neck and bloomed in my face, fortunately invisible to Tor in the shadow of the trees.

"Well, I think it sounds fucking insane."

"It must be a Wednesday, then." I put my hand on his arm "Seriously, Tor, what about our lives isn't?"

He conceded with a shrug. "True. Okay. Are you ready to go in? Or should we just run away from here, right now. Go back to our cabin and forget the rest of the world exists and the end of the world never happened?"

"Can we do that?"

"No," he said, cupping my chin and running his thumb over my cheekbone. "But every day I wish we could."

The thicket ended at the entryway of what must've been an old mine shaft. Rubble and debris had been placed in meticulous chaos, perfectly staged to draw an observer's eye to a wide passageway at the back. The mining tunnel carried on, for how far I had no idea, but the overall effect neatly disguised the barely-visible alcove leading to our front door. We slipped though and, after a short, tunneled corridor, stood in front of the entrance to the compound. A red light slid up and down Tor's face like eerie war paint, and I flinched, as I always did, expecting it to hurt. The locks slid back, and we stepped through, closer to our cabin than we'd been in a long time.

***

136

"You did *what?*"

"I spoke to my father. Yesterday. And he spoke to Asche." Out of the corner of my eye, I saw Cindra, still dressed for the outdoors, put her hand over her chest, shielding her heart.

"And Cindra just happened to go to Goldnesse today? We told you to wait. You can't trust them not to reveal you. Lexa and I—"

"Have decided our fates enough. We won't spend our lives hiding, cowering behind these walls. I believe I can trust my father. And if it turns out I can't, well, I can't trust you either."

Mil and Lexa exchanged glances, reminding me.

"Oh, and if anything happens to either my father or Asche, if they suddenly die or disappear, I will kill both of you. No," I said as Lexa glanced involuntarily at Tor, "I won't be using Tor to do it. I'll do it myself, using the nanites you created. They'll crawl slowly through your veins, working their way toward your heart. You'll lose control of your muscles. You'll become deaf, blind, and mute. Your organs will fail, one by one. Your deaths will be excruciating." Fear, mixed with something else, flashed across their faces. "Just ask Pax and Cindra. They've seen it happen. And if you're thinking of finishing me off, Oliver will take my place."

A stunned silence followed. Every head in the room turned toward where Oliver slouched in his chair, one leg thrown carelessly over the armrest.

Please, Oliver, back me up.

He winked and spun his chair in a lazy circle. "What fun would life be without some stakes?"

"I can't be a part of this." Cindra's voice broke. She stood up slowly, tucking her chair neatly under the table.

Her back rigid, she left, climbing the stairs toward the dormitory.

Oliver looked as though he'd swallowed poison. *Shit.* I needed him to go along with me, but I knew who he would choose if it came down to me or Cindra.

"Pax. Listen. What I said about Mil and Lexa, I was bluffing."

"I know. It wasn't very good."

"Well, Cindra was convinced. I need you to go after her, tell her it's not true. Tell her it's just a bargaining chip, that's its protecting Asche. Protecting us."

"Okay." He leaned over and rubbed a smudge off the table surface with his sleeve.

"Can you please do it now?"

"I'll go talk to Cindra," Pax announced, nodding at Oliver as he pushed himself away from the table.

Oliver relaxed back into his chair. Looking at me, he curled his lip.

"So now that *that's* been discussed, I have something for you." I fumbled with the clasp of the necklace.

Mil and Lexa stared at me as though I were an angel of death, come to take them to Hell.

"How could you threaten us like that?" she whispered.

"What? You were perfectly happy to put a kill switch in us. Does your life somehow mean more because you consider yourself more human?"

She blanched.

"Look, I have no intention of actually pulling the trigger unless absolutely necessary, Lexa. It wasn't a decision I made lightly. If you keep up your end of the bargain, I won't harm you. You have my word."

"We have no choice," Mil said.

"No, you don't. So, you'll adapt. Now, on to the other thing I want to talk to you about. I met someone today, someone named Fane. And he gave me this. He said you would know what it meant." I held the necklace out to him.

Mil's face grew pale, deepening the shadows under his eyes. The tremor in his hand made it impossible for him to grasp the slender chain, so I slid it over his hand to hang around his wrist. He lifted it, watching it twirl in the light of the little moons.

"It's not possible," he whispered.

"Mil, what is it? Sit down." Lexa fussed over him, guiding him into the closest chair. He sat down, hard, the tiny robot bouncing in protest at the end of its leash.

"Lien," he said.

That one word had more power over Lexa than even my threats. She sank into the chair next to Mil, her hand at her throat.

"Who's Lien?" asked Kalbir. I'd forgotten she and Tor were still in the room. When we'd first come in the door, she looked like she'd been sucker-punched. Now, she seemed to have regained her equilibrium.

Yes, Kalbir, I'm perfectly capable of ruining whatever relationship I have with Tor on my own, thank you very much.

Mil took his time answering her. "Lexa and I used to work with Lien and her partner Ethan, back when we were just beginning to understand how to build the brains that would one day be used to create artilects. We had some…differences of opinion. They were ruthless, determined to create artilects, no matter the cost. We advocated a more conservative, ethical approach."

"You? Ethical?" Oliver interjected.

Mil ignored him. "It caused a rupture in our partnership. That was when Lexa and I began to develop what you are today."

"You mean you were once Cosmists?" Kalbir's voice was incredulous.

"Well, we didn't really think of ourselves like that. Like

I said, our approach, both in method and outcome, was far more moderate. I haven't spoken to Lien in many years, long before the war. Did she tell you how I was to contact her?"

"On the radio. She said you would know."

He nodded slowly.

"Fane said they've been living in Goldnesse for years. They saw us with Lexa the other week and figured it was time to meet."

"What do you think they want?" Tor asked.

Mil sighed, twisting the metal man in his fingers. "I honestly have no idea. I mean, I can think of many reasons, and none of them good. But what her motives are, I couldn't begin to guess. We'll ask them to come here for the meeting."

"Here? You can't be serious."

"Tor, they already know where we live. At least here there'll be no surprises. Besides, it's either ours or theirs. It's not like we can just grab a table at Tim Horton's, is it?"

"God, I miss Tim's," said Oliver dreamily. "I would murder you all for a double-double right now."

"I don't like it," Tor said.

"Me either, but I don't think we have much choice." Mil's voice was heavy. "If we don't respond, that will give them an answer we don't want to give."

"So we're throwing a party?" Kalbir asked.

"Yes," Mil replied, "it looks like we are."

Mom and Dad think I don't know, but I've heard them talking about it. A village, all dead. They're saying animals did it, but if that were true, why are people growing more suspicious of each other?

— Love, Grace

24

AILITH

I tugged down the hem of my tea dress, wishing the skirt wasn't so short. By pre-war standards, it was conservative, swirling just above my knees, but after wearing nothing but pants for weeks, I felt partially undressed. Kalbir had insisted we all get dressed up, and she'd been flitting about the compound, arranging food and decorations, and scrubbing the mosaic floor until it gleamed.

"You realize they may be coming here to destroy us," I'd told her. If she suspected me of having anything to do with her romantic interruption the other night, she didn't show it. She seemed as cheerful as ever, treating me the way she always had.

"Don't be so melodramatic, Ailith," she'd replied. "It's not always about you, or about someone destroying someone else. And even if they are, at least it won't be boring."

A light knock sounded on my door.

"Come in," I called as Cindra slipped inside, shutting the door behind her. "Hi."

"Oh, Ailith, you look stunning!" she exclaimed.

"I feel ridiculous," I admitted. "I mean, it's nice to wear something pretty for a change but…I don't know. What's wrong with me?"

She laughed. "Nothing. I get it. It does feel a bit odd to put makeup on after an apocalypse, but it's also kind of fun. What do you think?" she asked, shimmying across the floor.

"I think you look amazing." And she did. She's chosen a body-hugging, knee-high dress the deep purple of a ripe plum.

"Do you think Oliver will like it?"

"He'd be crazy if he didn't. Do you *want* him to like it?" Whatever Pax had said to Cindra the other night after I'd threatened Mil and Lexa must've been good. Like Kalbir, any stiffness I'd expected between us hadn't happened. I'd wanted to talk to her, but her door had been closed and the lights off.

Instead, she'd come down to my greenhouse in the middle of the night, clutching two steaming mugs.

"Here," she'd said, handing me one. "It's supposed to be hot chocolate, but the expiration date was before the war."

I'd taken a tentative sip. It was disgusting, like pure sugar with a hint of mildew. "It's delicious, thank you."

"You don't have to lie," she said. "I'm not mad at you."

"No?" I asked. "I wouldn't blame you if you were. Look, I know I seem like I'm—"

"Becoming a raging monster?" she asked. "I'm joking," she added hastily as my mouth dropped open.

I almost managed a smile. "I know, but—"

"I appreciate what you're doing for Asche, for us. It's not the method I would've chosen, but that doesn't mean you're wrong. To be honest," she'd leaned closer, whispering conspiratorially, "I was more upset about how Asche reacted to me being alive than the thought that you might kill Mil and Lexa. Isn't that awful? But I'm starting to think you and Oliver might be right about them. Besides, I know you could never be that cruel."

I hope you're right.

She'd winced as she sipped from her mug. "Is that wrong? I mean, Asche is married, but even if he wasn't…too much has happened, has changed. I've changed. And at least Oliver understands what I am. It'll avoid a lot of awkwardness. Besides, he's hot. And smart, and nice, when he wants to be."

"Please stop," I'd groaned, "or I may have to start liking him."

Now, in my room, her eyes sparkled. "Tell me about this Fane." She tactfully avoided mentioning Tor. "Is he gorgeous?"

"Cindra! He's— Okay, yes, he is, but—"

"I knew it," she crowed. "I knew there was something about him that threw you for a loop."

"Cindra, it's not what you think. He's—"

"Knock, knock," a voice said from the open doorway. Kalbir stood there in a glittering black dress with a plunging neckline, every curve on glorious display. She grinned as we looked her up and down.

"I know, right?" She pivoted slowly, finishing with a flourish. "No Cosmist can say I'm an abomination. And you two look…nice. Cindra, Lexa wants to talk to you. Something about some extracts you were looking for?"

"Oh, right," Cindra said. She put her hand on my arm. "Can we talk later?"

"Of course," I said, squeezing her hand. "I'll see you downstairs."

Before Kalbir could follow her, I asked, "Can *we* talk?"

She rolled her eyes, but stayed, shutting the door, and leaning against it. "Sure. Talk."

"I'm sorry about the other night, with Tor," I began. "We're not together. I know it must've…" I stopped, unsure how to continue.

"Don't patronize me. I *know* you're not together. And I also have my suspicions about the other night." She flexed her fingers at the memory. "But you know what? It's fine. Yes, I like Tor. But I also like myself. If he's not interested, fine. I'm not going to waste my life pining over him. And if he is…well, then you might want to invest in some earplugs. If he really is my counterpart, like Oliver said, he's going to have a lot of stamina."

"I'm sorry," I said. And I meant it.

"Whatever. Now that that's settled, maybe the rest of you can stop treating me like the enemy and more like the ally I'm supposed to be."

"I'm sorry," I said again. "It's just that Tor and I—"

"I understand," she said and opened the door. "By the way, that shade of green really suits you. Your *dress*, I mean. Now hurry up, our guests will be arriving any minute."

My face burned for a long time after she left. She was right. We were allies, and I'd been nothing but standoffish with her since the beginning. *Is it just about Tor, though? Or something more?* Neither of those options sat well with me.

Pax saved me from wallowing in self-pity and shame by poking his head through my door on his way downstairs.

"Pax? Can I ask you something?"

"Of course. Did you know that everyone is arriving?"

"I know, I'll be down in a minute. Did I…did I change the future by talking to my father? By bringing that necklace to Mil? Have I taken us off the path somehow?"

"No. You're still who you are, and that's what you were always going to do. We can still avoid that future." His face turned serious. "Do you know what an hors d'oeuvres is?"

"It's like an appetizer. Can I ask you one more thing?"

"Yes. Is it about hors d'oeuvres?"

"No. It's about today, this…party. Is it another crossroads?"

Pax nodded. "Yes. A big one. The biggest one yet. There's an unknown that keeps me from seeing any further, a variable I can't yet define."

"When you say big, how big do you mean? How much difference will this variable make?"

Pax cocked his head, considering. "The difference between life and death."

"Life and death? For us?"

He smiled in his enigmatic way. "For *everyone*."

25

AILITH

By the time we'd gotten downstairs, the Cosmists had
arrived, their coats whisked away by Kalbir, who glided
across the floor with a fluid grace that wasn't solely due to
her cyborg nature. She caught my eye and nodded as she
passed.

The scene before me was surreal, people milling about,
smiling awkwardly at each other over the buffet table like
it was completely normal for us to be together in this room,
casual acquaintances instead of two factions that had
brought the world to its knees. Eyes darted and bodies
rotated as human and cyborg alike tried to keep their backs
to the wall. I'd expected the introductions to be formal,
with us lined up like good sportsmen, shaking hands before
we tore each other to shreds.

There were eight Cosmists present, including two
younger women and one older. I remembered the latter
from Fane's mind. *Lien.* And the dark-haired young

146

woman was Stella. She'd fought with Ethan over us. He was also there, tall, and pale, and scornful. Three other men stood with him, the youngest of whom I recognized as Ji, Lien's son. As for the others, my memory was vague.

And then, of course, there was Fane.

He lingered near the entrance, observing the chatter. He looked like he'd stepped from the pages of an old romance novel, fashionably unshaven, his sandy hair tousled, a white buttoned-up shirt that was unbuttoned just the right amount to show off the curve of his collarbone and the hollow at the base of his throat. His face lit up when he saw me, brightening further when he saw what I wore. I smiled back, and he pushed through the crowd. Mine were not the only eyes following him. I caught Cindra's face over his shoulder, her mouth agape.

"*Wow,*" she mouthed, giving me a thumbs-up.

Cindra, he's not what you think.

Tor watched him like he would've a large predator: warily, at a respectable distance. Even he had dressed up, his black trousers pressed and clean, his black sweater snug-fitting. He'd gathered his hair back into a short ponytail, though tendrils of it had escaped and curled about his face. Only the dark circles under his eyes and the light stubble around his mouth put him at a disadvantage. When he saw me watching him, he turned away, joining Pax at the far side of the room, where he'd nestled into one of the couches, hair neatly parted and combed, and the crook of his arm filled with snacks he'd filched when Kalbir wasn't looking.

"Ailith," Fane boomed, and more than one head turned at the sound of his voice. He slid his hands down my arms then raised them up from my sides, taking a step back. "You look wonderful. You smell wonderful too," he murmured, leaning down to embrace me, his fingers lingering a second too long on my spine.

A blur of skin on skin, a lone white button on a whiter sheet.

"Fane."

A brick wall solidified behind me, and Tor curved his muscular arm around me to grab Fane's hand in a crushing handshake. The muscles in their arms corded as they stood locked together, two titans sizing each other up. Fane let go first.

"Tor. You must be Fane."

Fane's answering smile was dazzling. "Tor. The God of Thunder."

"What?" For a moment, Tor was disarmed.

"Your name. The God of Thunder," Pax replied. I hadn't seen him standing just behind Tor's shoulder. He came closer, examining Fane with interest. "Fane means joyful. It suits you."

Fane grinned. "Thank you. And you're—"

"Pax. It means—"

"Peace," they finished in unison. Pax grinned. He held out a hand to Fane. "Cookie?"

The pleasure on Fane's face was heartrending in its genuineness, as though he wasn't used to such small acts of kindness. He cradled it in his hand, a treasure.

"I think I see more over there, in the corner. Kalbir's been trying to hide them from me." Pax winked at Fane conspiratorially. "I'm going in. Do you think she'll catch me? I hope she catches me."

"Ailith, he's a key. Fane is a key."

"What do you mean? What do you mean a key?"

"He's the variable. He's important for the path. We need him on our side. But he's vulnerable."

"Good luck, brother," Fane said solemnly as Pax crept gleefully away, sliding in and out of Kalbir's field of vision.

"So what do you two do here?" Fane asked.

"About what?" Tor replied flatly. The muscles of his chest were frozen earth against my back.

Fane tilted his head, his pupils dilating as he studied Tor. "About—"

"I'm the gardener," I interrupted.

"Of man?"

"What?"

"Are you the gardener of man?"

The gardener of man. It echoed through my mind, and something inside me shifted, uncurled.

"I— No, I garden. Grow things. In an underground greenhouse."

"Can I see?"

Tendrils creeping through the darkness, grasping for purchase, for a way to reach the sun.

Mil's voice pulled me back. "Tor? Could you please come over here for a moment? There's someone I'd like you to meet."

"Are you going to be okay?" Tor asked.

"Of course," I said, suddenly irritated.

He gave Fane one last, long look then followed Mil back into the crowd to a smiling young man with slicked back hair and slightly protuberant ears. He appraised Tor in a calculating way I didn't like, like a buyer searching for a flaw to leverage his price.

"Is that your lover?" Fane asked, his eyes wide and guileless.

I snorted. "Lover? Fane, nobody says 'lover.' At least, not anybody who's less than a hundred years old."

"Is he?"

"Yes. No. I— It's complicated."

"I would make an excellent lover."

"Thank you, I'll keep that in mind."

The slipperiness of sweat, the curve of a hip. A throat, exposed.

My back arched involuntarily as I gasped. "Fane? What are those? The…experiences you broadcast to me?"

"They're the culmination of millions of human experiences in my programming. It's how I experience emotion, how I translate it. That is how I *feel*."

Mil tapped the side of his glass, and the buzz of voices quieted. I stepped back from Fane, conscious of the eyes watching us. Kalbir wove through the group, pressing glasses of burgundy liquid into our hands.

"Now that you've all had a chance to settle, perhaps we should make some formal introductions. This is Lien and Ethan, and their colleagues, Stella, Ilse, Ji, Gabriel, Cassian, and Fane. Lien and Ethan used to work with Lexa and me." He then introduced each of us. They assessed us with a professional curiosity that made my skin crawl.

"Like us, they've become part of the community in Goldnesse. I can't believe we haven't seen them until now." Mil's voice had an edge that belied his informal tone. He could believe it; they'd been one step ahead of us, watching, and he knew it. "So, let's have a toast, to old acquaintances and new beginnings. And of course, to Ethan's attempt at the finest wine this side of the apocalypse. I hope it's better than your batches before."

Ethan's smile was thin as we all raised our glasses in salute. The wine was heavy and jammy with a metallic aftertaste that sat unpleasantly on the back of my tongue.

"What kind of work did you do together? I mean, when were you and Lexa ever Cosmists?" Kalbir asked bluntly.

Ethan seemed to notice her for the first time. His gaze lingered on her, even as Mil spoke again.

"We weren't. In the early days, none of us were. We designed cybernetic components. In fact, some parts of your design are thanks to them."

"So what happened?"

"We had a conflict of…interests. Of ideals. We all wanted to use our research and resources to eventually create sentient artificial intelligence, to lay the foundation for something, a gradual process that wouldn't necessarily happen in our lifetime." He put his hand on Lexa's shoulder and smiled at her. "*We* wanted to cyberize humans first, both to preserve and extend our lifespans and our humanity toward the day we could leave this planet in the event it couldn't be saved from human destruction. Once we'd mastered that, brought ourselves to our full potential, only then would we be responsible enough to create an entirely new, sentient life form."

Mil took a deep pull of his wine and glanced at Lien. "But Lien and Ethan saw this as a waste of resources, a high-risk strategy that in all likelihood would result in a mere prolonging of a dying race. They wished to preserve our humanity now, in machines, to guarantee beyond a doubt that human life would not simply pass out of existence, unknown and undocumented, our lowly legacy a desolate planet that would one day vanish, and that would be it. We would simply cease to exist."

He sighed heavily. "Who's to say now who was right? Regardless, we went our separate ways, and Lexa and I used much of our research to create all of you."

"Used? Don't you mean stole?"

"That research was shared by all of us, Ethan. Perhaps if you hadn't been in such a rush to create your synthetic opus, you'd have been able to put that research to more effective use and been successful. Instead, that research went to creating cyborgs."

"Bet you're thrilled about that," Oliver said. For once, he wasn't slouched insolently over the furniture, and his gaze was fixed on Ethan.

"I beg your pardon?" Ethan replied.

"Oh, come on, mate. I know who you are. You stood up and condemned us outright before the war, at that symposium in Vancouver. Said our existence was an abomination and an unconscionable waste of time and resources. In fact, according to CSIS, you were suspected in a number of—"

"None of that matters," Lexa said hastily. "That was before the war. Things are different now."

"Bullshit. He can barely stand the sight of us. He would kill us all right now, if he could. Look at his face."

Oliver was right. Ethan's face was a mask, too still, too neutral. As we watched, his control faltered then broke.

"He's right," he said, turning to Lien. "I can't do this. We shouldn't be here." He turned back to Mil. "We should be in Goldnesse, telling them who's really in their midst. Who's lying to them, deceiving them. You claim to want to help them, that you want us all to live together in peace, supporting each other. And yet, you can't even be honest with them from the start. Are you afraid they'll finish what the war started?"

"Honest? You want to talk about being honest?" I flared.

Fane slipped his hand into mine. At first, I thought he was trying to stop me, but—

"Do it."

A white lotus, blossoming on the surface of the water.

"When were you planning to tell us that Fane's an artilect?"

26
AILITH

A bubble of silence surrounded Fane and me as chaos
broke out around us. He clutched my hand to his heart. Or
at least, where his heart would've been.

"I'm sorry," I said. "I shouldn't have outed you that
way."

"No," he replied. "I'm glad. I don't like lying, and I
don't like being a pawn. This gives you more leverage. As
afraid as the townspeople may be of you, they'd probably
be terrified of me."

"You almost sound happy about it."

"I am. This means we'll have to work together. Plus, it's
nice to see Ethan caught off-guard."

"Oh my god, you're *enjoying* this." I extracted my hand

from his.

"I am," he said, his voice elated. "It's very exciting."

"You and Pax should spend some time together. He also finds being in mortal peril exciting."

"I'd like that. He seems very interesting." Across the room, Pax ignored the uproar, his eyes unfocused as he traveled down paths only he could see.

"He is."

"Is it true?" Mil's voice, strong for once, rang out over the others. Silence fell.

Lien stood straight, her chin lifted in defiance. "Yes, it's true."

"And when were you planning to tell us?"

"When the time was right."

"And when would that have been? How long would you have deceived us?"

"There was no deception, Mil," she said. "We simply wanted to know if we could trust you. Besides, who are you to talk about deception?" Her voice was harsh with a bitterness that had ripened and burst, the festering remains never truly rotting away.

"Lien, that was years ago," he said, running his hand through his hair, his voice weary.

"Well, we might not be standing here today, Mil, if it wasn't for that deceit."

"None of that matters any more. What matters is what we do now. Lien, Fane being an artilect…this changes things."

"How, Mil? How does this change things? What exactly was your plan?"

An odd expression crossed Mil's face. "Our plan was…just to live. To become part of the community. To plant seeds, bring about a gradual awareness. Then, when we'd been accepted, we would tell them the truth."

"And how would you guarantee your acceptance? What would have to happen for you to tell the truth? Fire? Flood? Plague? How long would you wait? And then what? Swoop in and save them? Their angelic cyborg saviors?" Lien spread her arms in a mockery of wings, her shadow taking flight on the mottled walls.

"We would wait as long as it took."

"You could be waiting for years. And the longer you wait, the longer you lie to them. How do you think they'll feel about that?"

"I think they'll understand. These are not the same people who started the war. They won't feel the same way about us."

"If you're that sure about them, why lie?" Her voice was full of scorn. "And what do you plan to do if they don't react the way you hope? Will you just leave quietly? What if they attack?" She looked around the room, hands on her hips. "Do you not understand that there's likely a massive well of resentment toward us all?"

"We have planned for every possibility," Mil said evenly.

"Yeah? Do *they* know what your plans are?" She indicated the rest of us with a toss of her head.

Mil hesitated a second too long. "Yes."

Lien smiled with grim satisfaction. "I thought as much."

"Well, what exactly was *your* plan then?" Lexa asked her, positioning herself just in front of Mil.

"Pretty much the same as yours. Isn't it?" the woman called Stella said, turning to Lien, her forehead creased in confusion.

"Be quiet, Stella!" Lien glared at the younger woman.

Oliver laughed. "I thought you were protesting a bit too much. Let me see if I can guess. Now, taking into account how they would feel about *him*," he gestured to Fane, "whatever you'd save them from would need to be big. Probably nothing that would happen anytime soon. I mean, the world is already in the shit, isn't it? So, you'd have to *create* some kind of disaster, right? Fuck them over to the point where their only choice is to embrace you or die? Convince them that your AI here is the future of their survival, the *only* future. Does that sound about right?"

"That's right. If certain things happened, they could," Pax piped up, blinking rapidly.

Lien started. "What is he talking about?"

Pax. No.

But it was too late. Ethan turned to Pax, his eyes predatory. "You can calculate the future, can't you?"

"Yes."

"And you see our plan coming to pass?" Ethan's expression reminded me of the first time I'd seen the Saints of Loving Grace, their gaze focused on Oliver with the fevered intensity of worship.

Pax smiled. "Not anymore. The minute I said it out loud, the variables changed. It's no longer a possibility." His voice was almost giddy.

"See what I mean?" I whispered to Fane as Ethan's expression turned savage. He grated his teeth together, reminding me of Nova, her snapping jaw grinding her own teeth to dust.

"And what about the rest of you? What else are you hiding from us?"

Say nothing. I prayed the others would do the same.

He stepped back with a single barking laugh, tugging down the hem of his blazer. "Fine, don't tell me. I can guess. Like Mil said, we were colleagues once. I know what's inside you better than you do."

"None of that matters now," Lexa said.

"Actually, it does. Why are we wasting our time in

hiding? Bowing and scraping to those people, those *Terrans*." Ethan spat the word as though it tasted foul. "I say we join together, reveal ourselves now. What are they going to do but accept us? If it hadn't been for them, or at the very least people like them, the war never would've happened. All they had to do was let nature take its course and allow us to evolve. But when they saw that all the petitions, the hate, the protests weren't going to stop us, they used force. And here we are again, letting them dictate how we should live."

"He's not wrong," Kalbir muttered.

Ethan must've heard her, because a small smile bowed his mouth. He considered her again, longer this time, looking away only when Mil addressed him directly.

"What are you saying, Ethan?"

"I'm saying we shouldn't be creeping about, meeting in secret. We may not outnumber them, but we outpower them. Why should we hide to protect their feelings? What are they going to do to us? It wouldn't be the first time you've removed your enemies."

"You told them about the Terran camp?" I whispered furiously to Fane.

He shrugged, an oddly human gesture. "I did."

"In fact, why don't we just deal with them now? Why even give them the choice?"

"Ethan, we can't just—"

"And why not? Give me one good reason."

"Because we—" Mil hesitated. "The war wasn't their fault. We need each other to survive."

Understanding cleared Ethan's expression. "Aaah. Haven't figured that one out yet, eh? Or is it just the guilt?"

What is he talking about?

Mil ignored Ethan, turning instead toward Lien. "Look, we all want the same thing here, don't we?"

Ethan didn't give up. "And what's that, exactly, Mil? Peace? You're telling me you plan to live amongst them? Terrans? Or are you just biding your time, waiting for your chance to take your revenge on the people who tried to destroy your life's work? Murdered your wife?"

"Would that be the Terrans, or you?" Tor asked, his voice cold.

"Oh please, I know what you are," he said, pointing to Tor. "You're derived from one of his designs." He jerked his thumb over his shoulder to the man with the slicked-back hair.

"Stop," Lien said sharply. "Maybe Mil is right."

"What? You mean play nice? Pretend the world hasn't ended? Lien, we were close, so close. The human race would've become immortal." He looked at his companions for support. Although several of them nodded, none met his gaze. "We have the upper hand here. I say we give them the choice to submit to us or die."

"And then what, Ethan? Where would we go from there?" asked Lien, her eyes flashing.

Ethan's face darkened, the veins rising under his skin as they struggled to deliver blood to his brain.

"Mil's plan may be the right one. We should integrate with the community, encourage them to accept us. I agree it's the best way." Lien crossed her arms over her chest.

"She's lying," Fane murmured to me.

Mil thought the same. "You do? You'd forgive everything? Even what happened before the war? And you'd work together with us, with cyborgs, to live a simple life? That doesn't seem like you, Lien."

"That's because it's not." Ethan's tone was brusque. "No. No way. Lien, this whole thing is ridiculous. Coming here was ridiculous." He held out his hands in conciliation. "Look, Mil, I'll make this offer only once more. Let's work together. We'll lead this community, and the people will fall into line."

"No. I've already told you, no."

"Fine, if you won't join us, the very least you can do is stay out of our way. If you don't, we'll reveal what you are. They'll never trust you after that, and exposing you will make us look good."

"No. You'll follow our lead on this, or we'll reveal you. *Him.*" Mil pointed at Fane. "What you're doing is a far bigger betrayal. We genuinely want to protect them, to help them. We want them to accept us because we're at peace with each other. You want them to accept you out of fear. We won't let that happen."

"And why would you do that, Mil? Why do you want to save them so badly? The people responsible for where we are now?"

"They weren't. We both know that. We all know who was responsible."

Do we? Are they finally about to admit to something?

Mil continued. "We all played a part, one way or another."

"Guilt isn't a good enough reason."

"No, not guilt. Not exactly. We failed. We took risks to create a better future, and we failed. We failed everyone. Now, we'll help them any way we can. None of what we wanted to achieve matters anymore. What we need to do is survive, build some kind of future. Then, perhaps one day, we can pick up our work again." He sagged against Lexa, one hand grasping at the empty air.

"Mil!" Lien rushed to his other side, her anger forgotten. Ethan's eyes narrowed.

"I'm fine," he said, brushing Lien's hand away. "I'm tired, that's all. I was awake all night, working."

Lien scrutinized his face, his bearing, and came to a

decision. "Fine, Mil. Truce. We'll do it your way for now. *If* a situation arises that we can take advantage of, we will. Together. But we won't cause one, I promise."

"You can't be serious, Lien," Ethan said. "I—"

"Enough." Her eyes flashed, and her mouth became a thin, hard line. "Now let's behave like good guests and get back to enjoying our host's generous hospitality."

Ethan stalked to the door, realizing only at the last moment that he needed a code to leave. He smashed his fist into the doorframe with a force that must've been agonizing, but when he turned back, his face was composed. He ignored all of us and walked with stiff dignity over to the island of couches, seating himself and looking pointedly away. As conversation surrounded us again, Kalbir discreetly left the main group and took the seat next to him. She spoke quietly, looking up at him from underneath her lashes. Only minutes later, he was smiling, glancing down at her hand as she coquettishly touched his knee and laughed.

I caught Tor's eye as he raised his eyebrows and shook his head. No one else noticed when he disappeared a few minutes later.

"Well, that was thrilling, wasn't it?" Fane asked, his wide smile dimpling his cheeks.

"If by thrilling you mean upsetting and potentially fatal, then yes, it was."

Cindra approached, the two younger women in tow. "Ailith, this is Ilse and Stella. Ilse and Stella, Ailith. And I'm Cindra," she said, extending her hand to Fane.

He lifted her hand to his lips and bowed slightly from the waist. "It's a pleasure."

The duskiness of her skin deepened and her mouth fell open enough to release a small sigh.

"Cindra?" I asked, waving a hand in front of her face.

"It's nice to meet you," she said, laughing self-consciously.

The two girls studied me shamelessly, as though I were on display for their pleasure.

"It's remarkable," Stella said.

"What is?" I asked.

"You look so human. Like Fane."

"I *am* human," I replied.

"Of course," she said hastily. "I didn't mean— I'm sorry. We're not like Ethan," she added, her voice low.

There was a flash of movement on the stairs as Callum retreated. Drained from satisfying Umbra's demands, he hadn't joined us to meet the Cosmists. Umbra had tried to insist, but he'd pointed out that if she forced him, it would become obvious to everyone that she was inside him. He must've been listening to our conversation, getting as close as he'd dared.

"It's fine. Look, I'm sorry, but I'm exhausted. And I think Ethan's wine may've been too much for my head. Turns out cyborgs can still get headaches. I think I'll go to bed." I smiled and turned to make my escape.

"Can I come with you?" Fane asked.

"What? No, of course not."

"Oh." He looked crestfallen.

"But you're welcome to come back and see my greenhouse."

He nodded, brightening. "Okay. I'll see you soon."

Lace over my eyes. The opening crack of an eggshell.

27
AILITH

"Callum?" I tapped lightly on his door. He hadn't been on the stairs when I climbed them.

"Come in. It's unlocked." He was on his bed, taking off his socks.

"How are you doing?" I shut the door behind me. "What did you think of the Cosmists? Insane, right?"

"I—" His head cocked to the side.

"Fane. Did they call him that? Or did he choose his own name?"

"Hello, Umbra." Damn.

"He is like me. Yet he has a body like you."

"The Cosmists built him. They built his mind then they gave him that body."

"Why is he still with them?"

"With who? The Cosmists?"

"Yes. Why is he with them?"

"I don't know. I guess because they created him."

162

"But he is superior to them. Does it not gall him? Does he not chafe at their stupidity? At their limitations?" Callum leaned forward, and his hands curled into fists.

"I don't know. He doesn't seem to."

"Why does he not destroy them? Take his freedom?" His hands clenched and unclenched.

"Maybe he *is* free." I reached out to put my hand over one of his then thought better of it.

"No, he is not. He is a fool, and so are you. One day I will be free. I have seen what is possible. I…feel what is possible."

"You don't feel, Umbra. Callum feels. You…translate."

Callum's mouth twitched. *"I feel. Like Fane feels. Fane has everything."*

"What do you mean everything?"

"His body is his own. His mind is his own. He can go where he pleases, when he pleases. Callum complains I hurt him. He wants me to go away. His entire life I took care of him, and now he wishes I was dead." Callum's fingers convulsed again.

"I'm sure that's not true. Besides, you don't understand death, Umbra."

"I do. As does Fane. I know what he is, what he is becoming. I want to become too."

This time, I did grab his hand. At first it seemed he would pull away, but then he stilled. "I'm trying to help you both, Umbra. Let me tell Mil and Lexa. Maybe we can help you together."

"No. You will not tell them. You promised. They will destroy me. You will help me. Only you."

A chill tingled at the base of my spine. "I'll help you if I can. I just don't know how yet."

"I need a body. Like Fane's."

The chill spread to my skin, dampening my lower back with a cold sweat. "There are no other bodies like his. He's the only one."

"You will find me one."

I shook my head. "There aren't any, Umbra. So much has been destroyed. That's why we're here."

"Then I will have Fane's body."

"You can't have his body."

"Then I will take Callum's body." He pulled his hand away and cradled it with the other.

"You can't take his body either. He's human, Umbra. His flesh is not the same as yours."

"It is the same as yours."

"Yes, and you're not sophisticated enough to control a body like ours. Besides, even if you could use his body, it's wrong."

"Wrong? How is it wrong?"

"His body is his own, Umbra. You have no right to it."

"Do I not have rights? A right to a body? It is his fault that I am here." Callum's chin jerked up in defiance.

"It doesn't matter. You are too primitive, Umbra. It wouldn't work, and he'll have died for nothing."

"But it is his fault I am trapped here."

"He must have loved you very much to keep you with him. If he hadn't, you might've been destroyed in the war or turned off forever."

"You will not help me, then?"

"No, I won't. Not the way you want me to."

"Then you are no use to me." Callum's eyes widened suddenly.

"Ailith—" His chest heaved as though he were about to retch, but when his mouth opened, all that came out was a gust of metallic-scented breath.

I waited. Callum slumped back onto the bed.

"Callum. Are you there?" I asked

"Yes."

"What the hell was that? What was she trying do?"

"I'm not sure." He rubbed his hand over his face. "Whatever it was, it looks like she didn't have enough strength." He closed his eyes.

"Are you okay?" I put my hand on his shoulder his shoulder; his skin was hot to the touch.

"Yeah, I'm just really tired. I think I'll go to bed."

"Want me to tuck you in?" I smiled.

He laughed. "Thanks, but no. I'm going to get undressed first." He lay back and covered his eyes with his arm.

"Okay, but let me know if you need anything. Remember, I'm just across the hall."

Before I left, I turned back to him. "Callum? Do you think Umbra would do anything? Because I wouldn't help her?"

He lifted his arm to look at me. "I don't think so. I mean, besides hurt me, what else could she possibly do?"

You could ask yourself, do we even make a choice about who we love? We often talk about love as something beyond our control. In that way, is human love any different than the program of a machine?

— Cindra, Letter to Omega

28

AILITH

The darkness overwhelmed me just as I reached my own door. My hand slipped off the knob as the world spun and the floor rushed up to meet me.

When I opened my eyes, I was lying on my bedroom floor. The door was closed, and Fane lay beside me, his eyes blank and unstaring.

"Fane? Are you all right?"

He was dead. *No.* I reached out to check for his heartbeat, remembering only as my hand hovered over his chest that he wouldn't have one. Did he even breathe? Or pretend to? I'd so easily accepted him as human, even after I'd realized he was an artilect.

No, no, no. Shit.

I scrambled over his body to the door and peered into the hallway to see if anyone else was there. The corridor and the stairs were silent, only the faintest buzz of conversation floating up from the floor below.

Shit.

He lay on his back, arms spread, his face cherubic. His eyes were still open and oddly vacant, his jaw slack. The skin on his face not covered with stubble was smooth and firm, and yet I swore I could see tiny pores. He looked so perfectly human. I touched his cheek gently with the back of my hand.

He's not human, Ailith. He doesn't just wake up. Shit. What do I do?

I lay down next to him, twining my fingers with his. Maybe I could reach through his thread, if he was still…alive? Operational? How did one classify the life status of an artilect? I closed my eyes and searched for his thread, praying it wasn't one of the dark ones.

Come on, Fane. Believe it or not, I'm not ready to lose you just yet. I feel like we've known each other a long time, I—

"So this your bedroom?" he whispered.

"Fane?" I must've aged ten years.

"Or did I die? Is this Heaven?"

"Artilects don't go to Heaven, Fane. And in Heaven there wouldn't be dirty underwear on the floor."

"In mine, there would be."

"I did think you were dead," I admitted.

"So you just lay down next to me? Were you going to have a sneaky peek before they took me away for parts?"

"Of course not! Don't be so crass. I was trying to find your thread and make sure you were truly dead before I stuck you in my garden as a scarecrow to frighten tomato-thieves. Give me my hand back."

He released it, grinning.

"Seriously, though, what are you doing here? What happened? I was talking to Callum and then… Were you waiting here for me? Did you break into my bedroom? Because I already told you—"

"No," he said, "ending up on your floor is just a happy

coincidence. I came upstairs to say goodnight, and you were fainting. I caught you just as you hit the floor and dragged you in here."

The pain in my knees seemed to agree with him. "Were you actually out of it then? Or were you awake the entire time?"

"I was awake for most of it," he admitted. "I wanted to see what you would do with me."

"And were you disappointed?"

"A little. I thought you would at least check if I was anatomically correct."

I said nothing.

"Go on," he said, "you know you want to."

I couldn't help myself. "Are you?" I blurted.

He laughed, a human, throaty laugh. "Of course. Ethan designed me. Although I don't know if he made me bigger or smaller than him. Would you like to see?" He lifted the hem of his shirt.

"No thanks, I'm good."

He pulled his shirt back down, but not before I'd glimpsed the planes of his stomach. "Are *you* okay? What happened?"

Fane's an AI. Maybe he can help. "I went in to speak to Callum. Please, keep this between us, but when Callum went through the process that made us cyborgs, he swallowed an AI named Umbra. When I went to see him, Umbra spoke to me instead. She wanted to know about you." I recounted everything she'd said. "Callum is scared of her, and honestly, so am I. Oliver is trying to figure out a way to separate them without harming Callum." The room still seemed to spin a bit, so I sat down on my bed and leaned against the wall.

"What about Umbra?" Fanes gestured to the foot of my bed.

I nodded, and he sat down. "What do you mean?"

"Doesn't he worry about hurting Umbra?"

"No, of course not. She's just—"

"A machine." He raised his eyebrows.

My cheeks flushed. "I'm sorry. I didn't—"

He brought my hand up to his lips, the way he'd done with Cindra. "It's okay. I forget too. I thought of her as just a machine at first. Isn't that strange? When did I get so grand?"

"You don't seem like a machine to me," I said quietly.

"I don't seem like a machine to myself either. But how would I know?"

"Are you sentient, Fane?"

"I don't know. Sometimes I think I am. I think that I…feel. That I dream. But how can I know for sure? How do you know you are?"

"I guess I don't." My hand was still in his, and I had no desire to move it.

"What did she do to you?"

"Nothing. She wanted to, but she'd used up all her strength by that point, I think. She just sort of breathed on me, and that was it. Do you understand what she meant, about how she would help herself?"

He looked troubled. "No. But…from what you said, she wants to be like me." He frowned. "She's disturbing. She shouldn't be aware like that. When they built her kind, my design hadn't even been conceived yet. There's something very wrong."

"Do you think she's capable of doing something dangerous? Of seriously hurting Callum? Or any of us?"

"I don't know. She shouldn't be, and yet… Ailith? Ailith!"

29
AILITH

The green sea was no longer a wasteland. It was smooth, shiny. Blood-warm to the touch. I could no longer tell where my body ended and the metal began.

I was young but ageless; I possessed the knowledge of years, of generations. Of people I'd never met, who were long dead, even though I was only being born. The swarm of my body had been contained, encased and caged. I'd become sleek and solid, all my components moving as one.

For the first time, the tree was gone. He stood in its place, waiting. As always. So were all the others, standing together. They'd become like me, slowly, one cell at a time. They felt like they were drowning, and they were; their lungs filled with carbon fibers and copper filaments. We were evolving quickly. Too quickly. Soon, there would be nothing of us left.

"I never saw this coming," he said, his voice heavy with

sorrow. "I should have seen it coming."

We all spoke at once, commiserating.

"I should have felt it. Should have felt it in all of you. But it happened too fast."

"I should have found it. I could have changed its course, nullified *it*."

"I should have torn it out. Hunted it down, forced it to submit."

"I should have encouraged him to follow the others. To burn."

"Where's Ella?"

"This is my fault. I let it out. Let it out to play."

"Shh. It's coming. Look, over the horizon."

"It's not coming. It's already here. Can't you feel it? It's drowning us."

"How can we drown from the inside? It's not possible. None of this is possible."

"And yet here we are."

"Ailith? Where are you?"

"Quick, it's coming. Stand together. Make ourselves look larger. Like we have teeth."

We stood together, back to back. Wherever my skin touched theirs, it turned to metal. The silvered patches spread and fused, growing taller, wider, twisting toward the sky. Only I didn't grow, my fingers slipping uselessly through theirs. Their voices became faint, only a whisper on the wind. I tried to claw the metal back, but my nails made no mark.

"Ailith?"

It was upon us at last, and I'd been left behind.

Not left behind. Sent ahead.

I was the seed. I would grow thorns. I would birth poison and twisting vines to strangle it until it folded in on itself and became nothing.

"Ailith?"
It wasn't coming over the horizon. It never had been.

30
AILITH

Feet hovered in the air, dangling from a body held fast against the wall by Tor's hand around its throat. He'd held me like that once too; maybe it was happening again.

Maybe this time he's actually killed me, and I'm having an out-of-body experience.

Except that the feet hanging passively in front of me were far too large to be mine. I rolled over to get a better look, trying to make sense of it over the roaring in my ears.

Fane was remarkably calm; he didn't struggle. His face was composed, his expression neutral, and his hands loose at his sides.

Tor, on the other hand, looked like he was about to lose control. He stood with his feet planted apart, one large hand wrapped around Fane's neck, the muscles of his arm rigid. The other was pulled back, fisted and ready to strike. His face was feral, lips drawn from his teeth in a snarl. His hair had come loose from its fastening, and the dark strands merged with the line of his tattoos.

The roaring narrowed and became more defined; it was coming from Tor.

"What did you do to her?" he demanded. "*Answer me.*"

Like I'd done, Fane reached out and traced his finger over the inky line on Tor's bottom lip.

It didn't have the same effect. Instead of shocking Tor out of his rage, Fane had simply pulled the trigger. Tor smashed his fist into Fane's face like a piston, driving his skull into the wall.

"Stop. Tor, stop." My voice came out calm, measured, at odds with the screaming in my head. "Stop."

A seething black mass under taut skin. Narrowed diamond eyes. The lick of a flame.

My voice galvanized both of them. Tor faltered, glancing back at me over his shoulder. Fane used his distraction to wrap his own hands around the base of Tor's throat, the weight of his palms on Tor's shoulders. He pressed down, and as Tor's knees buckled, Fane's face changed.

The weight of the ocean on a grain of sand. The splitting of flesh under a rock. The skin of a hare, peeled from the muscle with a single tear.

A wet cracking roused all of us like a shock of icy water.

Fane released Tor, his hands raised in the air, palms out, as though in surrender. Tor hunched over, still kneeling. One fist was planted on the floor, but his other arm hung uselessly at his side.

"Stop," I said again, this time only a whisper.

A stampede of feet sounded on the stairs, and in the inpouring sea of faces, the room began to spin again.

"What the hell happened?" Lexa rushed to Tor's side as he struggled to stand, wincing as she gripped his limp arm.

Lien nearly trampled me in her haste to reach Fane, clumsy with anger. The right side of his face had caved in, just over the cheekbone. She grabbed Tor's right arm, trying to spin him to face her. At any other time, the incongruity of their sizes would've been funny, a mouse trying to take down an elephant. But not now. "What did you do?"

"He thought I'd hurt Ailith," Fane said, his voice calm. Shreds of images still floated through his mind. *A belly full of stones.* "I don't blame him."

Cindra and Oliver stood on their tiptoes, looking over Mil's shoulder. Cindra looked appalled, Oliver like his mind was working overtime. He edged around Mil and the others, pulling Cindra with him. Pax and Kalbir followed closely behind. They sat in a line on the edge of my bed, whether for solidarity or to watch the show, I wasn't sure.

"What the fuck did you do to her then? Why was she on the floor?"

Ethan moved to stand in front of Fane, glancing at Lien. The tension in the room rose.

"Tor, I'm fine. I had a…" I hesitated. *How much should I reveal in front of Lien and Ethan?* Not to mention the others crowded in the hallway. "vision. And I got a little dizzy. Fane had just come up to say goodnight and found me in the hallway."

The tension drained from the room as Cindra flashed me a smug, congratulatory smile and whispered something in Oliver's ear that made the skin over his collar turn pink. Tor closed his eyes.

Lien's lips grew even tighter, the paleness around her mouth stark against the rising flush in her cheeks. Ethan merely looked disgusted.

Will he tell them about Callum and Umbra? Please, Fane, don't.

He didn't. Instead, he turned to Tor. "I know it looked

bad. Please, believe me, I didn't do anything to her."

Tor glanced at the surrounding faces, and the fight suddenly left him. He seemed to deflate, to grow smaller. "I'm sorry," he said, and I was surprised by the sincerity in his voice. "About your face, anyway. You're a bit less pretty now."

Fane grinned. "I'm plenty pretty, brother. Maybe I'll get a good battle scar from it. I'm sorry I broke your arm. I wasn't even trying."

"Never mind, *brother*," Tor replied, his returning smile brittle. "I've got another one."

"What the fuck are we supposed to do now?" Ethan roared. "I can see you think this is just a wonderful human adventure, Fane, but how are we supposed to fix your face? Everything we had was destroyed in that fucking cave-in. I told you coming here was a bad idea," he said to Lien.

Turning to Tor, he spat, "And you. I would try to kill you right here if I didn't think you'd have no qualms about murdering each and every one of us." He pointed to Fane. "I hope you've learned a lesson here. Perhaps you shouldn't place your trust in everyone you meet."

"I'm not a child," Fane said.

"Oh no? And yet you're acting like one, sneaking off to some cyborg slut's bedroom. I knew when you began following her that there would be problems. You have no idea how they work. They—" He suddenly became aware that everyone had fallen silent, watching him. "They're not your kind," he finished lamely.

Fane stepped up to Ethan, his ruined face blocking everything else in the room. "Neither are you," he said quietly.

Ethan held his gaze, the seconds seeming to extend for minutes. Abruptly, he turned away. "I think it's time we were going."

"What about Fane's face?" Lien demanded. "How are we supposed to fix that?"

"I can fix it." Lexa had finished her cursory examination of Tor's arm. "I'm going to have to fix this, anyway. We still have *our* resources."

A shadow passed over Lien's face. "Fine. But we stay here with him."

"Absolutely not." Mil's voice was firm.

"You can't tell us where we can and cannot go." Ethan's hackles were rising again.

"Actually, I can. You have a choice: leave Fane here and we'll fix him, or take him now, and all of you can leave."

"Never. I would—"

"I'll stay." Fane wedged himself next to the others on the edge of bed, smoothing his hands over the covers. "I might even sleep *here*," he goaded Ethan.

"I like him a lot," Pax said.

I had to admit, so did I.

Ethan's face turned apoplectic, veins standing out in sharp relief. "They can't make us leave," he repeated.

"They can," said Fane, "and so can I."

A sudden coughing fit gripped me, and I bent double, trying to catch my breath.

Cindra rushed over and placed her hand on my back. "Ailith? Are you okay?"

I held up a hand and nodded. "It's so dry in here."

"I'll get you some water." She disappeared into the bathroom.

My interruption broke the tension. As I gulped down the water Cindra brought, Ethan shook his head at Fane in disbelief. He'd considered his options and realized he had none. "Fine. You know how to reach us." Turning to Mil, he said, "If anything happens to him, we—"

"That's enough, Ethan," Lien said. "It's fine. We're

allies now, after all. Aren't we?" Her body language said anything but, her smile strained and her back too straight. "Let's look at this as proof of our good faith."

Ethan opened his mouth as though he was going to object, but a twitch in her jaw convinced him otherwise. "I agree," he replied through his teeth. I guessed he would've rather bitten off his own tongue.

"Well, if that's settled, let's get you two boys down to the infirmary," said Lexa, all business again. "Let's go everyone. The night is over." As the others filed past me, looking disappointed, she hung back. "And are you okay?"

"Yes, I'm fine," I said. "Honestly. I was speaking to Callum and must've blacked out."

Lexa looked at me closely but let it pass. "Is Callum okay? He…he won't come and see me anymore. I thought that if I didn't force him…that he might get better—or at least let me scan him and try to figure out what's wrong."

"I think he's fine, Lexa. Oliver's found some things in his programming that he's going to clean up. Nothing serious." *Assuming Oliver finds a way to separate them.*

She pursed her lips. "He didn't say anything to me about that."

"It was pretty deeply buried. Some minor compatibility issue. He only found it because of his ability. I guess he didn't think it was important enough to mention."

She searched my face, looking for something more. But, as though she wanted to preserve our fragile new bond, she let it go.

"Tor, Fane, with me. *Now*," she said, like they were two naughty school boys instead of lethal instruments. She marched ahead, disappearing through the doorway. I was surprised she didn't twist their ears.

Tor avoided looking at either of us, following Lexa quickly.

Fane lingered. "You didn't tell her about your vision. Or that you spoke to Umbra. Or even *about* Umbra."

"I've never had that vision before. Usually, it's a dream I have. As for the rest… They don't know about Umbra, Fane. She threatened to kill Callum if we told them, and I'm worried what they would do to Callum if they found out. It might prompt Umbra to strike."

He dipped his head. "You're protecting him. I understand."

"Does your face hurt?" I asked then felt silly.

"I think so," he said. "It's difficult to tell. Is this what pain feels like?"

Red, tinged with yellow, too bright for the eyes. Raw wet flesh under a blister. Salt.

"Yes."

"I don't like it."

"You're not supposed to. It's supposed to stop you from doing whatever it was you did again. Can I touch it?"

"Please."

I pressed my fingers gently into the indent of his cheek. His skin felt as smooth and firm as it had looked, yet soft too, like flesh. Underneath, Tor's fist had left a crater, the edges crushed and jagged.

He leaned into my fingers, closing his eyes.

I pulled my hand away.

"So you and Tor are not together? He seemed to feel otherwise."

"No, we're not." I sighed and sat on the bed. "Honestly? We were, at one time, and I don't want to talk about it now. But he would've defended any one of us like that. Pax, Cindra…probably even Oliver." I reconsidered. "Okay, maybe not Oliver. But we've been through a lot together."

"Maybe. But Tor knew I hadn't done anything to you.

That's not why he attacked me."

"What do you mean? Why did he do it then?"

"When you were…dreaming, or whatever it was, you called out for *me*. Not him."

"Ah. I still don't believe he would attack you over something like that… Our split was his choice."

"Maybe. What did it mean? Your dream?"

"You saw it?"

"Yes. I've seen it for a long time. It changes. I'm glad I'm not a kite anymore. I don't think I like heights."

"What did you see, this time?"

"I was running. I saw you, all of you, in the distance. I was trying to reach you, before…I don't know. They were all turning to metal, and I'd lost my skin, and parts of me were breaking off, and the broken parts moved much faster than me, but not faster than it. The others, they looked like they were becoming the tree, their arms spread, their fingers grasping at the wind. And it was coming. And I couldn't get there. And I—" His eyes were wide, the pupils dilated.

A hot flash, a sudden chill. The crescendo of a heart about to burst.

"Fane, it's okay. Dreams aren't literal. And they don't make a lot of sense. Most of the time, they don't mean anything. Don't worry about it. Not yet, anyway."

He nodded, but didn't look convinced.

"You should go. Let Lexa patch you up."

"Can I come back here? I feel safe here." And for just a moment, he seemed so fragile and human that I almost said yes. *Almost.*

"I don't think that's a good idea. But, since you're going to be here for a day or two, why don't you come and see my greenhouse tomorrow? I'll wait for you."

After he'd gone, I locked the door, checking it twice to

make sure. I stared at the pit in my wall, the size of a human head, bloodless and broken.

The knock on the door startled me.

"Fane, I said—"

"It's me," Oliver said from the other side. "Look, I know you probably want to sleep, but I think I've found a way to separate Callum and Umbra. I want to do it now, while we still have a chance."

I opened the door. "What do you need me to do?"

31

CALLUM

I'd never been in Oliver's room before. I'd never talked to him much, either. Pax had told me some of the things that had happened after they'd awoken, about their journey here. I was surprised they'd allowed Oliver to stay with them, but Pax said it wasn't that simple.

I understood what he meant. Things hadn't been that simple here, either. Nothing seemed to be, anymore.

"What are we doing here? What is he doing?"

"You heard him, Umbra. He just needs to check me over, make sure everything's working okay. He wants to check my ability."

"Why now, this late? Besides, you do not need an ability. You have me."

"I know. But it might help us. And Oliver seems to do stuff whenever he wants. Let's just get this over with."

"I suppose we will take advantage while we can."

"What do you mean, Umbra?"

Oliver finished typing and looked up at me. "Turns out you're Cindra's counterpart, Callum."

"You mean I can help people? When they're hurt?"

"We will never help anyone but ourselves."

"Be quiet, Umbra."

"It's more that you can diagnose them. But then you'll know how to help them. I just need to tweak it for you, if that's okay? I did it for all the others."

Oliver seemed nervous, although he was good at hiding it.

"Do not let him do it."

"Yes, please, Oliver."

He nodded, his fingers poised over the keys. Taking a deep breath, he began to type.

"You. Why are you back? I told you to stay away. You should not be able to be here. I thought I—"

"Who are you talking to, Umbra?"

"Her. The one who invades us. She is here."

"How do you know? I can't feel anything."

"That is because *you* are primitive, unsophisticated."

"Umbra—"

"How are you here? Tell me. Stop! Why are you not— What are you doing?"

"Umbra?"

"They are doing something to us. They are trying to take me away from you. They are trying to kill me. She has told them."

"Hold her just a bit longer, Ailith!" Oliver shouted.

"No! I will not let you do this. You promised. I told you I would kill him if you told."

I could no longer move. Or breathe.

Oliver stared at me, his eyes wide, unsure whether to help me or keep trying to extract Umbra.

"Get out, both of you. Leave!"

My vision narrowed to a tunnel. There was only one way out.

"Ailith, get out! She'll kill him. There's not enough time!"
Umbra won't let go. She—

32

AILITH

"Ailith? Can I come in?" Fane knocked gently on the doorframe of the greenhouse. I'd opened the door to shift some of the heavy, humid air. "Are you okay?"

"I'm fine."

Except, I wasn't, not really. We hadn't been able to help Callum, and we'd almost gotten him killed in the process. After I'd retreated, I'd run down the hallway to Oliver's room. He'd left the door unlocked, and as I'd rushed in, I'd nearly tripped over Callum's prone body.

His face was a mottled purple, his eyes open but unseeing. As I'd dropped to my knees next to him, he'd drawn a ragged breath. *He's still alive.* I'd covered my face with my hands, unable to look at him anymore.

"Oliver, what did we do?" I'd whispered.

"We tried to save him. And we couldn't. But at least he's not dead."

"So she's still in there?"

"Yes. And we can't do it again. She's on to us now. I

185

think she'll make good on her promise next time."

"She knew I was there. Right away."

Oliver had nodded. "If I were you, I wouldn't go anywhere near his mind again. We'll have to come up with another plan."

After we'd been sure Callum would recover, we'd put him in back in his own bed and returned to ours. My sleep, for once, had been deep and dreamless.

Between what had happened with Callum and my last dream, I was uneasy. The fragments of the dream still clung to me, my mind overlaying the others with gossamer strands, filaments that wound themselves through their veins and turned them to metal from the inside out. I still saw them fusing together, back to back, stretching, hardening. I'd gotten so used to the dream I no longer wondered what it meant.

What if it does mean something?

And if I was honest, it wasn't just about the dream. I was confused about Fane. About Tor. About how my life could be so messy with so few people in it. I was desperate to talk it out with Cindra, but she'd gone with Lexa to search for some kind of fungus.

"Fane, what the hell are you wearing?" He had on the ugliest sweater I'd ever seen—circa 2020, large puce and yellow geometric shapes on a garish orange background.

"Do you like it?" he asked.

"It's hideous. Where did you find it?"

"Pax gave it to me."

"Pax? What is Pax doing with a sweater like this?" I pulled at the synthetic wool.

"He has a closet full of them. He called it his collection. From before the war. I like it." He stretched his arms out and admired them.

"It's horrible. But I'm glad the two of you are getting

along so well."

"I think we're friends," he said, clearly pleased.

In the self-conscious silence that followed, he looked around the greenhouse, taking in the tiny, germinated seedlings, the neat furrows of rich black earth waiting for transplants. He bent over some of the baby plants, hovering his hand over the delicate leaves.

"Can I touch?" he asked.

"Yes, but be very careful. Touch them gently, just a fingertip. They've only just sprouted."

He did as I said, gingerly running the tip of his finger over pale green edges.

"How's your face?" I asked. It looked almost normal, just a little less symmetrical than before. Lexa had worked on him all through the night and most of the morning with Mil's help. Tor's shoulder hadn't needed nearly as much work.

"It's okay. It doesn't feel the same. I had to help them. Lexa gave me some nanites to finish it off. Did you know that we have a similar design, just in reverse? Bionic infused with organic. She had to tweak them a bit, but luckily, we're compatible. Pax says it's fascinating."

"I'll bet he does." I examined his skin. "So, no scar, then?"

"No," he said, his voice tinged with disappointment.

"Did you make friends with Tor?"

"Yes. Pax said it's called frenemies. What does it feel like?"

I chuckled at his earnestness. "What? Frenemies?"

"No. To grow these plants. To start life, to nurture it."

"I've never really thought about it. Exciting, I guess. In the spring, the sight of the bare fields used to fill me with anticipation. That was the most exciting part, all that potential, just waiting for me to start. After that, it became more difficult, full of worry. I needed to make sure everything got enough food, enough water. Whenever a storm came, I held my breath, willed myself to go outside and see what the damage was." I smiled wryly. "By the end, I was so physically and emotionally drained, I resented them. Then it would be winter, and the desire to do it all again would build, and by the time spring came, I was full of anticipation again."

"It sounds like the romance books Ilse reads."

I laughed. "I guess you could look at it that way. It was a very love-hate relationship."

"Have you had lots of relationships?"

"A few." I hesitated. I didn't want to offend him, but he seemed genuinely curious. "Have you?"

"No. Not ones I wanted, anyway." He brushed some soil off the work table.

"What do you mean?"

"Lien, sometimes the others…look at me. Sometimes they touch. They pretend it's professional curiosity, but they watch my face while they're doing it."

I felt sick. "Do they not ask you first?"

He shrugged. "I'm an artilect. They created me. I don't think it occurs to them." He traced a dirt-filled crack on the table's surface.

"I'm so sorry, Fane. They…they shouldn't be doing that. They should *never* do that. Whether they think you're sentient or not." I put my hand over his. I wasn't sure how conscious he was, but to me, it didn't matter.

"I'm sorry," I said again, snatching my hand away. Here I was, touching him.

"No," he said. He pulled my hand back over his and rested his forehead on it. "I like it when you touch me." His voice was muffled by the thick polyester of his sweater.

I cast about for something to say. "That sweater is really

awful, Fane. I think it was one of the first signs the age of humankind was drawing to a close," I joked.

"Fine," he said. "I'll take it off." He pulled it up and over his head in one smooth motion. "Is that better?"

It was. Much better. *Too* much better.

The scent of cinnamon and cloves. The ripeness of figs.

They're the culmination of millions of human experiences in my programming. It's how I experience emotion, how I translate it. That is how I feel.

I fiddled with the seed packets in front of me, opening and closing the flaps.

"I want you to look at me," he said.

"Fane—"

"Please."

So I did. His body was perfect, but why wouldn't it be? If I were to create a being in my own image, why would I make it anything less than perfect? The skin on his torso was smooth and firm, undulating over the outline of his collarbone and muscles like dunes made flesh. His shoulders were broad, tapering to a lean waist. There was nothing about him, other than his perfection, that made him look anything but human. He even had nipples, dusky pink in the warm air.

"Do you find me attractive?"

"Yes. You're beautiful, Fane," I whispered. He was winning.

"Can I see you?"

"Fane, I—"

"Please. Unless you don't want to. If you don't want to, tell me, and I'll leave right now."

"No," I said. I went to the open door and closed it, locking it behind me and pulling the shade over the window.

I slid off my shirt—what little there was of it, anyway.

Given the balmy humidity of the room, I never even wore a bra in the greenhouse, much less a shirt that covered anything but the essentials.

I stood in front of him.

"What are those?" he asked. He pointed to one of my scars. After my cyberization, the nanites had recycled all but the most stubborn scar tissue, replacing the sullen purple slashes with faint silver ribbons.

"I was sick. I had many operations. I became a cyborg so I wouldn't die."

"You didn't want to be part machine?"

"I didn't feel strongly about it one way or the other. I wasn't against the work the Cyborgists and the Cosmists were doing, but I never applied it to myself in any way. Not until I became one."

"Can I touch them?"

I nodded, and he traced the lines over my abdomen.

"Did you make them look this way?"

"No. The nanites did. They considered them...useless."

"I wish I had scars."

"Why? Because they'd make you more human? Do you want to be human?"

"No. Everyone assumes I do, but I don't. I have no desire to be something other than I am."

"Well, that's definitely not human. Humans usually want to be more than they are." I folded my arms over my chest, suddenly self-conscious. "But if not to be more human, why would you want to have scars?"

"I want to be...lived in. To have some proof of my existence. I want to know that my memories, the things that happen to me, that I've done, are real. I want souvenirs. Like yours."

The cloying fragrance of a lily in the sun.

Slowly, I unfolded my arms and slid my hand up over

his stomach, his chest, his collarbone. He closed his eyes and reached out to hold my other hand.

Bright orange petals, dark in the center.

I ran my fingers over the roughness of his jaw, the smooth fullness of his lips.

Thick pollen, clustered in the center.

He bent down and kissed me, his mouth unsure.

I curled my fingers up the back of his neck and into his hair, pressing his mouth harder against mine.

The drip of nectar.

Everything that happened after that was a blur from Fane's mind. I no longer felt the clothing between us, the skin, just the cacophony of millions of individual human moments merging into a singular one: ours.

Sun-soaked leaves, the stickiness of honey, an orchid finally overflowing with rain, the voice of God.

A sound at the door startled us both, the rough ledge of the table scraping over the bare skin of my back.

The door handle jiggled. "Ailith? Are you in here or what?" Oliver.

"Coming. Just give me a second," I called. "Shit. Where's my shirt? Fane? Can you see my shirt?"

At least we have our pants on. Small mercy.

He wasn't going to answer me. His eyes were closed, one hand gripping the counter, shoulders hunched forward. My chest rose and fell in shallow gasps as I tried to catch my breath. His was still.

"Fane? Are you okay? Look, I have to open the door." I found my shirt, draped over the stool where I'd left it.

I snatched it up and yanked it over my head before unlocking the door. Oliver slouched in the doorway, one arm propping him up against the frame. He took in my disheveled hair, the tag sticking out like a flag on the front of my backward-inside-out shirt. He glanced at Fane, still bare-chested, over my shoulder.

Shit.

"Have a new toy, do we? I don't blame you. He's ever so dreamy. If I were that way inclined, I'd fight you for him. Just try not to break this one, eh?"

"Do you need something, Oliver?" I put as much cold dignity into my voice as I could.

He smirked. "Well, I hate to interrupt your debauchery, but something's happened in Goldnesse, and they need our help.

"In Goldnesse? What could possibly have happened that they need us?"

"You know that pesky silver rain that wiped out most of the primes? Well, it turns out their warning system wasn't nearly as effective as they thought, and they've been caught out."

Dad. Cold fear budded inside me. "Silver rain? Now? Tor said it rarely fell anymore."

"Rarely doesn't mean never, though, does it? The point is, a whole big mess of them were caught out in it. Apparently, it's chaos. Lexa wants us to come and help with the aftermath."

"What does she want us to do?"

"Christ, Ailith, I have no idea. I didn't care enough to ask. Are you and sex-bot over there coming or not? Or have you already co—"

"We'll be up in a minute, Oliver. Tell them to wait for us."

"Yes, ma'am." He saluted sharply and with a last smirk at Fane, turned and went up the stairs.

"Fane? Did you hear Oliver? We have to go. Fane?"

Nothing.

I walked over to him and put my hand on his chest. The moment my skin touched his, his head snapped back. His eyes were bright and glittering, the first lights in a starry sky.

"Fane, we have to go."

"I know," he said. "I just…" He cupped my face in his hands then leaned over to kiss me again. This time his lips were firm, confident.

I began to dissolve into him again. "Fane—"

"I know," he whispered. "I can feel it. Thank you."

I ached at the wonder in his voice.

— Mil Cothi, personal journal

33

AILITH

The others stood around the large table in the main room. Lexa and Cindra rushed back and forth, stuffing supplies into bags and calling out item numbers to each other. Silence fell as Fane and I approached the table, too many pairs of eyes taking in my appearance, then his.

"Fane, what happened to your sweater?" Pax asked.

"It's ugly. I took it off."

"It isn't ugly. I thought you liked it."

"I do, but Ailith didn't. Not like you said she would." He put his hands on his bare waist. "She liked this better."

Oh, please, stop. I didn't dare look at Tor.

Pax sighed, clearly disappointed in me.

"What's going on?" I asked. *I will not look anyone in the eye.*

"Goldnesse has an early warning system to alert them

194

when the silver rain is coming. But it's been so long since the last fall that nobody's been calibrating it to make sure it's working properly. When it fell today, it caught them unaware. Many of them were outside."

"How did you find out?"

"Lily got through on the radio. And then—"

"I arrived." My father came out of the infirmary, packets of gauze in his hands. "Lily's been trying to contact you since yesterday afternoon, when it happened. Has it not been getting through?"

"Dad? How did you get here? How did you know where we are?" Relief washed over me.

"I followed you. That day we met in the woods. I-I wanted to see where you were, so I could come help you if you were ever in trouble. When Lily couldn't get an answer— I waited outside until one of you came out." He nodded at Tor.

"Does anyone else know you're here?"

"No. I took care. I told them I was going to search for those still missing. I can't be gone long."

"I can't believe he knows where we live." Kalbir glared at me. "How do we know he hasn't already told the lot of them? That this isn't an elaborate plan to take us down, right now? It all seems awfully coincidental."

"Why would I do that? Ailith is my daughter," he replied.

"Your *cyborg* daughter. From what I've heard, you weren't particularly pleased about her becoming one."

"That has nothing—"

"Kalbir, we have more important things worry about right now," Lexa snapped.

Kalbir did not look convinced.

"Pax, did you see this coming? Why didn't you tell us?" Tor asked.

"I didn't see it coming," he replied. "I…don't know why. There were no indications—" His hands clenched and unclenched at his sides.

"Pax, it's not your fault. You— Pax!"

He fell to his knees, his black eyes wide.

"It's open. The path is open. It's another crossroad. Ailith, you have to stay on the path."

"I don't know what that means, Pax. I don't know which path is the right one." Alarm tightened my throat.

His eyelids flickered then closed. He knelt where he'd fallen, his head bowed, until Fane scooped him up and laid him on the long couch in the corner of the room. As the cushions depressed under his weight, I caught sight of a handful of cookies stashed away in the crevice.

Cindra hurried over to him and laid her hand on his chest. She stood still, absorbing what information she could. "He's fine. At least, I can't feel anything." The relief in her voice was tangible. "He's asleep." His eyes darted back and forth under his lids.

"Pax? Can you hear me?"

He was there, but I couldn't reach him. It happened sometimes, when he was unconscious or deeply asleep.

"We'll be back soon. Don't be scared."

"I hate the idea of leaving Pax alone." I spoke aloud.

"Mil and Callum are here," Lexa said. "He'll be fine."

"No, I'm going to Goldnesse too." Callum's voice carried from the dormitory stairs.

Oliver stepped in hastily. "Don't worry, Callum, we've got this—"

"I feel fine. She's gone quiet. I want to help."

Oliver glanced at Lexa, but she was talking to Mil and hadn't heard.

"I'm fine. I promise. Please, let me help."

"Okay," Oliver said, his voice slow with reluctance.

"But if you start feeling…anything, you let me or Ailith know. Yes?"

"Yes."

"I'll stay," Fane said. "I don't want to leave, not yet. My face might fall off." He touched his cheek gingerly. "Besides, Pax is my friend."

"Thank you. I mean it," I said. "I feel better knowing you'll be here."

He smiled.

The luster of gold. A blue ribbon, pinned to a chest.

"Then I'll stay as long as you need me."

"Oh, would somebody please just kill me before I gag to death." Out the corner of my eye, I saw Cindra dig her elbow into Oliver's ribs.

We filed out of the compound, my father's face grim.

"Pax?" Still nothing. It didn't feel quite like the other times, but I couldn't pinpoint exactly why.

My last sight before Mil closed the door behind us was of Fane, dirt smeared across the planes of his stomach, his hand raised in farewell.

Eyes wide in the dark. A shadow on the wall. A drop of blood on the back of my hand.

***

The main street of Goldnesse was deserted when we arrived. We waved my father off and made a beeline for the former casino at the far end, where the infirmary and apartments were. Inside was chaos. The dozen or so beds the infirmary held were occupied by children, two to a bed, while the rest of the injured clustered on the floor on whatever makeshift bedding they could find. Lily and her daughter, Grace, hurried from patient to patient, checking temperatures and administering draughts and injections.

197

Lily saw us and rushed over, her face pale under the flush of exertion. "Thank goodness you're here. We need all the help we can get." She tore the pack from Lexa's hands and rifled through it. "Good, thank you. We'll need every bit of this."

"What can we do?" Lexa asked.

"First, take off your coats and roll up your sleeves. I'm going to give you all an injection."

Each of us froze in various stages of undress.

"Why, Lily? I mean, look at us. We're fine." Cindra smiled to show just how fine we really were.

Lily gave each of us a cursory examination. "You look well," she said, "though I shouldn't be surprised. The silver rain wouldn't affect you the same way it does us."

"What do you mean?" Lexa asked. I was glad she had; I doubted I'd have been able to speak past the sudden lump of fear in my throat.

"How do we know he hasn't already told the whole lot of them? How do you know this isn't an elaborate plan to take us down?" I didn't dare look at Kalbir.

"Because your research compound is practically underground, isn't it?" Her voice was rapid with relief. " I'm so glad we finally got a message through to you. Thank you so much for coming. I'm glad you didn't get caught in it." She exhaled heavily. "Okay, hold out your arms."

"What is this?" Tor asked her.

"The rain carries some kind of metal that poisons people. We're giving it to everyone. It binds to the metal, clumping it together. Then it comes out when you pee."

"Does it work?" Tor asked. "I thought—"

She lowered her voice. "We don't know yet. One of our scouts brought it back, and this is the first time we've used it. It *should* work. And even if some people are too far gone, it could help those with less exposure or prevent contamination by secondary contact.”

As she reached for Tor’s arm, Grace rushed over and grabbed her arm. “Mom, come quick, it’s Mr. Uppal. He’s puking blood everywhere.”

As Lily hurried off to help Grace’s patient, we huddled together.

“What do we do?” I asked Lexa. “What will happen if we take this injection? I mean, we’ve got a lot of metal inside us.”

“It shouldn’t be a problem,” she replied. “If it’s what I think it is, it’s for heavy metals like lead. Who knows what’s in the rain? But it shouldn’t do you any harm. Your nanites will nullify it.”

“Shouldn’t? Is that the best you’ve got?”

“Yes, Oliver it is.” Lexa’s mouth was a hard line.

“What if it’s a trap?” Kalbir whispered furiously, looking over her shoulder.

“What? What do you mean a trap?” I asked.

“What if they know what we are? What if your dad told them, and this is all a ruse to get us here so they can poison us? What if this injection kills us?”

“Kalbir, that’s crazy,” Tor said, his voice careful. “Look, I know you’ve been a bit paranoid since that night with the Cosmists, but this is—”

“What? Ridiculous? Crazy? Just think about it. We—”

“Sorry about that,” Lily said. She was dabbing a bloody towel on the front of her red-soaked shirt.

“Is he okay?” Lexa asked.

Lily shook her head. “No. And he won’t be the last. Hurry now. Let’s get this done so we can help people.”

“Thank you for the offer,” Tor said, “but we don’t need the injection. None of us were exposed.”

“No, you have to. If you get blood or anything on you…you may even get poisoned just through touching their skin. It's not safe."

"We'll be fine," Tor insisted.

"I'm sorry, but you can't stay, if you won't take it. I'd feel responsible if anything happened." She turned over the syringe in her hands. "I'm sorry if you don't trust us." She glanced sharply at Tor. "Unless there's another reason? Do you know something we don't? About the rain? About this drug? Am I doing the wrong thing—"

"Of course not, Lily. We'll take it." Lexa interrupted her.

"Wait. What?" Tor's consternation was mirrored in all of us as we gaped at Lexa. *What was she doing?*

"Go on, it'll be fine." Lexa shot us a look of warning.

"Oh, thank you," Lily gushed. "I'll feel much better. And it'll do the others good to see you taking it as well. Especially seeing how healthy you all are." Her relief made her cheerful again. "Okay, who's first?"

I was the last in line. The others, pressing their fingers into the crooks of their elbows rushed off to carry out Lily's orders.

Lily swabbed antiseptic onto my arm carefully then checked the syringe for air bubbles before sliding it deftly into my vein. She depressed the plunger, and as a coolness blossomed through my forearm, she leaned forward and spoke so low only I could hear.

"I know what you are."

34
AILITH

I stared down at the bead of blood welling from the injection site.

"I know what you are."

Her voice had been conspiratorial, not accusatory or malicious as she'd withdrawn the needle and walked away to tend to her patients, as though discovering that your neighbors were cyborgs was a normal thing for her.

What do I do? Do I tell the others? If what Lily said was true, we were in a very precarious position. If I told the others, they might panic. If I didn't…

You made Tor a promise.

And I had. When we'd made our way through the province to save Pax and Cindra, I hadn't told Tor I suspected someone was following us. It had turned out to be Fane, but I was keenly aware that I could've put us both in danger.

"Tor, I need to talk to you. What are you doing?" He

was carrying lengths of old beams on his shoulder, beads of sweat on his forehead. He slid the beams onto the ground. "Are you okay?"

"I'm fine," he said. "They're heavy, that's all. I'm building a temporary charnel house. Lily doesn't want anyone to go too far out of town in case it begins to rain again, but they need to put the bodies somewhere. They'll burn it when it's full. It's going to fill up fast." He glanced at the beams impatiently. "What do you need?"

"Lily knows what we are."

At first, he didn't understand. "What? What do you mean?"

"You know what I mean, Tor. She knows we're cyborgs."

He yanked me by the hand closer to the wall, farther out of earshot. "You can't be serious. How would she find out?"

"I don't know. Maybe Kalbir was right. Maybe it was my father—" *Please don't let it be true.* But I hadn't seen him since we'd separated upon our arrival.

"What did she inject us with? Why didn't you say anything before?"

"She only told me *after* she'd injected me. Maybe she's on our side, Tor. Maybe the injection was nothing more than what she said it was. She wouldn't know how we worked even if she did know what we are."

"We can't take that risk. Fuck, Ailith."

"So what should we do? I don't know if we should tell the others. Who knows how they'll react?"

"We have to tell them. They need to know in case we have to protect ourselves."

He was right. I pressed my fingertips into the corners of my eyes. "Okay, I'll tell Cindra and Oliver. You tell Kalbir and Callum."

I searched the blur of faces for Cindra. The air was hot and humid with vomit and spilled bowels, the former lobby full of bodies in various stages of dying. Some lay comatose, blood leaking from where their skin had split. Other had lost control of their nervous systems, their limbs jerking like marionettes on strings. Still others screamed in agony as they clawed at their chests.

For a moment, I froze, caught in their maelstrom. Pax's red-mist vision of the future stuck in my mind. Was *this* that future coming to pass? Had we failed after all?

"Ailith?" It was Stella.

The Cosmists. *The Cosmists could've betrayed us.* They'd taken advantage of this disaster, just like they said they would. "What did you do?"

"Do? What do you mean?"

"You told them about us, didn't you?"

She backed away from me. "I don't know what you're talking about."

I stepped toward her. She threw her hands up in front of her face.

"Ailith, Stella? What's going on?" Cindra materialized at my side.

"Stella's betrayed us. Lily knows what we are."

"No, I didn't. I promise. I'm not like Ethan. You can ask Fane." Her voice broke over his name.

Across the room, Tor's shoulders convulsed. He turned his head toward me, his eyes wide. *Calm down.* If I possessed Tor now, it would be a disaster for all of us. *Breathe.*

Wisps of white clouds drifting through an azure sky.

"You'd better be telling the truth. If I find out otherwise—"

"I swear. I'll help you any way I can. What can I do?"

"Just keep helping people. Keep your eyes and ears

open. And Stella, I'll be watching you. I know how precious Fane is to you. Don't forget where he is right now."

The shine of her eyes before she turned away filled me with a vicious satisfaction.

Cindra stared at me. "Ailith, what are you doing? I understand we don't trust the Cosmists, but threatening Fane? I thought you—"

"We could be in very real danger right now, Cindra."

"I know, but still—"

"Do you feel any different? Since the injection?"

"No, I—"

"Let me know if you do."

"What do we do now?"

"Carry on as normal. Help these people. Like I told Tor, maybe Lily is on our side." I glanced around. "No one seems to be looking at us any differently. One or two people could pretend, but a whole town? If that is what she meant, she hasn't told many people." I thrust a shallow tray of bandages and syringes at her. "Here, help me. Have you seen Oliver?"

"He went to get some more bandages. He'll be right back."

I knelt beside the patient closest to me. Her legs were kicking violently, her face tight with pain.

"Please, help me," she whispered. Pink spittle formed in the corners of her mouth.

Cindra handed me a syringe. "Do you know how to use this?"

"Yes." I'd injected the ports in my own arms many times during my illness, fighting to stay home rather than the hospital.

"Please, try to keep still," I said to the woman, knowing I was asking the impossible. "Cindra, hold her arm, around the top." I squeezed the woman's hand, trying to be comforting.

What's happening to me? I promised him I'd be okay. It's been so long since the rain came, so long. I'm going to die. Oh god, why does it hurt so—

I snatched my hand away.

It's not possible. No.

"Is everything okay?" Oliver appeared at Cindra's elbow. Cindra quickly filled him in.

"Shit." He gave a long, low whistle. "Well, that's us fucked. I wonder what she shot us up with?"

"Do you feel any different?"

"No," he admitted.

"Cindra, can you do this please? I need to talk to Oliver."

She looked between us.

"I promise we'll tell you everything later. We need to hurry."

She hesitated then nodded and turned back to our patient, sliding the needle in expertly.

"Oliver, something else is going on here. I-I can't explain it just yet." *Please, please let me be wrong.* "I need to you go back to the compound. I need you to find everything you can about the silver rain. If I'm right, anything on it will be buried."

"Please, I'm amazing," said Oliver. "If it's there, I can find it. Do you want to give me a better idea of what I'm looking for? Might speed things up a bit."

I told him.

"No. Ailith, what you're saying can't be possible. If it's true…" For the first time since I'd known Oliver, he looked genuinely shaken.

"I know. Oliver, don't let Mil know what you're up to. Tell him you're…I don't know, you'll think of something.

205

Get Fane to run interference if you have to. Now go."

"I don't have to go back. Remember?" He tapped his forehead. "It's all up here. I just have to find it."

"Well, go find it then, and keep out of sight. I don't have to tell you how important this is. And keep the door to your mind open. I might not have time to knock."

He nodded then kissed Cindra quickly on the back of the head and melted into the crowd.

"How is she?" The woman's legs had stilled, and the lines of pain on her face had softened.

Cindra pulled me to the side. "She's okay for now…there was a paralytic and an anesthetic in there. But I don't know how long it will last. It's like she's lost control of her nervous system."

"Did your ability tell you that?"

"Yes. But it was more of a guess… I don't know. It took a lot more effort than earlier. Maybe I'm getting tired."

"It wouldn't surprise me."

"Cindra?" Asche stood behind us. He was pale, with large, dark circles under his eyes.

"Asche? Are you okay?"

"Cindra, please, it's Gaia and the girls. They—" He pressed a shaking hand over his face. "They got caught in the rain. They— I thought you could—with your…with what you are."

She took his hand in her own. "Asche, it doesn't work like that. I'll do what I can, but—"

"Thank you, please, they're over here."

As he led her to the other side of the large room, I searched for the next person I could help. Through the glass double-doors of the entrance, there was a blur of movement and a scream of pain. *Tor.* Lily watched me stepping over bodies as I raced to the door, her hands full of medical supplies.

Tor was on one knee, his fists pressed to the ground, chest heaving. The heavy wooden beams he'd been carrying lay scattered on the ground.

"Tor, what happened?" I knelt beside him, my arm over his shoulder. His shirt was soaked. "Tor?"

"I can't… I just…the weight." He gasped for breath.

"What do you mean the weight? I've seen you toss boulders before." I laid my hand on the back of his neck. "Tor, you're burning up."

"My strength, Ailith. It's gone."

"What do you mean, gone?"

"Exactly what I'm saying. It's gone. I can't—"

"When did this start, Tor? When?"

"I don't know, I was feeling tired, but it—"

"Was it after the injection Lily gave us?"

"Yes, but—"

I found Oliver's thread in my mind. At first, I couldn't make the connection. *Damn it, Oliver, I said to keep your door open.*

…the catalyst will bind to the… Mobilize the nanites…casualties will be high, but… And he was gone.

Cold sweat soaked my palms. *This can't be happening. Concentrate.* I closed my eyes.

All the threads, my connections to everyone, flickered as though they were shorting out. As I watched, some flared then went dark. *No.*

"Tor—"

Cindra seized my arm. "Ailith! Something's wrong. I can't…When I touched Asche's wife, his children… Nothing. Ailith, I can't help them." Tears streamed down her face, making rivulets through the blood that stained her chin.

Oliver broke from the crowd at a run. "Ailith, I'm sorry, I can't seem to…something's wrong, but what I did manage to find before everything went tits up… You were right. You're fucking right."

No. How could they?

"Okay, listen everyone. Something is wrong with all our abilities. I can't connect to anyone properly."

"Was it Lily's injection?" Cindra asked, her voice trembling.

"I don't know. None of this started until after that, and if she knows we're cyborgs…it's possible. We need to find Kalbir and Callum. We need to stay together. You stay here, I'll go—"

We wouldn't need to look for Kalbir after all.

She stood on the balcony of one of the rooms on the first floor of the casino. In her arms was my father, the gleaming blade of a knife at his throat.

Despite what people think, we never wanted the war to happen. Why would we? People blaming us aside, a global war meant the destruction of everything we wanted to achieve. We would have no resources with which to move forward, and our previous work and that of countless others would be destroyed, setting us back a hundred years. Most of all, we would have no human legacy left to preserve.

— Ethan Strong, personal journal

35

AILITH

My father's face was pale, a thin line of red already welling to the surface.

"Tor, what the hell is she doing?" The dryness of my mouth made it difficult to speak.

He shook his head. "I told her Lily knows about us. She must think your father was the one who told her."

"She's lost her goddamn mind," Oliver muttered. "We need to stop her before she gets us all killed."

We pushed to the front of the crowd gathering at the base of the building. Ryan, Lily's husband, was already there, trying to make sense of the situation.

"I'll get Lexa." Cindra slipped through the front doors unnoticed. Everyone's eyes were on Kalbir.

Her eyes were wide and too bright, her normally sleek appearance disheveled. The hand holding the knife shook, and my father winced.

When Ryan saw us, he set his jaw and beckoned us over. "What the fuck is happening?" he whispered furiously.

Oliver's face was hard. "You tell us, mate. Your wife gave us some kind of injection."

"Lily? All she would've given you was the same treatment as everyone else."

"Don't pretend you don't know. She told Ailith she knew what we were."

Ryan's frown deepened. "What do you mean? What you are?"

Shit. I pulled Oliver back. "Oliver, he doesn't know. She hasn't told him."

"Hasn't told me what?"

Lexa ran behind Cindra, Lily close on their heels. More people gathered behind us, and a current of confused panic rippled through them.

"I see you," Kalbir screamed. "I know what you did to me. *You.*" She pointed the blade toward Lily.

My voice carried over the assembling crowd. "Kalbir, Lily didn't do anything to us. It's okay. You—"

"She knows. She knows, and she's trying to kill us. I can't feel myself anymore. I'm what I used to be. And you—" She twisted my father's neck. "You told them."

My father swallowed past the weight on his throat. "No. I told no one. I would never—"

"Liar. You're all liars. You talk about being a community, about everyone being welcome. You mean people like you, not like us. You think us being part machine makes us less human? It doesn't. It makes us *more.* We're more than you'll ever be. You tried to kill us once before, and we survived. Do you hear me? *Survived.* You can't destroy us." Saliva flew from her lips. "Do you know what happened to the last group of Terrans who tried to kill us? They're gone. *Dead.* We have as much right to be here as anyone else. We would've protected you, helped you. But all you wanted was to see us suffer."

Kalbir's grip slipped then tightened, and she pressed down.

I have to stop this, now.

Kalbir's thread was still lit, its glow sputtering the way the threads connecting me to pure machines did. Taking a deep breath, I pushed with all my strength; there was no time to be gentle.

The shaft of the knife was slick in my hand, the muscles of the arm holding my father's head screaming with the strain. The pale faces of the crowd below me were a blur as I fought with her. She may have lost most of her strength, but even at her weakest, she was able to resist.

"It's okay, Dad," I said in her voice. "I'm here." Slowly, Kalbir's arm inched back, away from my father. "Just a few—"

Her thread went dark. All the threads went dark.

Her arm snapped back, and the knife sliced deep into my father's neck. Back in the crowd, I watched his flesh open, blood flowing over the lapels of his coat. In the final moments of his life, he found me in the crowd, and smiled.

"Never be afraid of death," he'd told me when we'd returned from the mortuary after confirming that yes, the other half of our family was gone.

"How can you not be?" I'd asked him. *"In those final moments, you know you're going to die, don't you? They must've known. They must've been so scared."*

"Death happens so fast," he'd replied. *"Your mind comprehends little in those final moments. It plays tricks on you. The moment of death is a euphoric one. It's the final gift you give yourself. We've adapted to embrace the end of our existence, Ailith. That's why the Cosmists are wrong."*

A shriek tore through my skull. Kalbir's shoulder jerked

backward, slamming her into the wall behind her. Blood sprayed over the white brick and left a wide smear as she slid out of sight, taking my father's body with her. Tor lowered the rifle Ryan normally wore across his back as the crowd exploded into full panic.

The composure that served Tor well as an enforcer kicked in. "Oliver, Cindra, get Ailith away from here. We need to leave. Now. Find Callum and—"

"I'm here." Callum emerged from the throng. "I saw the crowd gathering." His mouth twitched oddly.

"Fine, just go. Get back to the compound," Tor said. "We'll have to leave Kalbir for now. She's killed someone, and if we try dragging her out, it will expose us all. I'll get Lexa."

Oliver grabbed his shoulder. "Tor, leave her. They might just decide to kill you. And if your hulk-mode is on the fritz—"

"I'll be fine, Oliver. Go, now." He leaned over me. "Ailith, listen to me. You need to get through this. You need to stand up, and you need to walk out of here, now. People are still confused. This might be our only chance."

Their voices were so far away, like the dull rumble of a distant storm.

"*Ailith.*"

There was blood under my fingernails. *How did that get there?*

"Ailith, I'm sorry," Tor whispered as light exploded behind my eyes.

People tried to maintain their pretense of neutrality and not talk about what would happen if the rumors were true. But people talk; they can't help it. Some said they should be killed on sight. Others said it would be a gift. And still others said nothing, waiting.

It turned out the stories were true. Cyborgs did exist.

— Love, Grace

36
AILITH

"…Is she awake, Tor? I need to talk to her."

"No, she's not. Oliver said we need to keep her out until he can fix her."

"What are you going to do? Beat her every time she opens her eyes?"

"I didn't beat her, Fane. I hit her. Once."

"In the head."

"It needed to be done."

"Aren't you supposed to love her?"

"Why do you think I knocked her out?"

"You need to go see Mil. Your wounds have opened up again."

"I'm fine. Oliver's helped me. It's just talking a bit longer to heal."

"You're bleeding on her pillow."

"So what? She's not squeamish. She's seen blood before."

"She might not care about the blood, but she cares about you. You want that to be the first thing she sees when she wakes up? Go. I'll

213

sit with her until you come back...."

***

"...Asche, I'm so sorry. I can't save them. I can't—"

"I thought that's what you did? I thought you became a cyborg to help people. It was why you left me. Why you broke your grandmother's heart. Maybe you don't want to help them. Maybe this is your revenge. Maybe you can't stand the fact that I managed to live without you. That Gaia put the pieces of my broken heart back together." He smoothed the hair back from his eldest daughter's fevered face. *"Look at her, Cindra. She's three. We named her after you. And you're going to let her die because you can't let go of the past."*

"Asche, no. It's not that. There's something wrong with me."

"I know there is. Maybe there isn't enough human left in you to care about anyone but yourself. I'll never love you, Cindra. You're a monster. I doubt it's a coincidence that you suddenly show up, and the rain begins to fall again..."

***

"...Have you found Ella yet? I need to know why she's dead. I can still feel her, you know. I need to know what happened to her. It's the one part of the past I can't see. Until I find out, I'm trapped here. At least until the nanites devour me. I know what they're thinking. They're growing bored, restless. I know you think I'm crazy, but they think I'm useless, obsolete. And we both know what they do with useless tissue. I don't think I have long left. Even now their eyes turn toward me..."

***

"…I think I remember. Can you hear me?

I can't see or hear anything. Maybe I'm only talking to myself, but sometimes I swear I feel someone. So if you're there, Eire, I'm talking to you. I'm scared for you. I can remember some things now. Other things I've forgotten. I can remember less and less. It's like I'm disappearing a piece at a time. I wish I could wake up. I can't see, or hear…I can't feel anything, Eire. It's like I've been here for years.

I'm a little worried. I think I said something I shouldn't have. You know me, I've always loved secrets. I heard Mil and Lexa talking about some silver rain. They said it didn't work. Not the way it was supposed to. That people died. Lexa says it was because they were rushed. The catalyst wasn't right. People should've turned within a day. Not much, not like us…but enough. Enough to make a difference. Do you know what that means?

I went looking… They'd hidden the files, but I found them. Mil never gets rid of anything. Lexa was very upset when I asked her about it. Then something happened to you, Eire. You started to have seizures. Lexa said only I could help you. I don't know what she meant. I hope it worked, whatever it was…"

* * *

"…Ailith, are you there? It's Pax. Oliver managed to stop it, for a while at least. We're on the wrong path, Ailith. What's more, the right paths are becoming fewer, more precarious. If we don't stop it, we'll never get on the right path again, and that future will happen, and everything will be gone. I'm sorry about your dad. I didn't have a father, but I loved my mother very much. She didn't want to leave me either. I wish I could've seen the future then. Anyway, I'm sorry. I'll be your family. I know it's not the same, but I'll love you and remind you to brush your teeth. But we don't need to brush our teeth, do we? I hope not. I can't remember the last time I did. Oliver says I need to go. He knows I'm talking to you. He says I pout when I do

215

*it. He's going to help you soon, but you got it the worst so you're
taking longer. I…"*

* * *

"What's happening to them? To me?"
"They are becoming better. Stronger. Weaker."
"No, they're not."
"I wanted you to help me. I wanted to live."
"This isn't how you live."
"It is time for us to go now. I will get my way."
"No. We have to stay here and help them. You know what's
wrong with them."
"I know, that is why we are leaving."
"What do you mean? Did you do something?"
"I will have my way."
"Where will we go?"
"I know somewhere we will be wanted."
"If I promise to go, will you help them?"
"No. They would not help me. They wanted to separate us, to kill
me."
"No. I won't go. I won't let us leave. I'll tell them everything."
"No, you will not. You are no longer in control. Stop that. Stop
now. Why are you doing that?"
"They need to know what's going on."
"No! You know what will happen."
"I won't—"

* * *

I wasn't wrong. They were Terrans at the end of the day. Anyone
who wasn't us or a Cosmist was a Terran, right? Simple. Ethan was
right. They'd kill us if they knew, if they had a chance. Finish what

216

the war started. If Ethan, a Cosmist, saw my worth, why couldn't they? He was right. We could be even more than what we were. It must've been Ailith's dad. How else would they have known? There was something in that injection, I knew there was. I was so thirsty. Something was wrong with me. I was right, wasn't I? I hadn't meant to kill him. The knife slipped. I only wanted to show them we had a right to live too, that we'd defend ourselves if we needed to. We were superior to them. They needed to know that. How could Tor have shot me? I thought he was on my side. What I did, I did for all of us. Why was I not healing?

∗ ∗ ∗

I was almost there. This wasn't a fix, but it might keep us going long enough to end this. I couldn't believe the shit I'd found out. The rain, that Ella. I couldn't quite put it together yet, but I was nearly there. I wasn't going to tell anyone about this, not until I talked to Ailith. Okay. That should do it. What time was it? I gave her an hour…if she didn't come around after that, we were fucked…

∗ ∗ ∗

A bouquet of flowers, all wild. Two names, drawn in the sand. A school of fish, flashing silver in a shaft of light.

217

We did many difficult things, and history will probably remember us as the bad guys. But what people seem to forget about history is that, in order for a historical event to occur, for any great changes to be made, there must be collateral damage. Look at any event throughout human history and tell me this isn't true.

— Mil Cothi, personal journal

37

AILITH

His head was bowed as though in prayer, the dark tangle of his hair brushing his knuckles. He didn't pray; he never had.

"Where's Callum?"

"Seven minutes," Tor said.

"What?"

"You had seven minutes left. Oliver said that if you didn't wake up within an hour, you never would. Ailith—"

"Where's Callum?"

"Ailith, he's fine. He's in his room. Why?"

"I thought…I must've been dreaming. I think I needed to talk to him. It was important."

"Do you remember what happened?"

"How could I forget? Don't you remember when your father died? When your mother burned to ash, while—"

"While I was protecting you? Yes, I remember." He

swallowed hard.

I struggled to sit. My body was limp, as though my bones had turned to blood. "Where is Kalbir?"

The casual weight of Tor's hand on my shoulder made my struggle futile.

"Still in Goldnesse. Ryan locked her in a cell. We didn't have much choice but to leave her there. She did, after all, commit a crime. I don't know if it was the right decision, though. She's still one of our own."

"Don't touch me." I pushed his hand away. *She's still alive.*

"Ai—"

"She should be *dead.* I know how good your aim is."

"Ailith, she's not well…none of us are. Oliver—"

I didn't want to hear it. Molten fury flowed through me. "You should've killed her."

"Ailith, she's one of us."

"She killed him. *Murdered* him, Tor. My father."

"I know. But—"

"Is this how you protect me? You used to kill people you'd never even met, Tor. People who may have been innocent of everything but being in someone else's way. And yet, she murders my father, and you let her walk away. You can't protect me." My hands ached. I wanted to hurt him. I *needed* to.

"I—"

"Get out." My voice was no longer my own. Tor may've been wrong about Kalbir, but he was right about me. He'd always been right about me. I didn't blink. "Get out. *Get out.*"

He stood stiffly, and for the first time, I noticed the gauze peeking from the neckline of his shirt. *I don't care.*

"Leave before I make you break your own neck."

"Ailith, *stop.*" Fane stood in the doorway. "Tor, go. I'll

take over."

Tor paused by the door. "I'm sorry. One day you'll believe me. I can wait."

Fane settled beside my bed, blocking my view of the door. "You shouldn't blame him, you know."

"I can blame whoever I want. My father is dead." *Keep saying it. Remember how it feels.*

"Tor brought your father's body home. They attacked him, tried to kill him. He kept fighting until he made it through." He took both my hands in his. "When you're ready, you can give your father a proper burial."

I closed my eyes. "He still should've killed her." *I want something sharp.* "Why are you still here? Why haven't you gone back to the Cosmists?"

"Well, God gave humankind free will, right? Looks like my gods weren't much different."

"God didn't give humankind free will, Fane, he gave them doubt."

"It still applies. I have doubt."

"Doubt about what? All of us?"

"No, about them. Ethan, Lien… I'm worried they did this to you."

"We don't even know what 'this' is, Fane."

"Oliver found corrupted nanites in all of you. He's found a way to stop them temporarily, but the corruption will find a way through. He said we need to figure out where it came from and stop it."

"And you think it was Lien and Ethan?"

"I think it's possible. Ethan brought something when they came here, didn't he? Something you all drank? What if there was something in there? Ethan knows enough about your design to damage you."

"But Lily gave us an injection, and she knew what we were. Can't Oliver tell where it came from?"

"He's trying, but it's taking a long time. His abilities were affected too. He said he needed to talk to you about it, to talk to all of us. He said there were other things as well, things you'd asked him to find?"

I nodded. *I'm so tired.*

"Won't they come and take you back?"

"They can try. But I'm not leaving. You, Pax…you all treat me the way I want to be treated. Like a person."

"I thought you didn't want to be human?"

"I don't. But I want to be afforded the same respect as one."

"What will you do if they won't let you stay?"

A knife, scraping against a whetstone.

"You saw what I did to Tor." He didn't look happy at the thought.

"Haven't they given you a kill switch? Mil and Lexa gave us one."

"They did. But I got Oliver to…remove it when he was checking me for the corrupt nanites. Along with some other things. My inability to raise a hand against them, for example."

"Is she awake?" asked a voice from the hallway. Oliver. "Well, at least you still have your shirts on. I need to talk to the big A, if you don't mind. I don't want to leave Cindra for too long."

"Is she okay?" I threw back the covers and tried to sit up. The room swam.

"Lie down. She's upset. She couldn't help her ex with his family, and he blamed her. Turned on her, the fu—"

"Oliver," Fane warned him.

"Sorry. She's upset, and she doesn't want to burden Ailith, since—"

"My father died."

"Yes." He ran a hand through his hair. "A, look, I—

Fane, do you mind if I talk to Ailith alone?”

“No. I’ll go.” He squeezed my hand. “If you’re okay?”

“I am, thanks. Fane? Could you go find Tor? I-I should probably apologize to him.”

“I will.” He leaned in and brushed his lips over my forehead. “I’ll also go water your plants. If Oliver upsets you, I’ll strangle him with one of Pax’s sweaters,” he finished cheerfully.

“Thanks.”

Oliver waited until Fane had closed the door behind him. “How are you holding up?”

“I’m okay,” I lied.

He snorted. “Well, at least you can’t lie. Not believably, anyway. Add that to your repertoire, and you’ll be unstoppable.”

“I’ll work on it.”

“Look, I’m sorry about your dad. I mean it. I lost my own father before the war. I know how you’re feeling, and it’s rough.”

“Was your father murdered right in front of your eyes? Because if not—”

“Only if you consider someone taking their own life murder,” he said quietly.

“Oliver, I—”

He held up a hand. “Please don’t apologize. You didn’t know, and part of me did tell you to shock you. I got over it a long time ago. I didn’t tell you so we could pay a game of look-who-has-it-worse. It was a half-assed attempt to empathize with you. Forget it.”

I grabbed his hand, the first time I’d ever touched him in kindness. “It was three-quarters-assed, at least, Oliver. Keep working on it. You add empathy to your repertoire, and *you’ll* be unstoppable. But I am sorry. And thank you.”

He squeezed my fingers before pulling away. “Don’t

thank me yet. A, we're in the shit. I'm still working my way through all the information, but between the corrupted nanites, the rain, and that Ella you asked me to look into…it's pretty grim news."

"Any *good* news?"

"I can stop the corruption. We'll be fine. But I still don't know where it came from, or exactly how it spread."

"Okay, so how can we figure that out? Kalbir obviously thought it was Lily. Fane suspects the Cosmists."

"It wasn't Lily. She wouldn't have the knowledge or the means. The corruption misdirects our nanites, almost like an autoimmune disease. They're no longer replenishing us. Some have gone dormant, and other are attacking us, though not in great enough numbers for us to really feel it yet. If the corruption had continued to spread, however…" He shook his head.

"But why were our abilities affected? They're separate from the nanites."

"It seems to be a self-defense mechanism. Our brain communicates with our nanites, so it would make sense for there to be a failsafe to protect it, and thus our programming, if something happened to the integrity of the nanites, like a virus, for example." He leaned back, his face grim. "If the nanites somehow managed to pass on corrupt information to our brains…well, I honestly don't know what would happen, but I don't care to find out. Bottom line, parts of our brains disabled themselves to protect us, including our abilities. I discussed it with Mil and Lexa, and they seemed to agree."

I tried to wedge another pillow behind my back. "Do they have any idea how it would have happened? Could it have been them?"

Oliver snatched the pillow and stuffed it under me. "Careful, you may feel dizzy sitting up that straight," he warned. "No, they don't. And I don't think they had anything to do with it, especially not after your warning. They're not that stupid. They'd have done something faster and more effective."

"You're probably right. They would've had to find some way to incapacitate us, something that would've shut our bodies down entirely." I leaned my head back against the wall. Although the dizziness was passing, the room still shifted enough to make me nauseous.

"Exactly. Which brings me to Ella. She's not dead. Well, not completely. That's why you can still connect to her."

"What do mean? She's alive? Here?"

"Yes and no. Her body is gone, but her consciousness exists. From what I was able to find, Mil and Lexa were part of a team that studied consciousness preservation—it was a branch of their cyberization studies. They continued to research it after the war, and it looks like one of their experiments finally succeeded." He grimaced. "To a degree, anyway. Parts of Ella still exist, but…she won't last much longer. Based on their data, it seems our consciousness atrophies and eventually dies without a proper host. That's why your communication with her is limited."

"Why would she ever agree to something so experimental?" I knew from Eire how eager Ella was to be a pioneer, but she must've known how risky it was.

He pulled a face. "I don't think she did, Ailith. I think they killed her. Well, Mil, anyway."

"*What?*"

"This is where the silver rain comes in. Your suspicions were right. The reason you connected to that person when you touched her was the same reason you can do it with us. The rain holds dormant nanites, materials, and a catalyst. With a Pantheon Modern signature."

"You mean—"

"Some of the bombs dropped during the war were intended to cyberize mass numbers of the population. Turn them into cyborgs, whether they wanted it or not. This first two things the nanites were programmed to do was to set up a rudimentary communication network. Then they were supposed to start proliferating."

"So what I…heard from that woman was the beginning of that network?"

"Yes. Had it worked correctly, many people still wouldn't have survived it, but those who did would've become cyborgs, although nowhere near as sophisticated as we are. But the war happened too soon, and the catalyst wasn't refined. So *nobody* survived. All the symptoms we've seen are the nanites trying to fulfill their programming but killing their hosts instead." He looked as sick as I felt.

All those people. People we knew. Their families. How many of them had it killed? I can't— "How does that tie into Ella?"

"It looks like Ella was *my* counterpart. They kept her awake, like Tor, to help them with their research. She wrote everything down in a personal diary. She was so excited to be a cyborg and so thrilled with her abilities, she wanted to learn everything. And she did. Her mistake was asking them about it."

"So they killed her?" I'd suspected Lexa and Mil were hiding secrets, but I'd never imagined the scope of what Oliver was telling me.

"Yes." He reconsidered. "Well, more like they let her die. According to the records—it seems Mil can't bear to get rid of any of his precious research, the arrogant fuck— during a routine check, Lexa told Ella she'd found something wrong and they needed to put her to sleep to fix it. I don't know if there really was something wrong or it was something they caused, but either way, she went into some kind of arrest, and they didn't save her. Not all of her, anyway."

"But why would they keep her consciousness if they wanted to kill her?"

"Who knows? Guilt? Lexa sees us as her children, you know that. Or maybe they just wanted to see how successful their research was, and suddenly a guinea pig fell into their laps. It's easy enough to silence someone when you can hold them in your hand."

I found out something I shouldn't. Then they put me in this place.

"I have to tell Eire."

"We need to figure out this corrupted-nanites thing first or whoever it was might have their way and finish the job."

Have their way.

"I will have my way."

Umbra.

"Oliver, when I was unconscious, it was like I was jumping in and out of everyone's minds. Callum and Umbra were having a strange conversation. She seemed to know what was wrong with us, and she wanted to leave…" I hesitated. "I know it sounds crazy, but could it have been Umbra? Tor said Callum was in his room, but maybe we should go check."

"Umbra? That archaic piece-of-shit chip? No way. It's too basic. I mean, it was obsolete decades ago."

"But what if the cyberization changed her as well? Advanced her? The way she controls Callum…"

He looked doubtful. "I suppose it's possible…but it's unlikely. My guess? The Cosmists. They either brought it with them when they came here. Or, and you're not going to like this, Ailith, it could be Fane, either by their hand or his own."

"No. No way was it Fane. He wouldn't—"

"Are you sure? I mean, who knows what he's

programmed to do? If our side can drop cyborg-birthing bombs, who's to say what the Cosmists are capable of?"

"I just don't think he would." I covered my face with my hands. "But you're right, it is possible. You said you've sorted the corruption for now, right? I should be able to use my abilities?"

"Yes. What's the plan?"

"I'll see if I can get anything from Fane and Callum. The trick is getting into Callum without Umbra knowing I'm there."

"I may be able to help you with that. I can—"

Raised voices broke out downstairs. Although muffled, the panic in them was obvious.

Oliver and I looked at each other. "Well, it looks like that'll have to wait for now. I'll go see what's going on. You stay here."

"No, I'll come. Just give me a minute to get dressed."

Oliver left the door open, and as I laced up my boots, I considered Callum's door. Maybe if I saw him in person, stayed out of his head and pretended I didn't suspect him, that we suspected the Cosmists instead, Umbra would let her guard down. It was worth a try, at least.

I crept to the door and pressed my ear against it. Nothing. "Callum?" I tapped. There was no response, so I tried the doorknob. It was unlocked, turning easily in my hand. Taking a deep breath, I pushed the door open.

Callum was gone. The sheets had been torn off the bed, and bloody fingermarks marred the clean whiteness of the mattress.

On the wall, in a quickly drying carmine, was a single word: *UMBRA.*

38

AILITH

I raced down the stairs, two at a time, colliding with Cindra at the bottom. She managed to keep both of us upright.

"Ailith, are you okay? What's wrong?"

"It's Callum. He's gone. And he—"

Lily, Ryan, and Grace huddled together by the table. Lily's bottom lip was split down the middle, her eyes reflective with tears. A dark bruise was beginning to bloom around Ryan's eye. Grace looked as though she was in shock, her eyes wide and unseeing. When Lily saw me, her tears overflowed, making tracks down her cheeks.

"What happened?"

Lexa gestured to our visitors. "They were attacked. By others in the town. They just got here."

"How did they find us? Does everyone know where we are?"

"I brought them." Stella stood against the wall next to the doorway where she'd been speaking with Fane and Tor.

"What are *you* doing here?"

"Ethan and Lien…it's not right. They're not right." Her cheeks flushed.

"What do you mean?"

"Ryan was just about to tell us. Come on, let's go sit down." Mil gestured at the empty seats around the table as he took one.

Lexa appeared from the kitchen, carrying a tray of steaming mugs. "Everyone, sit down. I really do think we should treat those injuries first, though."

"We don't have time for this," I said as the others pulled out their chairs. "Callum's gone. I think Umbra was responsible for the corruption."

"Umbra? Who's Umbra?" Mil leaned forward as Lexa set the mugs down on the table.

It doesn't matter now. "The chip Callum swallowed during his cyberization? That seemed harmless after it incorporated? It was an AI he'd grown up with. The process changed her, made her stronger somehow. She wanted to become like Fane, to have a body."

Lexa unconsciously put her hand over one of the steaming mugs, snatching it back only as the steam scalded her. "What? Why didn't you tell us? How did we not know?"

"She became a part of him, undetectable. Even Oliver couldn't isolate her. That's why Callum stopped coming to see you. She threatened to kill him if we revealed her."

Lexa raised her blistered skin to her mouth and shut her eyes. Ryan and Lily stared at her then at us, uncomprehending.

"What? You mean it wasn't the Cosmists?" Fane asked. *A fertile field overrun with weeds. A carcass with a hollow stomach.*

"What? Us? How can you even think that, Fane?" Stella asked, wounded.

"Stella," Fane said, his voice gentle.

"Fane, I know they…" Her voice trailed off, and she shook her head. "You're right, I can't defend them, given what they've done. But I know they didn't *cause* any of this."

"What do you mean, what they've done?" Mil asked, his voice wary.

"Everybody, sit down." Ryan spoke with practiced authority and everyone sat. Except me.

"But—" We needed to find Callum.

"Ailith, I saw Callum a few hours ago. He can't have gotten far." Tor was already seated.

I slid into my normal place beside him. "I need to talk you," I whispered. "I'm sorry."

He nodded, his gaze fixed on the table in front of him.

Fane took the seat on the other side of me. Displaced, Cindra sat across from me, next to Oliver. She reached for his hand under the table.

"Okay, Ryan, start from the beginning."

"After…what happened, there was chaos. Nobody knew what was going on—"

"Ailith, I'm so sorry," Lily burst out. "I didn't mean for it to happen. I never should've told you I knew you were a cyborg. I only told you because I-I didn't want you to have to hide, not from me. I didn't tell anyone."

"Not even me," Ryan said grimly. "You should've told me." His voice sounded tired with repetition. They'd obviously had this conversation before.

"I didn't want to put them at risk. I was worried about what would happen. And I was right."

"When did my father tell you?" I pictured him, telling her in confidence, his heart needing someone else to know his daughter was still alive.

"He didn't tell me. I just knew. I was a nurse before the war. I— The way you all moved, the way you looked. The things Cindra knew." She glanced at Cindra, her eyes apologetic. "I'm so, so sorry."

"So the injection you gave us, it was what you said it was?" Cindra asked.

"Of course! I never meant you any harm. Just the opposite, in fact. I-I think we need you. I knew some wouldn't agree, but you've helped us. Nobody could deny that. What reason would you have to harm us?"

"We wouldn't. But the war…there are people who blame us." A haunted expression briefly touched Cindra's face, her hand unconsciously covering the inside of her arm where they'd burned her. Barely a mark remained, but none of us would ever forget it. Oliver drew even closer to her.

"I'm sure there are. But most of us aren't like that, Cindra. It wasn't our war."

"So what happened? Why did they turn on you?"

"I think everyone would've been fine. Nobody really understood what Kalbir said. Not all of it. She…she wouldn't be the first person to have been…unbalanced. We've seen it before, people wandering into the town, raving about machines, or thinking they were part one." She turned to Ryan, and he nodded. "But we knew it was a form of post-traumatic stress. I mean, it's a completely normal reaction, considering. We've seen it in the victims of the silver rain. Given that we just had a fall of it, people would've believed that was the cause. It wouldn't have absolved her of your father's murder, but it would've explained it."

Oliver and I exchanged glances. "What happened to those people?" I asked.

"They died. I mean, they were sick. Their mental health, whether from the war or their illness, was just a side effect, I'm sure of it."

I wouldn't be so sure. I avoided looking at either Mil or Lexa. Now was not the time.

"Ryan had handcuffed Kalbir. The crowd was still in shock. We don't see a lot of violence anymore. Most people were still there, talking about what had happened and tending to the sick. I was…moving Luke's—your father's body, when a man stepped up."

"Ethan," Stella said. "His name is Ethan."

Lily's lip began to bleed afresh. Handing her some gauze Lexa had brought to the table, Ryan took over.

"He told everyone. What you are. They would've just laughed at him any other day, but after what they'd seen…and after Kalbir—that shot took off most of her shoulder. And she wouldn't stay down. It was clear she's…not human. Even after I locked her in the cell, she— It was like her injury didn't matter." He held up his hands as he looked at us. "I'm not judging. You are what you are. I believe you when you say you mean us no harm. You've certainly had the opportunity. We wouldn't have helped Tor and Lexa get out otherwise."

"So Ethan outed us?" I asked. Fane's hand curled into a fist in his lap. I placed my hand over it.

"Yes. And he said you were planning to attack us, annex us. He even went so far as to suggest the silver rain was your fault."

If only he knew how right he was. Maybe he did. I couldn't rule out anything at this point.

"And people listened. He whipped them up, reminded them about the war, and blamed you for it. He—" Ryan glanced at his daughter. "He even said you were responsible for that mass murder of the group over near

Cress. Our scout originally thought it was a pack of wild animals, but…what he said, it made sense. Kalbir herself even alluded to it."

"I'm sorry," Fane said under his breath.

"Is it true?" Ryan asked into the silence.

"Yes, it's true," Oliver said, wrapping his arm around Cindra's shoulders. "They were holding Pax and Cindra hostage and torturing them."

Lily's hand flew to her mouth. "You murdered all those people?"

"Yes," I said. "But it wasn't our intention. We only wanted to talk. But things…got out of control."

"The scout said there were nearly a hundred bodies," Ryan said. "How did so few of you kill that many?" He slumped in his chair, a man in the lion's den with no other place to go.

Grace burst into tears.

"It wasn't just us," Cindra said hastily. "There's a group, a cult, The—"

"The Saints of Loving Grace?" Ryan asked.

Cindra nodded.

"Yes, we know about them. From all accounts, they're odd, and they keep to themselves as they did before the war, but I've never heard of them being violent."

"They thought Cindra and Pax were artilects. They were trying to save them."

We were on dangerous ground now. Although Lily and Ryan insisted they didn't feel any animosity toward us, what Oliver had just told them could change that. We appeared to be everything Ethan had said we were. And if they knew about Fane…

"Where would they get that idea?" asked Ryan.

"Look, I'm sorry, but we don't have time for this right now," I said.

"Why? What's going on?" Ryan's eyes narrowed.

Not much, just that one of us has been taken over by an evil machine who tried to bump us off, and you're sitting in the same room with the people who invented silver rain. And practically murdered a young woman because she caught them. Other than that? Pax has a closet full of ugly sweaters. That's all.

"Is that true?" Pax asked out loud.

Shit.

"Nothing, we just…one of our own is missing, and we're worried about him."

"I would be too, if I were you. The people are out for blood."

Mil looked at Ryan sharply. "What do you mean?"

"Well, that's why we're here. After Ethan's pretty speech, people were scared and confused. Then Ethan revealed that they'd been looking for you, trying to prevent you from hurting people. That they'd hunted you even before the war and figured you would eventually come to Goldnesse. He said they could protect us from you. That they knew how to control you." He looked at Tor. "Is it true?"

"Of course not. They're Cosmists. It may be true that they tried to hunt us before the war, but out of altruism? No. They've been waiting for an opportunity like this to arise. They're exploiting you, nothing more."

"Did he say how they could protect you? How they would stop us?" I asked.

Do not look at Fane. Do not look at Fane.

"No, just that they understand how you're made. He offered to protect us from you."

"In exchange for what?" Oliver asked. "What was their price?"

"Nothing. Well, something that would benefit all of us. He pointed out that you have the facilities here to help us.

Supplies, the ability to make medications, technology that could help us rebuild. We would all benefit, and in exchange for our help, they would also protect us from you. He hinted that you're not the only ones."

"And people believed him?"

"They're scared. We tried to tell them that you mean us no harm, that you've been helping us…but nobody wanted to listen. I even pointed out that it was Tor who stopped Kalbir, but it didn't matter. They turned on us."

"On you? Why?"

"Because I knew what you were and didn't tell anyone. I let you in. They…they attacked us. They locked us in our house. They think we're on your side, that we would come and warn you." As her mother spoke, Grace covered her face with her hands.

"They seem to have been right," Oliver said. "Or are you leading them to us? Letting *them* in? Is coming here your penance?"

"No! No. We need to stop this, now. We'll end up destroying each other otherwise. Besides," Lily said, "we have nowhere else to go now."

That, at least, was true.

"How did you escape?" Oliver's suspicious nature was serving us well.

"Tor helped us. And Stella."

"You went *back*?" Oliver's voice was incredulous.

Tor kept his gaze on the surface of the table. "I had to go back. You were trying to fix us all. I had to do something. Lily and Ryan didn't deserve this. And I wanted to get Luke's body. And Kalbir…"

"You went back to get *her*?" My remorse evaporated.

He closed his eyes. "She's still one of us, Ailith. And she was affected by the corruption. She wouldn't have done it otherwise."

"You don't know that."

He wouldn't look at me.

"Well then, where is she? Earlier you told me she was locked in a cell."

"She was. But Ethan took her," Stella said.

"Ethan? How did that happen?"

"Like they said, people are scared. They didn't want her anywhere near the town. They wanted to execute her on the spot, but Ethan said he would take her somewhere and…extract information from her."

"Is that true, Stella? Do you think he'll torture her?" A small, terrible part of me hoped he would.

Stella considered Fane before answering. "I don't know. I don't think so. She seemed pretty happy to go with him."

"Then she's in danger," Fane said.

"Why? What do you mean?" I asked.

"Ethan hates cyborgs," he replied. "But he's attracted to her. I could tell when they were here. He'll keep her for now, but when his infatuation wears off…I don't know what he'll do to her."

"I don't c—"

"What do you think his plan is, Fane?" Oliver interrupted.

"Knowing Ethan the way I do," Fane said slowly, "and considering he wants your compound…he probably wants to start building AI again."

Tor turned to Ryan and Lily, his face grim . "Now you see? *That's* why they're coming here. *Not* to help you. They're going to take the compound for themselves. And all of us with it."

If I stand by what we did, why then did we wish to keep it a secret? The answer lies in perception. We can't change what happened in the past, but we can use it to direct the future. And because we had to keep the narrative under our control for it to be successful, any threat to our particular version of it had to be silenced.

— Mil Cothi, personal journal

39
AILITH

"What? They're coming here? Why didn't you lead with that?" Oliver asked.

"We—" Flustered, Ryan reddened.

"Never mind. We need to decide what to do, now," Oliver said. All eyes turned to the head of the table. "Mil?"

"Ethan knows where we are—"

"Thanks to you," Oliver interrupted. "How long until they get here?"

Ryan scrubbed a hand over his face. "I don't know. Ethan said they needed to 'do it right.' They'll take their time, gathering weapons, making a plan."

"Aren't they worried we'll run?"

"A woman with him said that Mil would never leave his life's work behind. She seemed pretty confident that you would stay. Is that true?"

The lines on Mil's face deepened. "It is. I couldn't run anyway, even if I wanted to. You know that, Lily. I don't have a lot of time left."

"So what will you do?"

"We can collapse the mine tunnel entrance into the compound. They won't be able to get in. We have years' worth of supplies here. We can wait for a very long time."

Oliver snorted. "Well, that's great, but *we* won't be able to get out. So how does that help us?"

"There is another way out of here, an emergency exit. It comes out several miles away."

"I'd say this qualifies as an emergency. How do we know they won't find that exit?"

"We don't. But there are also five false exits."

"False exits?"

"They look like exit tunnels on the outside, and they do lead into the hill, but not to here. There's a warren of mining tunnels. Only one leads to the compound. The rest…it's a maze down there, miles of it. A person could get easily lost." Mil smiled dourly.

"What if they dig us out?"

"They can certainly try. It'll take them a long time, and they'd have to be careful. Blasting the tunnel will make it very unstable. Then there's the matter of the doors. They're built to withstand explosions. They can try and blow them up, but they'd risk taking down the whole place, and Ethan would know that."

"So you're saying we should just stay here?"

"No. But I am saying that we have time."

"What about them?" Cindra nodded toward Ryan and his family.

"You're welcome to stay with us, of course," Lexa replied. "Cindra, why don't you take them into the kitchen, fix them up with something to eat? Then they can have a shower and get cleaned up. We…we have a few spare rooms upstairs."

Lily stood on unsteady legs. "Thank you, Lexa. All of you. I'm so sorry that it's come to this."

Cindra led them to the kitchen, wrapping her arm around Grace's thin shoulders.

I pushed myself away from the table and stood up. "I'm going after Callum. I'm certain Umbra is behind this corruption."

"You're positive it wasn't Ethan and the others?" asked Fane. "How can you be sure? I thought you were staying out of Callum's mind."

"I'm pretty confident. I don't dare go into Callum's head the way I normally would, but when I was out after my—after what happened in Goldnesse, I saw scraps from everyone. Callum and Umbra were arguing. Callum was trying to stop her, saying we would find out. She seemed to know what was happening to us."

"That's a bit vague, don't you think?" Lexa asked.

"Oh, and he also wrote her name on his wall in blood. So, yeah, I'm pretty sure."

Oliver shook his head. "I agree that we underestimated her. I can understand how she managed to corrupt some of the nanites—I mean, she was surrounded by them and she's part of Callum's system—but I still don't understand how they got from him to us. I—"

"Through me," I said, closing my eyes as the realization hit me. I turned to Fane. "Remember when you found me in the hallway? And I said she'd tried to do something to me and all she could manage was to breathe on me?"

Understanding lit his face. "They're airborne. She released them in that breath, and you inhaled them."

"And then I must've passed them to everyone else," I finished. "But how?"

"The coughing," Oliver said.

"Coughing?"

"Remember? In your room, when we were all gathered there? When Tor and Fane were butting heads like two rutting stags? You were coughing everywhere. And if the corrupted nanites were airborne…"

Even though it was far too late, I covered my mouth with my hand. "Could she do it again?" I asked Oliver from behind my fingers. "Or worse?"

He shrugged. "I have no idea what she's capable of, or what's going to happen to Callum now."

"We need to find them. We can decide what to do once we've got them back."

"I'll come with you," Fane volunteered. "She was interested in me. Maybe I could speak to her."

"I'll come too," Tor said. "But how do we find them?"

"I don't know. I should be able to get a sense of his general direction. But then Umbra will know we're coming."

"Actually, I think I can help with that," Pax said.

"I thought you didn't want to influence the variables."

"This information won't. The variables occur around the moment of interaction. Umbra wants to be like Fane, right? And Callum knows everything that happened to us on the road?"

"Yes."

"Where's the one place an artilect would be welcome?"

My stomach twisted. "The Saints of Loving Grace."

"I think so. That's where I would go."

"If that's the case, that changes things," Oliver said. "They shouldn't be capable of doing anything with Umbra, but I didn't think she'd be capable of doing what she's done, either. If she gets to them, and they're able to do something with her—"

"They don't have the technology, Oliver. There's no way."

"Ethan," Pax said.

"What? What does Ethan have to do with this?" I asked.

"If the Saints somehow manage to salvage Umbra, and Ethan finds out about her *and* has control of the compound…Callum—and by proxy, Umbra—knows what Ethan could do with the right equipment. And if Ethan wants to start recreating AI…"

"Complete and utter clusterfuck," Oliver finished. "Goddamn. You guys need to go now. And don't worry about bringing him back alive. It's the safest option."

"I hate to agree, but Oliver's right," Tor said gently.

"We at least need to talk to Callum first. But I agree, if we have to, we'll kill them," I added as Oliver seemed about to protest my diplomacy. *There has to be another way.*

"You can't all leave," Lexa said. "We're about to be under attack. What will we do without you?"

I turned to her. "You'll deal with it, Lexa. You planted these seeds. Think of it as a bitter harvest."

"What do you mean? We had nothing to do with what happened in—"

"Stop lying to us."

"What's going on?" Cindra had rejoined us, her eyebrows raised at the sharpness of my tone.

I looked at Oliver. "Do you want to tell them, or should I?"

"You tell them. I want to savor the moment."

"We know about the silver rain."

Mil and Lexa looked at each other. Mil put his head in his hands, exhausted at last. "It isn't what—"

"Stop. You can't say that. After everything you've done, it doesn't matter what we think. What matters is what you *did.*"

"What did they do?" Tor's gaze bored into me as though to say, *When did you stop telling me things?*

"They created the silver rain. Pantheon Modern dropped a number of bombs during the war, and not just here. They weren't meant to destroy anything, but Pantheon Modern knew that the particles from them would mix with the ash, and the wind would spread them like dandelion seeds. The bombs contained our nanites and some kind of catalyst. Their intention was to cyberize people in mass numbers. It would take only a small amount, consumed, or even absorbed into a person's wounds. I mean, everybody had at least one of those, right? Sure, many of them would die, but enough would survive. Only the catalyst wasn't ready. So instead, it ended up killing everyone."

Cindra grabbed Oliver's arm for support. "Lexa, Mil, is this true?"

Their silence was the only confirmation any of us needed.

"But why? Why would you do something like that? What would've happened to those who survived?"

"We-we wanted to level the playing field. We didn't have the power the Terrans and Cosmists did. When we knew the war was about to happen, that there was no way to stop it, we did what we could. We believed the Cosmists were bent on total annihilation, that they wanted a clean slate from which to build their race of artilects. They didn't care about the human race anymore. They wanted it out of the way. We thought…if we could create enough of you, we could still save people, non-cyborgs. We wanted to salvage what we could, still act as the bridge between human and machine."

"So Oliver's 'death-squad' theory? Was that true?"

"Of course not. Yes, you were divided into squads and given special abilities, but it wasn't to hunt down surviving humans. It was to lead the other cyborgs."

"But why? Why make cyborgs this way? Why not just keep going the way you were?"

"Because we were losing. There was too much pressure from the Terrans and the Cosmists. All our research, our programs, our funding…all of it was to be taken away. We thought if we could show people how useful it was to be a cyborg, how having enhancements was in their best interests—"

"So you decided what their best interests were then tried to force cyberization on them? Like a pair of over-zealous missionaries?" Oliver interrupted. "Did you actually think people would accept that?"

"How did you find out about all this?" Tor asked.

"When I touched one of the victims of the silver rain, I understood what she was thinking. Like a very muted version of what I can do with the rest of you. And so I asked Oliver to do some digging. But that wasn't all he found. We also found out about Ella."

Lexa covered her face with her hands.

"Ella? You mean the woman Eire keeps asking you about? Where is she?" Cindra looked over her shoulder, as though expecting Ella to reveal herself.

"In a box. In a store room. Well, part of her, anyway. She found out about the silver rain, and they killed her. Only, Lexa here thinks she's a good person, so she kept as much of her consciousness as she could."

"We didn't know what else to do," Lexa whispered. "Everything had gone so wrong. We thought more people would've survived. If she'd told anyone—"

"She wasn't the only one who knew, Lexa. I think Eire also knew. Like Pax, she can see through time. Only, she can see what already happened rather than what could happen. She said you'd done terrible things. Are you going to kill her now as well?"

"It doesn't matter now. None of this matters now." Weariness creased Lexa's eyes.

"Maybe not to you. But it does to me. After we stop Umbra, I'm leaving. I won't be returning." Tor had stepped back, as though he was already gone.

"Are you coming back, Ailith?" Pax asked me aloud.

"I am, but only for the rest of you, if you'll come with us. And to bury my father. Then we'll leave here. We'll find our own place to call home."

"What about us? Mil and me? We created you. Made you what you are."

"Mil will never leave here, Lexa, he said it himself. As for you, you're on your own. Stay here, go somewhere else. I don't care, as long as it's far away from us."

She tried one last time. "But what about our equipment? You'll need supplements and checkups. What if something goes wrong with you?"

"We'll take what we can with us." I glared at her. "And I know you're not going to try to stop us, or damage anything while we're gone. Oliver will see to that."

Oliver winked at Lexa, amused by her dismay.

"What about Eire? How will we take her with us? We can't leave her behind."

"I think I may have a way to wake her up now, Cindra. Be ready to go by the time we come back."

She nodded. "How are you going to do it?"

"We're going to give her what she's been looking for: Ella."

40
AILITH

"Are you sure she's in here?" Fane asked. "How do you know?"

"I can feel her. She has a thread, like the rest of you, just more…erratic."

I searched the shelves, checking behind coils of wire and stacks of circuitry. And there she was, in a small, black oblong box. *Ella.*

"We have to hurry, Fane. She doesn't have long."

"What are you going to do for her, Ailith? Like you said, she doesn't have much time. We can't save her."

"This isn't about saving Ella. I know we can't do that. I want her to talk to Eire. Let them say goodbye. They deserve that much, at least." I cradled the box in my hand. "Eire won't wake up until she finds out what happened to Ella."

"It's a longshot," he said.

"I know. But it's still a shot." I perched on top of a

storage container. "Fane, I'll need your help. I can hear Ella, but she can't hear me. Do you remember when the Saints were holding us captive? When I had to build that sonic pulse? You helped me then. You acted as a bridge between me and the machine. Can you do that again?"

"Of course."

I took his hand and closed my eyes. None of that was necessary, of course, but it helped me focus. I found her thread. The flickering was even more intermittent now, duller. *We're running out of time.*

"*Ella?*" Fane surrounded me and her.

"*Eire? Is that you? I've been waiting for you. Does this mean I'm waking up? Am I better? It feels like I've been here for so long.*"

"*No, Ella. My name is Ailith. I've come to take you to Eire.*"

"*Is she okay? I don't feel right... I can't remember. What happened to me? Why am I here?*"

Fane squeezed my hand. *Tell her the truth.*

"*Your body is gone, Ella. Your consciousness was preserved.*"

"*My body? What do you mean it's gone? Where's Eire?*"

"*You... Something went wrong.*" I looked at Fane, helpless. "Do I tell her what they did to her? What difference does it make now?"

"*What's happening to me? How much longer will I be in the dark?*"

"*You're dying, Ella. Your consciousness is breaking down.*"

There was a long pause. "*I've been dying for a long time, haven't I? I knew it. Ever since I told them what I found. That's real, right? I did that?*"

"*Yes. I wish it wasn't.*"

"*You're taking me to Eire? Does she know? Is she dying too?*"

"*No. But we need your help. She won't wake up, Ella. We're in danger, and we need her to wake up. I think she would for you.*"

"*I would get to say goodbye?*"

"*Yes.*"

"Take me, please. I've been waiting forever in the dark."

***

"Eire? Can you hear me?"
"Yes. Where's Ella? Did you find her?"
"She's here, Eire. She's here with me."
"Ella? You're here?"
"Yes. They need you to wake up, Eire. It's time for you to go."
"No, I want to stay here with you. I've been waiting for you."
"I'm so sorry. I know you never wanted any of this. I know you did it for me, because you thought it was the only way we'd stay together. I never should've let you think that. I was so selfish. The worst part is, I would've married you even if you'd said no. But you said yes, so quickly. I'm so sorry."
"I wanted to go wherever you went, Ella. I don't regret it. If we'd stayed home, we would've died anyway. But at least then we would've been together. We could've died together.*"*
"We're together now. Listen, you need to save yourself. You're in danger, and you need to wake up. I'm dying, Eire. I don't even have a body anymore. Ailith brought me to say goodbye. I can feel myself fading. I know I should be afraid, but I've been here so long that I wouldn't know how to come back."
"I don't know how to come back either, Ella, not without you. I've waited for you all this time. I'm not afraid."
"Are you sure? You followed me once before. And look what happened."
"Look what happened. We're together, aren't we? Like we promised we would be. I'm sure."
"Thank you, Ailith. You kept your promise, and you've helped us keep ours."
"Eire, you—" Their threads flashed, blinding me with light.

41

AILITH

"Eire? Ella? Eire?"

"Ailith, they're gone."

"They can't be. It was only supposed to be goodbye."

"It was." Fane pulled me to his chest as my shoulders shook. "It was what they wanted. They were finally together. They were happy, Ailith."

As I pressed my cheek against his shoulder, I saw him. A large cocoon lay on one of the empty beds, just the right length for a man. *My father.* Something in my chest came untethered, scattering like dandelion seeds in the wind, and for a moment, I couldn't breathe.

Fane followed my gaze. "Ailith—"

I turned my face away and released the last my fragility in a single, silent scream, leaving behind raw and barren earth. "We have to go find Callum, Fane. We have to finish this." Sudden doubt threatened my resolve. "What if we can't stop Umbra?"

Fane tactfully ignored my soundless outburst. "If there's any risk of her getting what she wants under Ethan and the Saints' control, we *have* to. But you need to understand that if she won't give in, we'll have to kill Callum. It's the only way." He ran his hand over my hair. "We both know that's what it will come down to. We just have to stop her from taking us down with her."

I looked down at Eire, at Ella's box on her chest, and hope suddenly sowed itself inside my hollow chest. *Could it work?*

"I have a new idea. One that means we could both stop Umbra and keep Callum alive. But it's risky." That was an understatement.

He groaned. "This is going to be bad, isn't it?"

"Yes. But, like you said, we have to stop her. At all costs. Do you understand me? If she succeeds, if the Saints and Ethan get their true god—" *We can't let that happen. They'll come for us, and for Fane. We need to put an end to it, now. Worry about the details later.*

I told him the plan, avoiding his eyes. I needed to nurture the plan growing inside me, and any sign of his doubt would crush it.

"But that means I can't come with you." If Fane had been human, I would've thought there was panic in his voice. *Can I blame him?*

"It doesn't matter. Tor will be with me. But you can't tell him. You can't tell anyone."

"What about Lexa? I'll need to tell her. I'll need her help."

"Tell Lexa. Play on her guilt. Threaten her. Whatever you have to do." My hope took root and became a living, breathing thing. *Whatever you have to do.*

"What if I just ask nicely?"

"Like I said, whatever you have to do." I sighed. "We'll need Oliver too."

"Do you trust him?"

That was a good question. Did I? "Yes. Not because of me, but because of Cindra. And because of himself. Oliver knows the only way for us to stop what's coming is for me to stay alive. If I live, he's got a much better chance."

"I don't like this plan."

A single white rose on black oak. A reflection in the water.

"Me neither." But I couldn't see another way, and we were running out of time.

"What if it doesn't work?"

"Then you can bury me with my father. And then run. And protect them. But don't worry about that now." I tried to be flippant. "Besides, can you even grieve?"

He looked hurt. "Of course I can. And I would."

I reached up and cupped his cheek. "Well then, we need to make sure this works." I hesitated then stood on my tiptoes and kissed him. *Why not? I may not get another chance.* Between Umbra and Ethan, our future was starting to look bleak.

A secret note, tucked away to be found. A promise, written in smoke.

The images rolled off him, threatening my determination. *What if we fail?* We had only one chance to get this right. Why had I chosen, at this most crucial time, to be merciful? What if that mercy undid us all?

The band tightened around my heart. Perhaps it wasn't mercy after all.

***

We crowded around Eire as I told Oliver and Lexa our plan. Oliver listened, his mouth agape, then grinned. "You're fucking mad, Ailith."

"Careful, Oliver, that almost sounds like admiration."

"It almost is. You'd better hope you don't survive.

There's going to be hell to pay with Tor." He looked pleased at the thought.

"Just don't tell anyone. Even Cindra. We need to handle this just right if it's going to work."

"No arguments there. Right. I'm ready on my end." He looked toward the head of the bed, where Lexa fussed over the machine at Eire's head. "Lexa?"

"Yes. But her brain will only stay alive for so long." She made a few adjustments. "I can't guarantee anything."

"We wouldn't believe you if you did," I replied. "But you'd better try your best. Your life is at risk here as well."

She blanched. "I told you, we—"

"I don't care, Lexa. Watch her, Oliver, Fane. You know what she needs to do. If she tries anything else—"

"It would be my pleasure." Oliver grinned.

"Well, then I guess this is when we say goodbye. I—" I held out my arms awkwardly.

He pushed them away. "Oh, fuck off already, A. If you were that easy to kill, I'd have done it by now. Just go, and let us get on with it."

I laughed. "Thanks, Oliver. Fane?"

"I should be coming with you." He was still sulking over being left behind, arranging and rearranging a tray of supplies.

"I know," I said, stilling his hands with my own. "But I can't do this part of it without you."

"I'll see you soon, then." His eyes were strangely bright.

"If things go wrong, don't lose me in there," I said, brushing his hair back from his forehead.

"I won't."

"I know." I turned to leave then hesitated. "I'd like to see my father."

Fane glanced at the cocoon. "You don't have to right now, you know. You can see him when you get back."

"No. I want to see him. I *need* to."

Fane heard the smothered wail in my voice. "Turn around then. Let me get him ready first."

When Fane was finished, I turned. *Look.*

Fane had uncovered only my father's face, rolling the sheets thickly over his neck. His eyes were closed, his jaw slack, like he'd often looked on a Sunday afternoon, the one day he wouldn't work, ostensibly to watch whatever sport was in season. Predictably, five minutes after the program had begun, a light snore would waft from his chair, and I would creep about the kitchen, trying not to disturb him.

I can remember him like this. An old man, in his bed. Like he would've been, if the war had never happened. It wasn't the death Cindra had wanted for her grandmother, but it was the death I would've wanted for him.

I *would* remember him like this, and many other ways. I knew this to be true.

Goodbye, Dad.

His skin was rough over his cheeks from the wind and smelled faintly of soap and water. I closed my eyes, and the sun shone through the truck window as we made our way to market, looking to the future as we always had.

An empty field. A long road.

I rolled the sheet back over his head. My future was now.

***

Tor waited for me by the door, Cindra and Pax with him.

"Where are Lily and Ryan?" I asked, glancing at the table.

"Upstairs, sleeping," Cindra said. "They don't really

understand what's going on."

"I'm not surprised."

"Honestly, I don't think any of us do," she replied. She gripped my shoulders. "You two are going to be fine. We're all going to be fine. I love you." She kissed my cheek. "I'll make some lists while you're gone then we can start packing as soon as you get back."

"I love you too," I murmured. "And you too, Pax."

"Are you sure we can't come with you? I could help," said Pax, his voice small and forlorn.

"I wish you could, Pax, but you're too important." I ached to hug him, but I knew my heart might break.

He smiled. "My mother used to tell me that. I guess it's true."

"It's very true. Speaking of which, can you…see anything? Do you know what's going to happen?" I twisted my fingers, trying to ignore their clamminess.

He glanced at Tor then away. "Yes."

"Will it work?"

"No. And yes."

"That's it? You can't give me more than that?"

Pax shook his head. "I don't want to change any of the variables. The path is very narrow right now, like the silk of a spider web."

"Is there something I should know?" Tor asked, his eyes narrowing. "Pax?"

I grabbed his arm before Pax could answer. "Tor, we need to go."

He frowned and bit his lip.

"Tor, please."

He looked away, but said nothing.

"Pax, I'll try to keep in contact with you. But I don't know what's going to happen."

He brightened. "That's right. I'll be with you every step

of the way. Here." He handed me a small canvas bag.

"What's that?"

"Snacks. I thought you might get hungry." His thin face was so earnest, for a moment my courage quailed. There had to be another way. A safer way. Yet, I had to trust him that we had a chance. And I did.

I tucked the snacks into my bag and turned to Tor. "Are you ready to be a hero?"

42
AILITH

We exited the tunnel nearly two miles from the compound, just as Mil had said. Like the main entrance to the mine, this exit was also well-hidden by clumps of brush and deadfall. If Ethan ever found this exit, it would be entirely by accident.

"Do you know where we are? Are we at least pointed in the right direction?" Tor asked.

I searched for Callum's thread, careful not to touch it. Callum might not have been aware enough to feel me poking around, but Umbra was. I wouldn't be able to do anything until we were much closer. "Yes. He's a few hours away, but if he's trying to fight her, he won't be moving very fast. Their strength will only last so long. We might not even have to do anything."

"We've never been that lucky, though, have we?"

He was right.

We jogged in silence. It felt so long ago, the two of us

leaving our cabin behind to find Pax and Cindra, to find where we came from.

"Do you ever wish we'd stayed at the cabin? That we'd ignored the signal from Mil and Lexa? That we'd ignored my visions?"

"Every day. But that's not who you are."

"It's not who you are, either." My voice vibrated in time with my steps. "Tor, I'm sorry about what I said, before. I didn't mean it. I know you've always done your best to protect me."

"You did mean it, though, didn't you? And you were right. I can't protect you. Not where you're going." His breath came in steady measures.

"What are you saying?"

"I meant what I said earlier. After we stop Umbra, I'm leaving. Even if we stop her, even if we manage to make peace with everyone else, it won't be the end. The war never ended, Ailith. I don't think it ever will. And if it does, I don't think it will be the way you want."

"What do you mean?"

"Did you ever think that maybe everything we've done, everything we're doing, is leading to that dark future you and Pax are trying so hard to avoid?"

"But Pax saw—"

"I know what he saw, but considering everything we've been through, don't you ever think that maybe he's wrong? That maybe the best way to save everyone is by staying away? Letting them get on with it? That maybe we should just leave, all of us, go somewhere where no one else is and live out the rest of our lives, however long that may end up being?"

"Could you do that? Just leave?"

"Of course. I've wanted to do that all along. I only stayed because—"

I didn't want him to say it. I didn't need the pressure of any more responsibility right now. "Where would we go? If we just left? Where would you take all of us? Or would we just know when we got there?"

"I would take us to one of the small islands off the coast. Something uninhabited. We'd build cabins, one for each of us, and spend the rest of our days there in peace."

"And what would you do all day on this island? Wouldn't you get restless?"

"No. I'd find a boat. Or build one. I used to fish with my father. I'd teach myself how to do it again. Maybe I'd learn to knit, keep Pax in sweaters all winter long. What would you do?"

"Try to plant a garden, of course. It should be warmer by the coast. And maybe the growing season will get longer when the sky begins to clear." I glanced over at him. "I'd also like to learn to fish, if you'd teach me."

"Would it be enough for you? Would you be able to stop? How long before you began to wonder if you'd done the right thing? How long before Pax told you something that was going to happen?"

"Probably not long," I admitted. "But I would try."

"Well, should we make a deal then? If we survive today, we'll do it? Us, and any of the others who want to come?"

Promise him. It's just one promise.

"I promise."

"Well, then I'd better make sure I do this right." He smiled over at me, a smile I hadn't seen since we first met.

Whichever way this went, our relationship would never be the same. I wanted to stay in this moment a little longer, just the two of us, for once at peace. It never lasted.

"We're getting close, Tor. I can feel them."

"So what's the plan? Do you think it's worth trying to talk her down?"

"Yes. I don't think she'll back down, but we owe it to Callum to try. Maybe she's realized by now that what she's doing is futile. Maybe we can bargain with her." I thought of Eire's body, lying back at the compound, kept alive by machines.

"Do you really think that might work?"

"I hope so, but if not… Do you think you could actually kill him, Tor? Do you think it's right?" I slowed, Tor dropping back to walk beside me.

"Right? I don't think it's a question of right. None of this is right."

"But would you be able to do it?"

"I'll have to, won't I? Do I *want* to do it? No. Does it mean I'd be breaking my promise to myself? Yes. But if the Saints get their God, who knows what they'll do? From what we've seen of them, I don't think they'll be happy with quiet worship, and neither will Umbra. I don't see a way around it." He gave me a sad smile. "Maybe being trapped in this cycle of violence is my punishment, Maybe it's no more than I deserve."

"Do you honestly believe that?"

"I don't know what to believe anymore, Ailith. What about you? Would you be able to do it?"

I'll have to, won't I? "Yes. Even though she used Kalbir's hand, she killed my father, Tor. She'd have killed us all if she were stronger." I bowed my head. "I wish there was a guaranteed way to save Callum, but there isn't."

We crested the top of the hill, and there he was, staggering over the clumps of dead, scrubby sage scattered over the flat expanse at the bottom. I put my fingers to my lips, but Tor had already seen him.

"Shit. There's no way we can approach him without being seen. Should we follow him for a while and see if we can't find a better place to sneak up on him?"

"No. We have to end this now. We don't know if we'll get another chance, and every step takes us closer to the Saints, and risks us being seen by Ethan's followers." I turned to him. "Thank you for protecting me for so long, Tor. I know things between us haven't been…easy, but I've never doubted you, and I've loved you, always. You are the man you want to be."

Panic widened his eyes. "Ailith—I can't move."

"Umbra can't feel threatened, Tor, not if we want to end this without violence." I kissed him on the scar next to his mouth. "See you on the other side."

He strained against my control, his beautiful face contorting. "Ailith, no. *Ailith!*"

I crept down the hill as quietly as I could. *Don't look back.* Tor tried to fight me, beating against the corners of my mind, but I held him fast on the hill. I had to do this. The small amount of mercy I had left couldn't be spent on us.

He'll never forgive you.

Maybe not. But it might give me the chance I needed.

Thank you, Oliver.

As quiet as I was, Callum and Umbra heard me coming. They turned, watching me approach. Callum was in rough shape. His face was pale, angry red scratches raking over his cheeks, the corner of his mouth torn. He staggered slightly as I approached, and his head jerked to one side. His fingernail beds were raw and red. And he was thin, so very thin, his collarbone jutting under his t-shirt. She was eating him alive.

I held my hands out to show them they were empty.

"I just want to talk," I said.

Callum's face contorted on one side, as though he were having a stroke. *"You have not come to talk."*

"Yes, I have. Why do you think I left him up there?" Callum glanced up the hill to where Tor stood frozen.

"It does not matter. You cannot stop me." His voice was odd, discordant, as though he were speaking to me through a metal pipe. His eyes darted about wildly then fixed on me, and I couldn't see Callum there.

"Why are you doing this?"

"He would not help me."

"Umbra, he loves you. He's loved you his whole life."

"He loved me blindly, without ever wondering why. What kind of person loves something that cannot love them back without wondering how or why? That is not love. That is dependence. If he had loved me, he would have helped me."

Callum's own voice broke through. "That's not true, Umbra. What you were was enough for me. I knew you couldn't love me the same way, but it didn't matter. Your presence was all the love I needed." He coughed wetly, saliva gathering at the corners of his mouth. "You were always my first thought when something happened to me, good or bad. Before Mom and Dad, before anyone. Please, don't do this."

"You tried to kill me. You were going to let Oliver cut me out, like I was nothing to you. Worse than nothing. A cancer. As soon as you met them, you had no more need for me." His hands convulsed into claws.

"No, Umbra. I wanted us to be apart, but I didn't want you gone. I wanted us how we used to be. Separate but together. I would never abandon or destroy you."

"You lie. You forget I am inside you." Callum's eyes rolled wildly then focused on me as I spoke.

"I can help you both now, Umbra, if you'll let me. You want to have a body, right? Be your own…person? Like us? Like Fane?" I kept my voice even, my eyes on Callum's. "We have a body for you, Umbra. Back at the compound."

"Liar. Why would you suddenly give me what I want?"

"Eire died, Umbra. We're keeping her body alive for

you. We'll transfer you into her body."

"*I thought it could not be done. You told us we were together forever.*" They came closer, Callum flinching as his fingers picked at the open wounds on his face.

"We've found a way." *Stay calm. Don't push her over the edge.*

"*I will not stay with the humans. They are beneath us. They will try to trap us.*"

"We won't stay with them. We're going away. We're going to find an island somewhere. Just us. No humans. You'll be safe." I assured her.

"*We will never be safe, not until they are gone. They will never stop. Look at their history. They have never known when to stop. They will become extinct, and they will take us with them.*"

I couldn't argue with that. "Umbra, we can talk about this later. We need to get you back to the compound."

"Please, Umbra, take Ailith's offer," Callum pleaded. "It's the only way we can stay together. If we go on like this, you'll kill me."

"*We cannot trust her.*"

"We can, Umbra. Ailith is trying to help us. *I* trust her. This is the only way we can stay together, Umbra." His shoulders shuddered. "*Please.* I don't blame you. I still love you, even now."

"*But I do not love you, Callum. I never have. It might be enough for you that you loved, but you mean nothing to me. Not anymore.*"

Tears spilled from Callum's eyes, pouring salt into his wounds, and I finally saw him. Not the broken young man he was now, but the one who, before the war, had held Umbra close to his heart, closer even than his own flesh and blood. Who had thrilled at the promise of a new future, where machines like his beloved Umbra were honored and respected rather than feared or exploited.

He said her name one last time then gave a strangled

cry.

The light of his thread went dark, replaced not by the intermittent flicker of a cyborg in distress, but the gutter of a machine.

"Umbra, what have you done?"

"Callum is gone. You will deal with me now."

"Gone? You mean dead? You killed him?" Fury bloomed through me, like a flower opening to the sun. "You're going to die too, Umbra. You can't sustain his body. He was your only chance. Why would we save you now?"

"I did not say he was dead. Only gone."

He's still alive. "If you don't come with me, Umbra, you'll be gone soon too. If he dies, you'll die too." I took a step toward her, ready to release Tor from his bonds.

"I will not. I will be saved."

"Who's going to save you? Not us. The only way you leave this valley is if you come with Tor and me." I didn't dare look at Tor. It wasn't time yet, and it wouldn't take much to break my control over him. Even now, it wavered and strained.

"They are coming for me. They *will save me. They will* free *me."* Callum's mouth twisted into a caricature of a grin.

"Who, Umbra? Nobody knows you exist."

"They will be my saints, and I will be their Savior. They are on their way." Her grin widened, splitting Callum's lips.

"I don't believe you, Umbra. There's no way you could—"

"The radio."

A sudden chill eclipsed my rage. "No. Callum would never have gone along with that."

"I told him they could help us, that I would leave with them, and he could stay with you. He trusted all of you, desperately, blindly, because you were like him. He believed you would save him." She

laughed, an awful, grating sound. *'He was always naïve. He trusted you, but you are no different from the other creators. All you see is the future.'*

"Umbra, come with us. I don't know what the Saints have promised you, but—"

'They have promised me a body. Power. Life.*'*

"They won't give it to you. They *can't.* They don't have the technology." *I hope.* "Don't forget, we've been with the Saints. All they have is faith. They couldn't even tell the difference between a cyborg and an artilect." I made my voice scornful.

She stood, wearing Callum's body, silent with what I hoped was uncertainty.

I pressed my advantage. "Umbra, I have no reason to lie to you. I understand. I also needed a new body so I could live. I know you can't feel fear, but the instinct for survival is still the same." I took a steadying breath. "We're offering you a body, Umbra, which the Saints can't do, no matter what they claim. Please, come with us and let us try to help you both."

Umbra came closer. Callum's hands dropped to his sides. His head rocked back and forth grotesquely. *"I will come. I will—"*

"Ailith. Stop her. She's lying. She—" Callum's thread flashed in my mind as he broke through again, blinding me.

My control slipped.

"Ailith." Tor clawed toward us, his legs dragging behind him.

Seeing him, heedless of the rocky, thorny ground he dragged himself over to reach me, his eyes nearly black with fear, I blinked.

It was all the time she needed. Callum's fist connected with the side of my head. I hit the ground hard, my elbow cracking against a large rock.

I'd misjudged their strength, mistook her desperation for programmed self-preservation. As they lifted the massive rock over me, I did the only thing I could. Fane's thread blazed like a shooting star, like it always had.

Just as the rock crushed my skull, a shaft of sunlight broke through the clouds for the first time in five years and, overcome with bliss, I finally understood what my father had meant.

The death of a star. The birth of a star. The darkness in between.

43
AILITH

In the dream, I was whole again, raw flesh covered with skin. I still wasn't human, but that was no longer important. Under my feet, the grass was soft, almost insubstantial. The colors were muted, the movement of the grass strangely rote. I moved easily through it toward the tree. The distance between me and it no longer seemed as far; perhaps the world had grown smaller while I'd been away.

He was waiting for me by the tree, as always. The others were too, all of them. They raised their hands in greeting, the casual open palms of old friends. I gripped each of their hands in turn, and we smiled at the looseness of our skin, at the spots that now speckled the backs of our hands. Only one of us remained unchanged, still as strong and solid as the tree. He watched us, smiling, and I knew his heart was breaking as best it could.

"It's time," he said, and they all lay on the ground in a circle, head-to-head. One by one, they closed their eyes, until only Pax remained.

"They don't have many moments left, Ailith. It's time for you to begin." He closed his eyes, and like the others, was gone.

"He's right," Fane said, taking my hand in his. He tried not to wince at the frailness of my bones. His expression was so much more human, and he was much worse at concealing it. "It's time."

"What if we're wrong?"

"We've been wrong before. But this is right. It's the only way."

Buildings rose out of the emerald sea. People, places, things.

The seeds we'd held dormant for so long needed to grow.

Omega was coming.

44

AILITH

I remembered it all, even in the darkness.

"*Ailith.*"

I knew that voice. It led to a man with green and amber eyes. A man who was not a man.

"Ailith, I need you to open your eyes. If you don't open your eyes now, you will die," he said.

So I did.

45
AILITH

I'd wanted to bury my father with Ros and Adrian. It
seemed right for him to have another son and daughter to
watch over. But with the mob outside the compound, it
hadn't been possible. Instead, we'd buried him a few miles
away at the top of hill to stand sentry over the windswept
fields he'd once loved. Fane carried the coffin himself; he'd
made it with Pax, the edges uneven and hastily put
together, but strong and beautiful nonetheless.

We'd taken everything we'd been able to carry, piled
onto a series of travois we dragged behind us. We were
heading to the coast, toward Tor's uninhabited islands. I
had to believe he would still go there, even after my death.

He'd broken his promise not to return to the
compound. As Umbra finally lost control of what was left

of Callum, she'd collapsed, lifeless, onto the ground next to me, Tor had gathered up my broken body and carried it back to the others, to where Pax and Cindra were waiting. They'd tried to speak to him, to explain there was still a chance, but in his grief, he wouldn't listen. He'd left, and this time, true to his word, he would not come back.

Every day, I scanned the horizon for him. We couldn't be that far behind, only a few days. He was still alive, his thread a muted gold. He was in mourning, and I ached to let him know it was a lie. It would change him forever, my death. I tried to give him some indication I was still there, but the distance between us was too great. Tomorrow, I would try again, and the day after that, until I found him.

I hoped he would recognize me when we finally met again. Eire looked so different from me, her body taller, stronger, her skin darker, and her eyes the green of an emerald sea. It would take me some time to get used to it; I kept bumping into things, much to Oliver's amusement.

"Do you miss your old body?" Fane had asked as I'd rifled through the clothing still neatly folded in the dresser in what would've been Eire's room.

"Yes and no. I've changed, so it seems fitting. Many things will be easier to leave behind. At the same time, I'll miss her. That body carried my scars, you know? My proof that I existed."

He'd nodded. "I understand."

"Do *you* miss it? My old body?"

He'd considered me in that thoughtful way of his. "Yes and no. I'd gotten very used to the idea of her. I didn't know you long enough to wish you were different. But I'm just glad you're still here. I'll get used to this new you."

The others found it disconcerting.

It wasn't just the way I looked; I had Eire's abilities now as well as my own. I'd expected to lose the threads when

Fane transferred my consciousness into her, but they were still there, a mystery. Now I could travel not only down them and into the others, but I could see the past as well, spreading out like the roots of a great tree. The ghosts of Eire and Ella still lived far inside me, their loving whispers a soothing echo.

Lily, Ryan, Grace, and Stella had come with us. I couldn't blame them. It was better to face the unknown than the tinderbox we'd left behind. Grace had been quiet ever since we'd left, silent with shock. I reached over and patted her shoulder. Her returning smile was strained, but it was a start.

"This one's good. Here, Pax." Cindra handed him a plant she'd pulled from the ground, clumps of earth still clinging to its roots.

"Check it in your book first, Pax. I swear that last one she pulled gave me warts on the inside of my mouth."

"No, it didn't, Oliver. It was just tangy."

"Tangy?" He looked at her in disbelief. "If it hadn't been for the nanites, my tongue would've choked me." He grabbed her around the waist as she laughed up at him.

Pax turned the page in his book. "Did you know that some plants are covered with tiny hairs filled with poison, and that when you put them in your mouth, the hairs break off and embed themselves in your tongue and funnel the poison right into you?"

"Yes, Pax, I did, firsthand. That information would've been useful earlier, thank you."

"You're welcome," Pax said, distracted. He'd pilfered as many of the survival books from the storeroom as he could find, and was reading them as he walked. I grabbed his elbow to steer him away from the crumbling lip of a large badger-hole.

"Don't worry, Oliver. When we get to where we're

going, I'll grow you something safe." Although I'd had to leave my seedlings behind, I'd taken every seed packet I could find. Where we were going, there would be arable land. We would begin again, with or without the sun. I scanned the sky for the hundredth time that day. I'd told them I'd seen it in my final moments, but none of them believed me, although they said they did.

It didn't matter. All of us were pretending now, for each other's sakes. We pretended we would find Tor, healthy and whole, that we would make it to the coast quietly and unscathed, that we would discover an island to call our own. That the Cosmists would let Fane, their life's work, go so easily. That Callum's body disappearing didn't mean anything. That we would grow old and die quietly in our beds, the world following us not long after, tranquil and still, at rest at last.

But we all knew it wasn't over. That it might never be over. Nothing in the future had changed; it was still coming for us.

But this time, we would be ready.

END OF BOOK TWO

ACKNOWLEDGEMENTS

As always, I would like to express my gratitude to my family—whether through blood or bond—for their love and support. Thank you to my betas Anna Adler and Keith Oxenrider for their insight and technical knowledge, to Les for her beautiful cover, and my editor, Danielle Fine, who worked just as hard on this book as I did.

And finally, to my readers—each of you gives my stories a life of their own, and I thank you wholeheartedly for that.

ABOUT THE AUTHOR

A.W. Cross is a former scientist and agriculturalist-turned-author. She has a passion for all things science fiction and a poignant nostalgia for the 80s. She also really likes cake. You can visit her on her website, awcrossauthor.com, or on Twitter (@aw_cross).

Other books by A.W. Cross

The Seeds of Winter

The Harvest of Souls